Praise for 7

"Brunsvold animates each of her well-drawn characters with palpable, deeply rooted emotion."

Publishers Weekly

"In the empathetic and uplifting novel *The Divine Proverb of Streusel*, a woman at a crossroads is drenched in family nostalgia and considers forgiveness."

Foreword Reviews

"*The Divine Proverb of Streusel* is a sweetly satisfying novel with layers of heartbreak and healing, forgiveness and family, homey wisdom . . . and recipes! You'll want to slow down and savor this one."

Julie Klassen, bestselling author of *The Sisters of Sea View*

"Sara Brunsvold's *The Divine Proverb of Streusel* is a lovely novel filled with faith, love, and honesty. With its sweet details, memorable characters, and much-loved recipes, readers are sure to savor each page."

Shelley Shepard Gray, *New York Times* and *USA Today* bestselling author of *Her Heart's Desire*

Praise for *The Extraordinary Deaths of Mrs. Kip*

"This heartfelt portrait of a life simply but generously lived is testament to the deep significance of individual influence and a legacy of goodness."

Booklist

"An uplifting debut. Inspirational fans will want to snap this up."

"A story that pulls at the heartstrings and captivates readers from the very beginning!"

The
ATLAS of
UNTOLD
STORIES

Books by Sara Brunsvold

The Extraordinary Deaths of Mrs. Kip
The Divine Proverb of Streusel
The Atlas of Untold Stories

The ATLAS of UNTOLD STORIES

SARA BRUNSVOLD

Revell

a division of Baker Publishing Group
Grand Rapids, Michigan

© 2025 by Sara B. Brunsvold

Published by Revell
a division of Baker Publishing Group
Grand Rapids, Michigan
RevellBooks.com

Printed in the United States of America

Library of Congress Cataloging-in-Publication Data
Names: Brunsvold, Sara, 1979– author.
Title: The atlas of untold stories / Sara Brunsvold.
Description: Grand Rapids, Michigan : Revell, a division of Baker Publishing Group, 2025.
Identifiers: LCCN 2024044180 | ISBN 9780800746124 (paperback) | ISBN 9780800747046 (casebound) | ISBN 9781493450541 (ebook)
Subjects: LCGFT: Christian fiction. | Domestic fiction. | Novels.
Classification: LCC PS3602.R865 A94 2025 | DDC 813/.6—dc23/eng/20241001
LC record available at https://lccn.loc.gov/2024044180

Cover illustration by Kimberly Glyder

Published in association with Books & Such Literary Management, BooksAndSuch .com.

Baker Publishing Group publications use paper produced from sustainable forestry practices and postconsumer waste whenever possible.

25 26 27 28 29 30 31   7 6 5 4 3 2 1

For my daughters.
Who teach each other,
and who teach me.

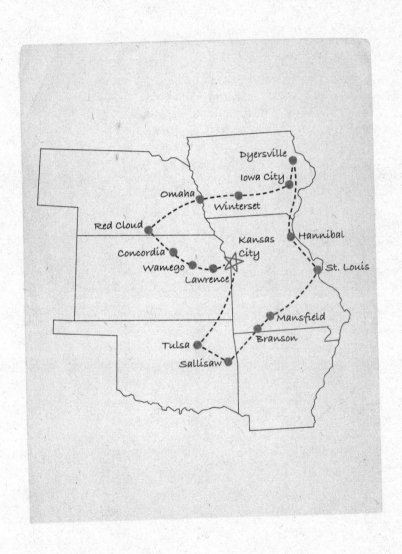

1

Strange how an empty room could be haunted by sound, especially a sound as whispery and distant as the *shiff* of sand between the bowls of an hourglass. Tendrils of the memory prickled Edie Vance's skin. She hugged her arms to her stomach. The Persian rug under her feet still bore the indents from the weight of her mother's grand mahogany desk. Her spirit zapped back to those afternoons decades prior.

Her eight-year-old form in the wingback chair in the corner, in the room but out of the way, the chair far too big for her body, and the book open on her lap far too dense for her comprehension. Across the room, in the soft touch of light from the bay window, her only remaining parent sat bent over an English major's research paper, red pen scratching across it. Between them was the antique hourglass, enthroned on the corner of the imposing desk. She could not see her mother without first seeing it. Every grain that fell was one second less of her time allotted in her mother's presence. The sand ran faster than her eyes across the page. The page could never hold her attention for long anyway. None of the books in her mother's ample collection lining the walls ever had pictures.

And none of those minutes measured out by the hourglass included a glance from her mother, not until the last grain had slipped to the bottom bowl.

"Did you enjoy your book, Edith?" her mother would ask. *Your book*, as if Edie had any rights to it.

Edie took her time answering. The longer the wait, the longer her mother's eyes had rested upon her.

Many decades removed from those afternoons, Edie stood freely in the middle of the study and breathed in what once was so real in that space. The desk, the books, the wingback chair, the silent cascade of sand were all gone. The last grain had fallen, for good. Still she waited for her mother's eyes to fall upon her. Could her mother see her now, through the veil between eternity and present?

A knock on the open door drew her attention.

"Me," Grant said. "It's quarter to two. Don't want to be late."

"Coming, dear."

He adjusted his bifocals on the bridge of his nose and swept his gaze across the room. "Seems bigger now that it's empty."

"Bigger in so many ways," she murmured.

"Want me to take the rug downstairs, put it with everything else?"

The plush piling cushioned the soles of her flats. She curled her toes as if attempting to root herself in deeper. The ornate gold and burgundy paisley had elevated the richness of the wood furniture with which her mother once surrounded herself with pride, a victory statement after being left with nothing when her husband abandoned her and their two small children. The rug was all that remained of the Moria Mondell dynasty. The walls bore scars from the dismantled bookshelves. The books, once so prized, faced an unknown fate at the estate sale.

"I'll bring it down later," she replied to his offer.

"Meet you downstairs." Promise given, he headed back toward the stairs.

His occasional habit of shortening sentences, leaving off the subject and sometimes the predicate, had been the first hash mark against him on her mother's mental scorecard. The second, his openness to any financial advice other than Warren Buffett's.

She squeezed her arms tighter, traced her fingertips along her sides. If given the choice between her husband and her mother, she would always choose her husband.

So why did she still dream of those afternoons?

2

----

*C*hloe Vance traced her Pitt pen along the penciled sketch marks she had made earlier on the page, angling the ultra-fine point down and to the left. She then carefully cross-hatched over the dark line to convey the softness of the jawline she had known all of her twenty-six years. The softness of her mom's jaw complemented the delicate nature of her fingertips, which always bore some dainty shade of pink or red. Maybe only artists noticed such details.

The framed photo of her mom sat to the right of her sketch-book. Without question, the photo was the best Chloe had ever taken of her. It provided the perfect reference for what she had tried three times so far to bring to the page as a surprise parting gift for her mom. She needed something of great value to demonstrate that her talents and gifting could be a blessing to others, a way to help them notice the world, and themselves, in richer ways.

If only she could get her mom's eyes right. She could never quite capture all the nuance they possessed. The eyes contained the light of a person, a collision of past and future, with soul secrets that couldn't stay hidden entirely. Where words failed, drawings spoke. They could speak a language all their own. They held the striking tension of whimsy and reverence, hope and fear, longing and duty. To express all that required the right combinations of forms and shadows.

Maybe the fourth attempt would be different.

She sang along to the praise music rising from her phone. She worshiped with her voice as well as her pen, pouring out the talents her Creator had entrusted to her, believing that someday others would see it as wise stewardship as well. Others including those who shared her last name.

Her bearded dragon supervised from under his terrarium lights.

"What do you think so far, Jeremy?" She kept her eyes on the paper, guiding the pen with a loose wrist. "This time will be different," she said, more in a prayer of assurance than in conversation.

It had to be different. Because *everything* was about to be different.

A chime cut into the song, bringing her sketching to a momentary halt. The final of the three reminders she had set blazed across the screen of her phone, in all caps: FOR REAL THIS TIME: LEAVE.

She sighed. Time bore down on two o'clock, and getting to the Kansas City Central Library down Main Street would take more minutes than she had before her mom arrived, promptly as always. Of all the times not to ruffle her mom, the day she told her she was leaving the country was it.

She slipped her pen back among its cohorts in the Gates Bar-B-Q cup at the top of her desk, then tapped pause on her playlist. "She's going to be mad, Jeremy."

He flicked his tongue, wishing her luck.

"Thank you, bud." She stepped over to his abode and stroked her fingertips down his spiny back. "I think I'm ready. But probably not."

In the week she'd had to prepare for their Friday afternoon coffee date, she had tried on several potential ways to break the news of her acceptance of the elementary art instructor job at the Redeemer International School of Prague, even practiced a few with her dad, but none of them had held up against the imagined scrutiny of Edie Vance. Her mom hadn't traveled farther than the other side of Missouri. It was one thing to tell her mom she was going halfway around the world. It was another to tell her she would be gone for two years. Still another to reveal she had to raise her own salary to be on mission at RISP.

All the things she needed to say bucked her mom's idea of what Chloe's life should be like "by this point." That seemed to be one of Edie Vance's most-repeated phrases—"by this point"—a constant reminder to Chloe that she was in some way always missing a mark she'd never agreed to meet.

"I had been married for four years by this point"—said on Chloe's last birthday. "All the girls your age have an advanced degree by this point"—said the previous Thanksgiving. "Aren't you tired of being a barista by this point?"—said more than once. Her mom's measure of an adult had nothing to do with mastering the art of conveying a magnificent collision in another's eyes or the ability to teach others how to do it.

Chloe stopped in her kitchen before heading out the door. Two containers of protein balls waited on the counter. So simple and easy to make, and a runaway bestseller with her coworker Sori's MBA classmates, especially as spring finals approached. Thanks to Sori, she had learned that her customers' wallets opened widest when presented with a healthy, filling snack in the most stressful points of the semester. Two protein balls huddled together in adorable little cellophane bags, and each bag was adorned with a sticker featuring an inspirational quote. The added touch made the treats all the more sellable, Sori said. After two years, the joint endeavor had given Sori real-world business experience and Chloe a savings surplus that would cover her flight to Prague, with some to spare.

She tucked the containers into her backpack and paused at the small mirror by the front door. Red curls as gregarious as ever. Freckles a little darker after spending more time in the embrace of the outdoors. But her eyes—those eyes. Emerald glinting from a dream so close the taste never left her tongue.

So close, yet one giant mom-shaped step away.

My boldness is in you, God.

She pulled open the door, then trooped down the stairs of her fourplex.

Out on the porch, her landlord, Seymour Bove, looked up from his usual chair where he worked on his afternoon crossword puzzle. Thick-frame glasses dominated his face. His short white hair offset his deep bronze complexion.

"Afternoon, Seymour!"

"Purse," he reminded her.

Her shoe scuffed against the concrete as she came to a halt. "Right." She set down her backpack against the brick facade and hustled back up the stairs. Her purse hung on the hook Seymour had installed by that little mirror specifically to help her remember to take her purse. Most days, it worked. Other days, it took a village.

By the time she arrived back on the porch, Seymour had helped himself to a treat. He stood by the door holding her backpack, crumbs on his lips.

"You're eating my fundraising," she playfully reprimanded him.

"This batch is better," he replied as if not hearing. "What's that I taste?"

She turned toward her bike in the opposite corner of the porch. "Almond extract. Like it?"

"Not bad. You late for work again?"

"Late, yes, but to meet my mom at the library. Figured I'd drop off more product with Sori while I'm there. She's working the coffee shop today."

"You're late meeting your mom?" He gave a low whistle.

"I question my choices too." She unlocked her bike and wheeled it toward him.

"You have a car, you know." He nodded toward the bright yellow Xterra in the driveway, wedged between their fourplex and the neighboring one. "Four wheels're better'n two when you're late. Not to mention an engine."

"Goldie and I have an agreement. I only drive her on the weekends. Gotta make her last."

"Junkyard don't care if a car runs or not."

"She's got plenty of life left, Seymour. Something I'm sure you can appreciate."

He looked up at her over the rims of his glasses. "Just for that, I'm taking another package." He swiped a cellophane-wrapped treat, then handed her the backpack.

She chuckled and zipped the bag. If her mom had been there to witness his act, she would have been incredulous. But a ten-dollar bill would "somehow" appear under Chloe's door before she got home, more than three times the value of the snacks.

Chloe strapped on her backpack and lifted her bike down the stairs. "See you later, Seymour. Keep everyone in line while I'm gone."

"Don't have to tell me twice."

3

----

en. The number of years Lauren Vance had given to Universal Health Systems.

Three. The number of minutes they had given her to pack her personal effects into a box.

One. The number of mistakes she had made. Just one. It was too late to do anything about it.

Her shadow stretched due east, pulling her away from the main door of the Universal office tower and all the charts, timelines, dry-erase boards, sticky notes, chintzy motivational posters, and stoic furniture—her entire daytime world and work since college. Her sweat and sacrifice now the legal property of a corporation that had turned its back on her.

Leave it all, they had said. Leave, the operative word. She was left behind, left out, left to fend for herself. No severance, no continuation of benefits, no proper goodbye.

She trailed across the parking lot with her lone box, led by the thin, dark figure that moved only when she did, an extension of her that seemed so real yet could not be dominated.

Car doors shut back-to-back two rows over. Three coworkers from her division chatted as they glided back to the building, the product of their afternoon coffee run in their hands. Their voices, mixed with a dash of laughter, carried across the distance. The ID badges clipped to their front pockets showed names she had said hundreds of times. She had meshed with their personalities, bonded with them over many inside jokes.

They looked her way and instantly grew quiet.

She switched the box to her opposite hip, concealing it as much as possible, even though it was pointless to try. Everything in her wanted to call out to them, to ask if they knew. Did everyone know? Surely Duncan did, but he still hadn't replied to her "please call me" text.

The trio gave a furtive last look before averting their eyes.

She forced her chin to stay up and veered left, farther away from them, widening the berth. In the end, the bond with Universal and its people was not a bond at all. Their "family," no family. It was all a masquerade, and she had played the fool.

Was that why Duncan wouldn't reply? All those chat messages, the lunches at their favorite spot, the happy hour commiseration, the sharing of reels over DMs to try to make each other laugh during mind-numbing meetings, even the flirtatious looks and light touches on the shoulder that seemed to scream his interest—had it all meant so little?

Surely he knew it was his #cubeselfie Instagram challenge that morning that had started all of it. She had tagged him in her caption. Surely he saw that her selfie accidentally included the inspiration board she had created on the wall of her cube for the electronic health care records system they were creating—including the picture of the interface prototype. Why didn't he warn her? Why didn't he tell her to take the post down before anyone else saw it? HR had called her within an hour.

What a fool. An incredible fool.

Her shadow seeped across her Honda Civic. She opened the trunk and set her box inside. The succulent poked out the open top. It had been a birthday gift from her sister. Along the bottom of the pot, Chloe had hand-lettered, "Beauty grows even in the barren land." Chloe had faith like that and believed everyone else should have it too. Her little sister was too inexperienced, too naive and protected, to understand that beauty too often was only a masquerade.

Lauren shut the trunk lid a little harder than she meant to.

She got into the car and shut the door. Engine on. Hands on the wheel. The car was ready to go where she commanded, one of the few things she still had control over.

She had been so careful, so strategic. Attentive to every decision. She had gone to community college for gen eds before transferring to a university to keep student debt at bay. She had bought a used car, paid for in cash. Saved a half year's income in an emergency fund. Maxed her retirement plan match. Circled her sixty-fifth birthday on her mental calendar of the future.

She had made so many sacrifices and smart decisions. Where had it gotten her? Alone, in the cold stare of a building that had sucked the vast majority of her waking hours. Alone, with only a succulent and a text stuck on Read.

Hot tears pushed up to her eyes. She forced them back down. She couldn't cry. Not here. Not ever. In that, she still had power too.

She reversed from her parking spot, turned the wheel hard to the right, and drove toward the exit, into the blankness.

To people like her little sister, life was an open canvas, ripe to show the possible. But that was not the native tongue of people like Lauren, who from a young age had been expected to think in probable. Probable was the only language she knew. It had kept her safe and centered—respected—for more than thirty years.

She could not tell anyone that probable had let her down. No matter what, she would not let her foolishness show. Especially not to her mom.

4

The downtown library had architectural appeal, Edie would give it that. As she and Grant stood on the sidewalk before the main entrance, she tilted her head back to take in the palatial columns that guarded the gold-plated doors. A bronze placard secured to the exterior wall revealed the building's original identity as a bank.

"You look nervous," Grant said.

"That's probably because I am."

"Why?"

She turned to him. "Our daughter made me come downtown, for one thing. This place is the den of thieves."

"It's perfectly safe, my love."

"The FBI has regional headquarters here for a reason," she countered. "The mafia still has their spoons in the stew, if you know what I mean."

"Edie." His simple, soft way of telling her she had started to slip into full-on Moria Mondell. He had used that technique throughout the past two years when caregiving for her mother had weighed particularly heavy upon her.

She clasped her hands tightly. "At least tell me why Chloe wants to meet with me."

"Not my place to tell."

"I'm your wife. You're supposed to tell me everything. It was in your vows."

"Which you wrote."

"And I meant every word."

He chuckled and placed a hand on her shoulder. "Telling you everything includes telling you when you need to relax." His gray eyes glinted with that mischievousness their youngest daughter had inherited tenfold. One of many reasons she fell in love with him.

"You're too soft when it comes to Chloe," she replied. "You always have been."

"I think she's turned out just fine."

"Fine? She's almost twenty-seven and works as a barista at a library. She should have an actual career by this point. And don't get me started on her relationship prospects. No boyfriend, only that . . . reptile thing."

Her mother had first called out Chloe's waywardness when Chloe was seven. "That one's on the wrong course," she had warned. "Too full of fanciful notions that come to nothing. You're allowing that, Edith. Mark my words."

Edie had given all she knew how to give to get both her girls on the right track. The lost sleep, the money spent, the gasoline used, all in pursuit of setting them up for stable and productive lives of education, careers, husbands, security—the wants of any rational young woman.

Only half of her progeny seemed to understand.

"Chloe's doing fine." Grant let go of her shoulder and took her hand in both of his. "Promise you'll hear her out."

Even after thirty-five years, his gaze and his presence centered her in ways nothing else did. He had been a peace from the first time they sat next to each other in the overwhelming lecture hall for American History 101. Her mother had strong opinions on Grant's treatment of Chloe, opinions that collided head-on with the check in Edie's own soul. Knowing which voice to listen to still proved perplexing.

She sighed. "I promise."

He kissed her hand, then headed back to the car he had illegally parked along the curb, much to the irritation of the drivers passing by on 10th. With a final wave, he eased down the street, off to his favorite butcher shop to find the sausage his arteries (and wife) begged him to stop consuming.

She girded herself, then turned for the gold doors.

Proud marble columns held up an art deco–style ceiling two stories above the granite lobby floor. Majestic chandeliers floated above the long rows of solid-wood bookcases. The shelves were lined with mighty spines of books that would either counteract moral bankruptcy or invite it in, one bestseller at a time.

The aroma of roasted beans wafted from the corner of the lobby directly to her right. The high-gloss floors carried into the nook where her daughter's workplace resided. The finely polished wood chairs and tables matched the hue of the library shelves just steps away. The counter and its fixtures were adorned with brass and gold that synced to the aesthetic of the surroundings.

Behind the counter, a woman who appeared to be a few years younger than Chloe looked up from her task. She wore her straight dark hair half pulled back and primly clipped at the crown of her head.

"What can I get started for you?" she asked as Edie approached.

"Actually, I don't know if I'm ready to order yet. My daughter is meeting me here. Perhaps you know her—"

"You're Chloe's mom."

"I am."

"She told me you were coming. She texted me that she's on her way."

"I see." Her daughter had texted her coworker rather than her mom. That seemed the congenial thing to do, and completely in line with the way Chloe had been raised.

"You can order anything you like," the young woman said. "It's on the house today. Technically on Chloe's employee account, but free to you either way." She lifted her hand and brushed her hair behind her shoulder. The curtain of strands pulled off her name tag.

"Sori," Edie read. "That's not a name you hear often."

"It's Korean," the barista said.

"You're Korean."

"My name is Korean. I'm American. Three generations American. But I have Korean lineage." Despite her smile, the tightness of her answer came through.

Edie shifted her weight from one foot to the other. Kids of the modern world had a level of sensitivity older generations couldn't relate to. A simple invitation to tell a person more about themselves didn't have to be the minefield they made it.

"Beautiful name," Edie said as a way of apology for any offense.

The girl only stared at her, a stiff smile strung across her face.

Did that mean Edie was supposed to make the next move? Maybe a unifying comment on Kim Jong Un's rascality? The new generation was the hardest to figure out.

"Would you like something to drink?" Sori said at last, saving Edie from one debate and launching her into the next. The menu board above Sori's head listed a seemingly infinite number of options.

Before she could reply, a man's moan resounded from the far corner of the nook. Edie turned. The man had splayed his upper half across the table. His arms dangled toward the floor. His clothes carried the filth of many days and nights.

Edie clutched her purse strap and returned to the task at hand. "Do you have anything that is not caffeinated or sugary?"

"We have a nice passion fruit herbal tea."

Another moan. Longer and guttural, like a caged animal.

Edie fought the urge to do anything but retrieve her wallet. "I'll take a small, please."

"I can make it hot or iced," Sori continued, clearly unaffected by the animalistic sounds emanating from the corner.

"Hot would be fine." She leaned closer to Sori and added at a softer volume, "Is he okay?"

23

Sori rang up her order, smile intact. "He's harmless. He's here almost every day."

That didn't assuage any fears. If anything, it assaulted her senses all the more. How could her daughter possibly enjoy working in a place like this? A single young woman with little experience with the world should not be so careless. Maybe it was a good thing Alzheimer's had stolen her mother's ability to register reality, so Edie didn't have to try to explain Chloe's choices.

No one could explain them.

5

Only eight minutes late. Not bad for Chloe time. She paused at the bottom of the steps to the main entrance and waited for her pulse to calm after the three-plus-mile bike ride. Inside that building, her mom waited, probably checking her watch every five seconds and muttering disapproval.

She took a cleansing breath and then headed up the steps.

The coffee shop was empty, save for Darryl asleep at his preferred table and Sori behind the counter wiping down surfaces. The only other evidence of human presence was a single, mostly full mug at a table nearest the bookshelves, accompanied by three napkins. Three, in case of a spill. Her mom's signature.

Sori noticed her weaving through the tables. "It's about time you showed."

"I know. I'm sorry." Chloe lifted the bar flap and let herself in. "Where is she?"

"In the restroom."

"Vibe?"

"Displeasure with her order and literally everything else on the menu, three dirty looks toward Darryl, and one random reference to the mafia. It should make your big reveal more . . . lively."

"Yeah." She tapped the edge of her fist against her thigh. Her mom would come around the corner any second.

"Look at me." Sori locked Chloe's gaze. "You can do this. You will do this."

Chloe grinned. "I can. I will."

"You leave in September, so you have to do this. It's now or never."

"Right." It was already the first Friday of May. Time dwindled quickly.

Her friend pointed at the straps of Chloe's backpack. "Did you bring more protein balls?"

"Yes." Chloe slid out of the straps and handed Sori the backpack. "Help yourself to a pack as recompense for managing my mom."

"Won't be nearly enough, but I'll take it." Sori placed the bag on the counter and retrieved the containers. Her first order of business was to unwrap a snack for herself. "I have your take from the week's sales in my bag," she said between bites. "And wow, are these good. Did you do something different?"

"Seymour said the same thing. Taste okay?"

"More than okay, girl. No wonder these things sell out." Another bite, larger than the last.

High heels clacked against the marble. Chloe turned the same moment her mom glided into the nook. *Glide* was the only way to describe the way her mom walked, all perfect posture and clothes that hung stylishly loose on her frame. Even at Grandma Moria's funeral, she'd carried the air of a woman who never ate chips in bed. She had regained noticeable color since the services two months prior. The puffiness around her eyes had decreased. All indicators that Chloe's strategic waiting for a "better time" to break the news about Prague to her mom had arrived.

Chloe waved. Her mom lifted the corners of her mouth, but it was a smile only in the loosest sense.

"Chloe," she said. "Nice to see you."

"Hi, Mom."

For a moment, they stood there in each other's presence, a shade of peace between them.

Then her mom spoke. "I thought we said two o'clock."

So it began. She turned to Sori, who nodded an encouragement. She snagged a package of protein balls and met her mom at the table. "Sorry I'm late. I brought you this." She slid the treat onto the table next to her mom's mug.

"Thank you," her mom said. "Your dad enjoys those."

Chloe lowered into the chair facing the service counter. Sori filled the pastry case, glancing at their table every so often. "I made this batch differently. You should try them."

Her mom nodded. "They are selling okay, then?"

Her mom's measuring stick had a way of shifting. It was best not to mention a dollar figure. "They're doing better than I could ask for," Chloe replied.

"That's good." Her mom reached for the mug of tea, seemed to remember she was protesting it, and instead folded her hands on the table. Her snack remained untouched.

Once more, their eyes met. Those pale brown eyes eluded Chloe's ability to get them right on paper, a shade like coffee with a splash too much cream. Why were they so hard to read?

Darryl's whimper interrupted the moment.

Her mom looked over her shoulder at him, then back at her. "That man has been making feral noises the whole time I've been here."

"He's harmless, Mom."

"That's what your friend said." Her mom scooted the tea farther away, then reached into her purse to retrieve a piece of paper. She handed it to Chloe. "I found this online."

Another job posting. Chloe resisted the heavy sigh pushing up from her gut. Meddling and printing from the internet were two of her mom's favorite activities. "This is for a UX designer," she said.

"And?"

"Do you know what a UX designer is?"

"I know it's better than this." Her mom circled a finger in the air, indicating their setting. "You'd have benefits and security, and don't you dare say insurance is a scam."

"It *is* a scam."

"Says the one who's never had to face significant medical bills. You should have seen how much insurance absorbed of your grandmother's expenses. I'm not sure where we would have been without it."

Seeing Grandma Moria's private medical bills would have been as big of an improbability as hearing her actually say hello when Chloe walked into the room. Most things Grandma Moria kept to herself, and that was perfectly okay in Chloe's estimation.

Her mom pointed at the paper. "You could have any job you want at this point, Chloe Grace, if only you'd try."

Sori caught Chloe's eye and shook her head, refuting the insistence that Chloe hadn't "tried" for anything.

Chloe rested her forearms on the table. "I told you I'm not after the cubicle life."

"Is there something morally objectionable about the cubicle life, as you call it?"

Plenty, in fact. Every moment being tracked and recorded in some way. The temporary walls that could be cleaned off and torn down at a moment's notice, much like the employment status of the people who lived most of the week between them. The slow degradation of one's true sense of self and the dreams of a bigger purpose for their lives that once burned bright and hot within. Cubicle dwellers dreamed the dreams others told them to.

"Your father never saw anything wrong with cubicle life," her mom contended. "Your sister doesn't either, nor do millions of other responsible citizens."

The last two words were clearly meant to sting. Chloe picked up the ignored protein balls and fiddled with the ribbon securing the cellophane bag. "They have all done well for themselves, but it's not for me."

"What is for you, then?"

There it was—the perfect segue. The moment to launch into the well-rehearsed speech. Chloe wrapped the ribbon around her right index finger. "Mom," she began, "I want to tell you something." So far, so good.

Her mother tilted her head to the side.

Chloe's pulse kicked into higher gear. Pangs seared through her veins. She pulled the ribbon tighter around her finger. "Have you ever had something you've always wanted to do? An idea that wouldn't leave you alone? An experience you wanted to have that you were sure would make you feel alive and fully appreciate your time on earth in ways you can't even imagine?"

Her mom blinked. "What on earth are you talking about?"

"A dream, Mom. Have you ever had a dream?"

For a moment, her mom's eyes drifted to the expanse of the library behind Chloe. Perhaps she searched her memory, remembered some faded ambition of her younger self. But a firmness soon settled in her expression and tone. "Nothing I'm not glad I let go of."

Her chest hitched. The bulwark around her mom was thick and jagged.

"Chloe, what are you getting at? What is this all about?"

She unwound the ribbon and folded her hands together. Behind the counter, Sori gestured for her to speak, to say what she had come to say. But the strength of her argument faded by the second, too weak to survive the scale over the defensive barrier. She had no backup plan.

Lord, she prayed.

On the side wall of the coffee nook hung a row of large, framed prints honoring classic novels. The middle one depicted a family standing by a pickup truck loaded with their possessions. The Joad family of *The Grapes of Wrath*, a librarian had explained, on their way from Oklahoma to California, trying to escape the devastation of the dust bowl and Great Depression. They were setting off on the greatest adventure of their lives—to save their lives, to find their lives.

"I . . ." Chloe tried again. God bless, where were the words?

The watercolored Joads stared back at her. The artist had pulled off what she herself labored to do, revealing in their eyes the battle within their souls—the notes of fear combated surety that something better was out there, beyond their vision. They longed for that better, risked for that better, despite the odds against them. Out there on the road, surely their hope for the better would become their sight.

The road led to the better. The road led to changed perspective, changed fortunes. The road was an experience her mom had never had.

"Chloe?" her mom prompted.

The road! That was what her mom needed! Adventure had a way of shattering fear. Chloe could shake her mom free of the routine of life and awaken within her an understanding of the value of risking for the better. Because the better was out there, beyond their vision. If her mom tasted adventure, she would be more receptive to the idea of Prague. Surely she would!

Chloe grinned. "Let me take you on a road trip."

Her mom furrowed her brow. "I'm sorry?"

More words rolled off Chloe's tongue, surprising and inexplicable and somehow right. "A road trip. We could go together. The first week of June."

The folds across her mom's brow deepened. "Since when have you ever wanted to go on a road trip? More importantly, since when have I?"

Chloe's pulse thrummed as dot after dot connected. "We could have an adventure, just you and me. We could see what's out there, see how other people live, make memories all our own. And it would all be my treat." Whether her bank account agreed with that last promise was a matter for another time. The trip idea held so much potential, so many answers. She held her breath, waited.

Her mom leaned back in her chair and folded her arms. "A trip?"

"Yes."

"Is this really why you wanted to meet today?"

"Of course."

Her mom angled her chin down and peered at Chloe from under that tightened brow. "You couldn't have asked me this over the phone?"

"Well . . ."

Behind the counter, Sori could only shrug, as if to say, *You're on a different script now.* The characters on the prints looked on. Everyone stood by for an explanation, including Chloe.

And then it came, roaring forward with enough force to straighten her back. "Actually, downtown is the perfect place to get a little teaser for our trip. Come on, I'll show you." She rose and gathered her mom's unfinished tea.

"I have to see *more* of downtown?"

"It'll be worth it, trust me. Let me take care of this mug, and I'll be right back." Chloe scurried behind the counter and dumped the tea down the drain.

Sori came up to her and whispered, "A trip? Chloe, what are you getting yourself into?"

"No idea, but can I ask you for a favor?"

"Sure."

"Will you ask one of the librarians to make a list of all the book-related Midwest towns they can think of?"

6

Lauren pulled squarely into her designated carport, opened her door to double-check her positioning, then cut the engine. Box in hand, she trekked up to her third-floor condo. Quiet draped everything, a silent reminder that everyone else was gainfully employed. Still, she refused to let it dig into her mind and pry open what she held with fierceness. She would not cry.

Shoes off by the door, purse on the hook, box on the leather couch, phone on the armrest. All without a single blip of emotion. Not a single one. She could outrun it. She could be the kind of strong Duncan would regret letting slip through his fingers. Emotions were highly inconvenient things anyway.

She lifted the succulent from the box and settled it into its new home on the end table next to the glass balcony door. It added a certain charm to the room, a rustic-chic accent. A happy splash of green life to a mostly monotone room. A visual contrast that was almost Instagram worthy.

She smiled.

The wild wave of tears engulfed her without warning. The unstoppable torrent erased the smile, contracted her posture, brought her to a heap on the couch.

Why?

The question raged against the walls of her mind. *Why? Why? Why!*

She hugged her knees to her chest and buried her face in them. Her shoulders racked with sobs. Her own mistake was the only answer she had to live with. If only she had never followed him on Instagram. If only she had never followed him at all.

The streams of light through the balcony door offered a sliver of warmth in the great, cold alone. She curled into them, allowed the wave to crash as it would.

Eventually it tamed enough for the sobs to quiet to a hiccup. She lifted her head, wiped her face with the backs of her hands. Her condo seemed smaller, the vaulted ceilings lower than before. Everything constricted when the air was taken out of it.

A chime from her phone.

She grabbed it off the arm of the couch. Surely it was Duncan, at long last. But the message wasn't from him. It was from her dad. True to form, he had sent a GIF, his preferred mode of communication. The image was of a cartoon pig standing upright and holding two pinwheels. Bold letters arched above his head:

TGIF!

Though a grin sprouted on her lips, the innocent fun contrasted sharply with the pinch in her heart. It was not a Friday worth being thankful for. It was a Friday worth forgetting. Still, she sent back a GIF of a cat in a party hat tossing glitter. Underneath, she typed,

Hope you have fun plans for the weekend.

Her thumbs begged to add, *Can you talk?* A plea for her daddy to help her sort it out, like he did when she was young and they would talk over a drive around the city, maybe a stop for ice cream. But there was a significant difference between telling him she had done poorly on a test and telling him she had tanked her career. He couldn't rescue her from her grown-up problems, or from her mom's vapid disapproval if she found out.

She alone had to sort it out. To do so, she had to take back control over what she could. No more crying. Crying solved nothing.

"You're better than that, Lauren," she pronounced over herself. She sucked in a cleansing breath, pushed down the remaining tightness in her throat. "You'll figure it out. You always do."

She dried her face, rose to her feet. What she needed was to throw herself into what she could accomplish—fueled by Taylor Swift. She opened her playlist, cranked up the volume on her phone, and let the opening chords of "Ready for It?" drive her onward.

She grabbed the box from her cubicle. Everything inside needed a new place to roost. The framed picture of her parents went on her nightstand. The bronze hedgehog statuette complemented her mantel. And the suspense novel she had been working through on lunch breaks fit into the bookcase in the corner of her living room.

She paused at the shelves and ran her fingertips along the row of spines, all arranged by height and color. Many had been gifts from her mom as she cleaned out Grandma Moria's study, "because I know you'd appreciate them," she had said. Her mom had never actually asked what kinds of books she would appreciate. They were all well outside Lauren's preferred genres. Regardless, she had read every one in case her mom ever wanted to discuss them.

They sat on the shelf collecting dust and the admiring glances from her mom when she visited, but they never prompted a conversation.

There would be no admiring glances Lauren's way during her mom's planned visit the next day if news of her firing got out. Lauren couldn't let that happen. Not yet. Not until . . . until she could figure out what followed "until."

She turned from the shelves, skipped her playlist to "Shake It Off," and danced every remaining item in the box to a place in her condo. Then she played the song again. And again. And one more time.

By the end of the fourth play, she had unpacked and recycled the box, and deleted Instagram from her phone.

7

Chloe led her west along 10th and across a narrow street separating the library building's block from the next. Edie had to double-step to catch up to her daughter's breakneck strides.

"Chloe, slow down. We're not racehorses. Where are we going?"

"Not far," her daughter replied with a little too much glee.

The sidewalk was pocked with leaf-shaped decay and dark stains from liquid it was best not to know too much about. Edie carefully sidestepped the freshest-looking ones.

About thirty feet into the new block, her daughter came to a sudden halt. She spun on her heel to face Edie and spread her arms wide above her head. "Ta-da! We're here!"

Edie pulled down her brow. "We're where?"

"At the Community Bookshelf!" She gestured to the structure hovering over them.

Edie squared up to it. The facade of whatever building they stood in front of was decorated to look like a row of book spines, each two stories tall. The entire building from end to end boasted the larger-than-life works with titles that anyone with even a scant knowledge of the classics would have recognized. *O Pioneers!*,

Catch-22, Invisible Man, The Lord of the Rings, The Collected Poems of Langston Hughes. All taught in schools. All treasures from which her mother could have recited lines.

An involuntary "Oh" slipped from her lips. She quickly followed it up with "Look at that."

"It's something, isn't it?" Chloe settled her hands on her hips in obvious satisfaction. "This is actually the library parking garage. That's just a decorated privacy screen we're looking at."

The artwork would have been even more wonderful if someone hadn't planted trees in the flower beds right in front of it. The foliage blocked several of the spines. Edie craned her neck and could just make out the title of one of the hidden novels, *To Kill a Mockingbird*.

"What do you think?" Chloe asked.

"It's definitely something." All her life she had lived in Kansas City and had not been aware of the artwork's existence. Had her mother known about it?

"People come from all over to see this, and the library," Chloe said. "I meet lots of tourists."

That seemed a tad extreme, especially considering the ilk of some patrons in the library. Then again, book lovers had a perplexing devotion. Her mother had always dreamed of touring the English countryside in search of the worlds of Austen, Shakespeare, and other maestros.

"This, Mom, is what I wanted to show you. This represents the first stop of what I know will be an unforgettable adventure." Chloe's grin widened. "We're going to go on a bookish road trip!"

Edie blinked. "A what?"

"A bookish road trip," Chloe repeated, as if that helped in the slightest. She stepped in front of Edie and took her hands. "We'll go around to different towns that have a connection to a book or an author. Many of these books you're looking at have a connection to the Midwest in some way—that's why the community selected them to be part of the artwork. Like Willa Cather." She nodded over her shoulder toward *O Pioneers!* "She grew up in Nebraska. And Langston Hughes grew up in Kansas, and Mark Twain, who is somewhere up there, was from Missouri. Wouldn't that be fun to see their hometowns or the settings for their novels? I know how much you love books."

In contrast to the confident flow of words from her offspring, Edie struggled to find any herself. Especially to the contention that she loved books. She had never read out of love for *books*, not that either of her daughters knew that or needed to know. "I . . . am familiar with many of these works, yes. Your grandmother knew them better."

"Then what do you say? Let's go explore!"

The joy in her daughter's eyes, the eagerness with which she gripped Edie's hands, evoked the image of a freshly bathed little girl with a cherub face looking up at her from princess bedsheets, asking for "just one more chapter" from *Charlotte's Web*. So enthralled was that little redhead with what transpired between a young pig and a wise old spider. The book spine for that classic sat prime amid the bookshelf artwork too. Her daughters hadn't experienced the feeling of abandonment to a book they were too young to read alone, and it remained one of the few proud moments she had as a mother.

"It would all be my treat," her daughter reminded her. "My pleasure."

It wasn't Chloe's pleasure she was most hung up on. What did that say about her mothering? If only Grant were there to help her sort out all the things twisting inside her.

She wet her lips before responding. "Let's see what Dad has going on the first week of June and we'll discuss."

Her statement may as well have been a declaration that Jesus had returned, based on the way her daughter leaped in the air and laughed.

She indulged the response, even indulged her daughter's request to get a picture of her on the steps of the parking garage, which were designed to look like a stack of books. But the sense clung to her that the proposed trip was more than just adventure seeking. It was a shell over something unspoken, and shells almost always proved fragile.

8

The evening stretched out like a blank tundra, and Lauren stood alone at the very far edge of it. It was hard to convince the brain not to focus on the blaring empty space instead of what could be accomplished.

A run. A run would keep her mind and body busy in the right direction.

She laced up her sneakers and headed out the door. The Indian Creek Trail, which snaked for miles through the city, passed right by her complex. She joined up to the trail and pushed herself down the endless pavement.

Her breath settled into sync with the pump of her legs. She kept a ramrod-straight posture, abs in tight, and measured her momentum with the swing of her arms. The more calories she burned, the more the gloom of the day would wear away, slipping down her neck and back amid the streams of sweat. She could prove her dominance over it.

One mile bled into two, into three.

But the unanswerable questions kept pace. What next? Where did she turn? Who was going to hire someone who was fired? No amount of massaging the truth would explain why she was suddenly let go when she had clearly been on the leadership track.

How could she possibly polish enough to hide the fact she had been a fool?

A hard lump formed in her throat. She pushed herself another mile, harder than the three before it, until her legs were beat to a gelatin state and her sides cried for mercy.

Back at her condo, she showered, changed, and let her stomach cry. If her stomach cried, it meant she would not. She filled her largest water bottle to keep the strongest pangs quieted and settled on her couch to stream a movie. Dozens of options appeared on the screen. She scrolled through list after list until finally one thumbnail made her pause. *The Outsiders*, the movie that had been her company on countless Saturday nights as a teen.

She selected the film, curled around her water bottle, and laid her head on the pillow. The Francis Ford Coppola classic took her back into the reminiscent world she had first encountered on the pages of a required reading assignment.

Sleep drifted over her about the time Ponyboy and Johnny discovered their hideout from police consumed by flames. She startled awake at the cacophony of gunshots at the end. Sunlight still hung in the sky outside her balcony door, and she was still alone, left with only people who couldn't talk back.

This would be her life for the foreseeable future. She would slump toward the next bank of unfilled hours, unsure where to focus. If only she had someone, anyone, to tell her she was okay. That she was still acceptable.

If only she had someone who wouldn't turn their back because of a mistake.

9

- - - - - -

As evening gathered, Chloe stepped onto the porch of the fourplex carrying Jeremy in his terrarium and a tote bag of cleaning supplies. She breathed in deep. The aroma of meat wafted from the smoker in the side yard and hugged the building. To Seymour Bove, Friday nights were for barbecue. Smoked, grilled, roasted, basted, slathered, or dry-rubbed, it didn't matter the technique. In his own humble admission, he "didn't need an American Royal crown to know what makes a barbecue king."

The pitmaster played Solitaire in his usual chair, where he could oversee the smoker.

"What's on tonight?" she asked.

"Ribs. Be done in about thirty." He glanced up from his game and narrowed his brow at the terrarium. "You gotta do that out here? That lizard gives me the willies."

"It's the easiest place to wash it out. Besides, Jeremy likes to explore the grass." She descended the front steps and set the glass enclosure next to the sidewalk. Gently she lifted her bearded dragon from his perch on the climbing branch and set him in the grass, which was still warm despite the sun melting its yellows across the horizon like butter. She dropped his little beach ball in the grass next to him. He padded over and headbutted it. She laughed and pushed it back toward him.

"Like a cat, that thing," Seymour muttered as he smacked a card in place.

"You'd like him if you spent some time with him. He's very friendly."

He harrumphed. "Rather have a cat."

Her mom had said the same thing. Chloe chuckled and moved all the other items from the terrarium to the grass. "I suppose I shouldn't bother asking you to take care of him while I'm in Prague, then."

"I ain't taking no living thing from you, least of all that devil. Why you want to go to Prague anyway?"

"I told you, I got the job teaching art at the international school, and I might get a little side job teaching English to nationals."

"They ain't got a language over there already?"

"They do. It's . . . uh . . . something?"

He dipped his chin. "Seems you're the one needs some teachin'."

She grinned and carried the empty terrarium and bag of supplies to the side of the porch nearest the smoker, where a garden hose curled neatly under a spigot. "I do intend to learn as much as I teach when I'm there. Probably more."

"You really leaving in September for two years?" he asked.

She flipped on the faucet and aimed the spray at the glass. "Yes, sir. Got my visa and papers and everything."

"Your parents know?"

"My dad does."

"That's why you met your mom today? To break her heart?"

She turned off the water and doused the inside of the enclosure with Dawn dish soap. "Tried to tell her, actually, but it came out slightly different than I expected."

"How different?"

She set the bottle down. "I'm taking her on a road trip in a few weeks."

"What's a road trip got to do with telling your mom you're moving to another country?"

"I hope the road can tell me that, Seymour."

He tsked and snapped a card off the deck in his hand. "Lotsa teachin'," he mumbled. He wasn't wrong.

By the time Chloe had the terrarium cleaned and Jeremy bathed and back in her apartment, the ribs had reached fall-off-the-bone perfection. Seymour dished her up a generous portion alongside a slice of Tippin's apple pie, the only kind of store-bought pie he could tolerate. She joined him on the porch chairs, balancing her plastic plate on her lap as she ate.

The cool of the evening met them there, pleasing their skin as much as the smoky meat pleased their palettes. Sauce smeared on her cheeks and collected on her fingertips. Her company didn't bring up the topic of the trip, nor Prague, nor her mom. He ate and let eat. When she finished the last rib on her plate, he brought her another one.

"One to grow on," he claimed.

Later that night, Sori texted her a picture of a handwritten list of cities one of the librarians had compiled. Thirteen of those listed, when connected via Google Maps, created a crude circle through five states, with Kansas City as the hub.

Chloe grinned, then sat down to her sketchbook.

10

Y ou're really not going to tell me?" Edie switched off the bathroom light and headed to their bed.

Grant continued reading the Joel C. Rosenberg thriller in his hands. "Nothing more to say than I think you should go."

Two pumps—exactly two pumps—of lotion every night. She rubbed it into her forearms and hands with vigor, willing it to ward off the crepe and sag most women her age suffered. "She clearly clued you in on what she was planning to talk to me about. Can't you at least tell me if this trip was it?"

"Why do you question it?"

"Because I do. I question everything."

He glanced up at her. "So I've noticed."

"You stop while you're ahead, sir." She finished rubbing in the lotion and peeled back the covers. Her bare feet slid into the caress of the fresh Egyptian cotton, the best that Macy's carried. The kind her mother would approve. "Don't think I didn't see that little look of surprise when she told you she wants to take me on a trip."

"What look?"

"You're not fooling me, Grant Harris."

He laid his book in his lap, thumb marking his place. "If Chloe wanted to give you the Eiffel Tower, you'd insist she tell you how she got the money."

"Wouldn't you wonder?" She flapped the covers over her legs and settled against her pillows. "Our child is not exactly the most detail oriented, and it takes that kind of thinking to achieve such lofty goals."

"You mean like Lauren?" he asked.

"I didn't say that."

He twisted his mouth to the side and returned to his book.

"You think I'm wrong?" she pressed.

"I think Chloe's far more capable than you think."

"Explain."

In the methodical movements he always had when he geared up for a speech of some kind, he tucked a bookmark into the pages and laid his book and his bifocals on his nightstand. He turned to her, hands folded across his middle-age pudge. "Chloe is one of the most creative problem solvers I've ever known. She sees connections I never would have and further into the future than I ever could. She has an unshakable faith that what she believes in will come to pass. Those are qualities worth as much admiration as Lauren's abilities." He turned back for his lamp switch and added, "A little emulation also wouldn't hurt."

"Was that meant to be an insult?"

"I don't insult. I observe. Good night, my love." He switched off his lamp and pulled his pillow flat against the mattress before he lay down sideways, back turned to her.

Observation nothing. When it came to their youngest daughter, he was "too blind to know he was blind." That was what her mother used to say about people who couldn't see common sense if it was screaming in their face.

She switched off her own lamp and kneaded her pillows until they offered the right support in the right places, like she used to do for her mother in those final days when a second stroke was imminent. Those long, sleepless nights at her bedside. The longing for the things that would never be, the words that would never be spoken, the touch that had never—

She shook away the memories. They were the past. Nothing she could do about them now. Nothing she ever could have done, even if Alzheimer's and all its bruteness hadn't intruded.

She closed her eyes and willed sleep to outrun the recollections that rose with the moon.

11

The hours before Lauren's mom arrived at her condo were when its many flaws came into glaring light. Cobwebs appeared from nowhere in the corner of the living room. The stove's glass cooktop had a weird stain along the edge of the main burner. The kitchen sink had a faint odor from the garbage disposal. The baseboards in the hall bathroom needed a good scrub. She cleaned instead of eating breakfast, employed all her focus into what brought the greatest productivity.

She broke for half an hour to walk down the street to the farmers' market for red tulips. She arranged the striking stems in a Waterford vase and placed it on the coffee table between two coordinating serving bowls of raspberries and sliced apricots. As the minutes ticked down, she double-checked all sides of the two bone-china teacups and saucers and retrieved the carafe of freshly brewed coffee from the kitchen.

At nine o'clock sharp, her mom arrived at her door, long bob styled pin-neat, fingernails gleaming, and cardboard box in her hand.

"You look lovely this morning, Lauren," she said as she stepped inside.

"As do you." Lauren shut the door and followed her to the living room.

Her mom placed the box on the side table next to the succulent. "I brought some things for you from Grandma's house. I found them as I was preparing for the estate sale. Is this new?" She pointed at the succulent.

Lauren drew in her breath. "It was a gift." She held still, bracing for more prods.

Fortunately, her mom shifted her attention back to the box. She drew out a silver hairbrush and a matching handheld mirror, the gaudy antique kind with no practical modern use except maybe as elaborate decorative accents to a bedroom. "These were your grandmother's. She would have wanted them to go to someone who would appreciate them. These are heirloom quality, so they are worth something."

Worth something to whom wasn't clear.

"They are lovely," Lauren replied. Not once in her life would she ever use them.

Her mom put the items back, then motioned for them to move to the couch. "I also put aside her silver service set for you. Do you remember the set?"

Lauren emulated her mom's ramrod-straight posture as they sat on their respective cushions. "The one with the cream cup and sugar bowl she kept in her curio?"

"That's the one. It's a beautiful set, and it will prove useful someday when you entertain special guests, such as your in-laws." She punctuated the insinuation by raising her eyebrows.

Lauren pulled on a smile. "I'm sure it will. Coffee?"

"Yes, please." Her mom gave a once-over to the spread on the coffee table as Lauren poured the steaming liquid into their cups. A satisfied sigh hummed from her lips. Edie Vance's approval code wasn't that hard to crack.

Lauren pinched the edge of a saucer and brought it to her mom's waiting hands.

"Thank you." Her mom gripped the handle and paused before lifting the cup to her lips. "Speaking of in-laws, have you started seeing anyone?"

Their conversations were as predictable as the length of day. Lauren reached for the milk and added a splash to her own cup. Pale swirls blended into the dark. "Not at the moment."

"Are you meeting anyone?"

"I expect him along in three to five years."

Her mom arched an eyebrow. "You stole that from Chloe."

"With permission." She stirred stevia into her milky coffee.

"I don't understand why neither of you seem to be in much of a hurry. So many girls your age are mothers by this point."

"I'm focused on other things right now." It was the only truth she dared to speak. She tapped the spoon lightly on the cup's lip, the way she had watched Grandma Moria do. The way ladies were supposed to, especially ladies who wanted to be married and entertain their in-laws and keep a spotless home, a cadre of sophistication she might not ever belong to.

"You might rethink your focus areas," her mom said. "Thirty-two is not the new twenty."

Lauren took a long, slow drink. The sweetener took the edge off the bitterness of the coffee, but not of the comment. The only thing worse would be if her mom asked about her job, which was generally the follow-up when the marriage portion of the conversation ended.

She gently replaced her cup onto her saucer and guided the conversation to safe topics. "How are things coming with the estate sale preparations? Sounds like you're making progress."

"Your dad pesters me about hiring it out."

"Why don't you?"

"What else do I have to do? Your father's working most days. I have only so many women's ministry events to help plan. Besides, it's not like my sister wants to pitch in."

"Have you talked to Aunt Gab since the funeral?"

"Gabriella," her mom corrected, rebuffing the nickname everyone else in the family used. "No, I haven't."

Asking her mom if she had tried—aiming the same directness at her—would only make things worse. Lauren crossed her ankles. "Maybe Dad is right. Maybe you should hire out the estate sale. They would know how to organize and price everything."

"I don't want a stranger deciding what items are important enough to keep and what aren't."

"You can still go through everything first, Mom."

"Then I might as well price it too." Her mom punctuated the statement with another sip of her coffee.

Refusal played a big role in her mom's life. It had edged out rationality more than once.

The lull stretched to an uncomfortable length. The topic of Lauren's career, and all the related plans she was expected to have there too, inched closer. If only she could have a nice, long buffer from any prying questions, an assured break from her mom's prodding, at least until she could figure out what to do next.

Just as Lauren prepared to ask what other interesting finds her mom had discovered in Grandma Moria's house, her mom clinked her cup onto her saucer and announced, "I have news."

"Oh?"

Her mom slipped the chinaware onto the coffee table and retrieved her phone from her purse next to her feet. "Your dad also has a lot to say about this."

Lauren put her coffee aside and waited as her mom unlocked the screen and brought up a text conversation with Chloe.

In it was a picture of a hand-drawn map.

12

A road trip?" Her oldest daughter looked again at the image on Edie's phone.

On the map, a yellow star over Kansas City represented their beginning. Jutting due west from it was the start of a red dotted line that pinged between the proposed stops. First to Lawrence, Kansas, then onward west to Wamego. North to Concordia before driving into Red Cloud, Nebraska. A long, sharp cut northeast through Omaha. Eastward to Winterset, Iowa, then to Iowa City, then a quick trip up to Dyersville. South to Hannibal, Missouri, before hitting St. Louis. Next to the southwest quadrant of the state, to Mansfield and Branson. Then cutting through Arkansas to get to Sallisaw, Oklahoma, followed by Tulsa, then back home to Kansas City.

In all, nine days of travel.

"Chloe is convinced it will be a trip of a lifetime," Edie said.

Lauren tilted her head to the side. "Since when does our family do road trips?"

Edie huffed. She and her brunette beauty had always been in sync. She laid her phone in her lap. "Chloe said she wants to spend more time together, and by 'spend time together,' she apparently means trapping ourselves in her yellow jalopy and driving endless miles of back roads to see things with at least a mild association with books."

"I didn't know Chloe liked books so much. You, yes, but not her."

Across the room, her daughter's shelves displayed all the books that had migrated one by one from her mother's study. Edie had read only a few of them cover to cover. "Liking books has nothing to do with liking the thought of spending two days traversing Nebraska. What could possibly be so interesting in Nebraska?"

"Aunt Gab lives there. Maybe you could stop—"

"Absolutely not. I have no interest in seeing that ridiculous 'farm,' as she calls it." The weird collection of beasts her younger sister had amassed over the years perplexed everyone with a bit of sense and had never been far from their mother's lips when the subject of Gabriella was brought up.

Lauren reached for her coffee and took a drink. "What did Dad have to say about the trip?"

"He said it would be good for me to get away for a while. And that I need to give Chloe a chance and not offer any 'critiques' of her plans, including the jalopy part."

Her daughter nodded, clearly taking it all in. "Maybe he's right."

"Please, not you too."

Lauren held the saucer with both hands. "It does sound like a unique trip. Odd, but unique."

Everyone in her family had suddenly lost all rationality. How could she possibly be the only one who saw the risks of the trip that clearly had more to it than anyone wanted to tell her? She shook her head. "The trip is not the issue, per se. You know your sister, Lauren. We're likely to take a wrong turn and end up in Canada."

"She has GPS on her phone. That should be enough to prevent inadvertent border crossings."

"Now you definitely sound like your dad. It's almost like you all coordinated this to get me out of the—" She squared up to

Lauren. "There's something you're not telling me. Some reason why you're so eager for me to go on this trip."

Her daughter went still. "Why would you think that?"

"Because your dad knows the real reason behind this trip, and he refuses to tell me."

Lauren's shoulders relaxed. "I wouldn't know anything about that. I haven't talked to Chloe in a while."

"Maybe you need bonding time with Chloe more than I do, then." She righted. The idea was so brilliant it warmed her from head to toe. "You should come too!"

Lauren puckered her brow. "Me?"

"Yes! A girls' trip. We all get more time together, and you'll ensure we stay on course. It's a win-win."

Her daughter shook her head. "Chloe invited you. She didn't invite me."

"I'm inviting you."

"But—"

"*I* am inviting you. If Chloe wants me to go, then she needs to have both of us along."

Lauren quickly set down her coffee. "Mom, I can't—" Her words stopped there, her gaze stuck on the cup on the table.

"Can't what? Can't get the time off? I thought you said the other day you had no idea what you were going to do with all the time you had saved up."

"No, not that."

"Then what?"

Red tinted her daughter's cheeks. She flitted her eyes to Edie's, then back to her lap.

"Surely it's not finances." Lauren was far too careful for that to be the barrier. Besides, it wasn't a tour of England, it was a road trip around the heartland.

Lauren picked at her thumbnail, an uncouth habit since childhood.

"What's the problem?" Edie asked again.

Finally her daughter looked up and smiled. "It's nothing I can't sort out."

"Great. So I can tell Chloe you're going too?"

Her daughter nodded.

Relief swept through her. She picked up her coffee and took a grateful sip.

Grant would be thrilled. Chloe would be appeased. And she would be secure. Everyone would be happy. She had managed to find a way to weave disparate things together. Sometimes the difference between an idea and wisdom was a simple tweak.

13

"O f course." What else could Chloe say when her mom told her she would go only if Lauren came? Calling her mom out for obvious self-protection would only drive the woman's heels in deeper. So Chloe choked back the words and said, "Of course I'll book the hotels for three people."

"Of course," she said when her sister texted to say it wasn't her idea.

"Of course," she said to her dad when he called to ask if she was really okay with the revision. "I need to tell Lauren about Prague as well anyway." She smiled through the reply, pulling a positive tone into her words. But a weight tugged on her chest. If her mom didn't trust her to plan nine days in middle America, how would she ever believe she could plan an entire life in another country?

The verse she had studied that morning replayed in the back of her mind: *Only in his own hometown is a prophet without honor.* The belief of those closest to you was the hardest to earn. They knew too many of your sins and failures.

"Do you really have the leeway in your savings for this?" her dad asked. "I could loan you—"

"No, Popsie. This is not your responsibility. This was my idea, my plan. I can do this. Mom needs to see me do this. They both do. I'll never convince them otherwise."

"You don't have to prove anything to anyone."

"Yes," she said. "I do."

He sighed. "Are you sure you want to go through with this?"

She clung to hope, the only solid thing she had, and said, "Of course." Just because the prophet wasn't believed didn't mean he was wrong. Only time—and an altered perspective—changed how he was remembered.

The morning of the first Thursday in June, she stood on the porch of the fourplex with Jeremy's carrier in one hand and a tote bag in the other. She downloaded final instructions for her boy's care to Sori as Seymour wheeled her suitcase to the Xterra.

"Only use Dawn soap on his terrarium," she said. "All the food he can eat is on the list in this bag. Text me if you're ever in doubt."

"Got it."

"You're sure you don't mind keeping him for the week?" she asked, setting the carrier and bag aside.

"Not at all."

"If it goes well, maybe we could extend it by, say, two years?"

Sori arched an eyebrow. "Let's see how the week goes first."

"Fair enough. And you have the extra protein balls I made frozen and ready for summer session?"

"Got it covered." Sori glanced toward the old man loading the suitcase into the cargo area, shoving the bag into the spot next to the cooler of barbecue chicken he insisted Chloe take. "He's worried about your car holding up."

"I know. My dad too. I've been filling her with premium unleaded and prayers for a week. All I can do now is trust we'll be okay."

Sori shook her head and grinned. "Spoken like the Chloe I know."

"You mean illogical?"

"There's a fine line between illogical and faith. You straddle it well." She elbowed Chloe, eliciting a chuckle.

57

"I'll miss you, Sori."

"I'll miss you too."

Seymour shuffled through the grass in his house slippers. "You're loaded up. You best get goin', now."

"I'm headed that way," Chloe promised.

He hobbled up the steps, pulling himself forward with a strong grip on the handrail. "Sure will be quiet around here."

"I'll miss you too," she said.

"I didn't say nothin' about missin' nobody." His tone was curt, but he extended his hand to hers. Paper bills poked into her palm. He quickly pulled away, leaving them behind.

Chloe shook her head and pushed her hand back toward his. "I can't accept this."

"You already did. Besides, I know where you keep your extra protein things."

"Sori already took those to sell at the university." She wiggled her hand in the air in insistence he take back his money.

"Wasn't usin' future tense."

She paused. Realization dawned. He had a key to her apartment and an open welcome. She grinned. "You scoundrel."

"Not my fault you're lousy at bookkeepin'." He pointed a crooked finger at the bills. "Treat your mama right. She'll come round."

"Yes, sir."

For a long moment, they stood gaze to gaze.

"Is this where we hug?" she asked.

"Oh heck it ain't." He turned and shuffled to the morning paper that waited on his chair.

"Someday, Seymour," she said to his back.

He muttered something that sounded a lot like "Not even when I'm dead."

The big softie.

"I'll give you a hug," Sori said and wrapped her in an embrace. The squeeze was firm and centering. "Don't let them kick you around too much, okay? Stand your ground, and just . . ." Her friend pulled back, looked her in the eyes. "Be all that I know you are."

"Which is what?"

Sori gripped her shoulders. "I'm going to speak in alliteration."

"I love it when you do."

"Chloe Vance, you are loving and lionhearted and limitless and—"

"Late," Seymour cut in.

Sori playfully rolled her eyes. "He's such a mood killer."

Their shared laughter was the best parting gift.

After one last hug for Sori, she cooed goodbye to Jeremy, told him to be good, told her landlord to do the same, then climbed into her Xterra. She fired up the engine. Soon the road would be under them, coaxing them loose from the everyday they cloaked themselves with. What would they see then? What would be revealed? Would it be better than where they started?

She bowed her head, closed her eyes, and whispered one more time to the only ears that could hear, "Take us where we are meant to go."

14

The full sun blared directly into the commuters' windshields, bringing the morning rush into downtown to a crawl. Lauren's rideshare driver inched along with the traffic. She checked her Garmin watch. Still plenty of time before she was due at their meetup point, which, for reasons that baffled them all, Chloe had chosen to be a greasy spoon in the Crossroads district just south of the high-rises. She swiped up on her watch face, checking her current calorie burn. The effects of her morning run still churned, ticking the number higher.

She cleared out of the display and hugged her overnight bag. Her suitcase rode in the back seat next to her.

"We'll still be there by nine," her driver said over his shoulder.

"No worries," she told him. If only she could believe her own assurance. She'd packed more misgivings than changes of clothes. Why was she doing this? Bigger things needed her undivided attention.

Their lane, the middle of three, seemed to be the slowest. A woman in a Jeep Cherokee came even with her window. She wore a suit jacket and drank from a metal tumbler, clearly preparing for the day ahead of being powerful and productive. Employed people had the privilege of being both.

Lauren fiddled with the side seam of her bag. Nearly four weeks of scouring online for job leads, attending any networking event she could find, and sending out résumés, and all she had gotten was one screening interview that ended with a promise they would let her know by early the following week if she was selected to move on to the next round. She was left to wait for a group of strangers to determine her professional worth, because no one at Universal apparently assigned her much value, including Duncan. "I think it's best if we both move on" was his only response to her text. None of her other coworkers had reached out. The bond was no bond at all.

For the next nine days she would have to pretend that all was well in front of her mom and sister, that she didn't have a constant rock in her stomach or dreams of sinking. The veil hung wisp-thin over the truth.

Her driver crept forward.

Focus on what you can accomplish—that was the plan she had to stick to. She closed her eyes and ran through the meticulous details she had written out in her Notes app for the trip. When she hadn't been consumed with her job search, she had created a list of the cities, the times and distances between them, the names of their hotels along with backup hotels, research notes about the authors and sites they aimed to visit, and a list of the books, some of which she still needed to read. Alternate routes. Recommended restaurants and what she would order at each. Nearby grocery stores and laundromats, because preparation was the key to security. Thorough plans equaled thorough command. With every item she ticked, her breath steadied.

With two minutes to spare, her driver pulled up to the curb at the foot of the restaurant. The squat building sat at the tip of a wedge intersection. The three-story buildings behind it were towers by comparison. She thanked the driver, sent a tip through the app, then stepped out onto the sidewalk.

The vents of the eatery spewed the scent of fried meat and

potatoes into the air. It hailed down upon her and her luggage. The front windows allowed a clear view inside. Her family was not among the patrons.

"Lauren!"

She turned to the familiar male voice. Her dad waved from between two cars at the edge of the restaurant's small parking lot.

"We're over here!"

Her mom appeared beside him, saw her, and gave a quick wave as well.

Lauren pulled up the telescoping handle of her suitcase and headed their direction.

"Hey, kiddo." Her dad's bright smile enveloped her first, then his arms.

"Hi, Dad." His touch was the first she'd had in weeks. She started to lean deeper into him, started to melt inside his comfort, but she restrained. If she let herself go too far, lingered too long there against his chest, the tears would come and not stop, and the veil would be blown away before they even left Kansas City. She cleared her throat and stepped out of his arms. "Chloe's not here yet?" she asked.

"Do you really expect her to be on time?" Her mom shielded her eyes and looked over Lauren's luggage. "That's all you brought?"

"Your mom has three bags," her dad explained. "Three very heavy bags."

"They are not that bad, Grant. Stop."

He winked at Lauren. "So why didn't you call us for a ride? We could have picked you up."

"That would have been so far out of your way. A rideshare works great."

"You didn't have him pick you up at your condo, did you?" Her mom's mouth pinched. "You know that's how some criminals learn who is not at home."

"I don't share my unit number, Mom. He wouldn't have much to go on. It's fine." Though a new fear unlocked. From that point forward, she would have drivers pick her up at the grocery store next to her complex.

"Would anyone care for a cup of coffee to go? My treat." Her dad motioned toward the restaurant.

"I'd rather not smell like a grease trap the remainder of the day," her mom replied.

Lauren waved off the offer as well. "They probably never change the coffee filters in that place."

"Isn't that the truth," her mom agreed.

Lauren grinned and crossed her arms, covertly placing a hand on her lower abdomen. The pudge had gone down the past several weeks, but not enough.

They waited in her parents' Buick, luggage in the trunk and doors open to the gentle morning.

Ten minutes later, well after their appointed time, Chloe's yellow Xterra finally whipped into the parking lot. They assembled at the back bumper of the car as she nested her vehicle into the last remaining spot at the end of the lot. Chloe burst out, red curls thick and loose around her ivory face, and pumped both fists into the air. "Road trip!" The last syllable elongated into three beats.

Their dad chuckled and met her halfway across the lot. The two of them collided into a bear hug, him lifting her off her feet.

Lauren locked her arms across her stomach and trailed behind their mom.

Freed from the hug, Chloe smoothed her T-shirt, a black tie-dyed variety with a graphic of praying hands overlapping a mountain. Arched over the image were the words "Watch what happens." The same boldness exuded from the irrepressible glow of her sister's face. Chloe always looked like she reflected the sun, an improbability Lauren could never quite decrypt.

"Have any trouble getting here?" Chloe asked their parents.

"Not at all," their dad replied. "Though I've been craving bacon and eggs for twenty minutes now."

"I fed you before we left." Their mom settled in at his side and nodded hello to Chloe. "We are wondering what's so special about this place you had us meet."

"And I can't wait to show you. But first . . ." Chloe turned to Lauren. Her smile broadened. "Morning, Laur. Been a while."

Lauren took a step forward, primed to give a quick, congenial embrace. Her sister, however, closed the distance between them and flung her arms around Lauren's neck. Chloe's hair partially curtained Lauren's face, filling her nostrils with a sweet aroma and her mind with visions of her kid sister jumping into her arms when she walked in the door on a weekend visit from college. Chloe would stay up late with her to find out "every little thing about being a big shot." The scent of her hair, the touch of her arms, the proximity of pure welcome tore at the veil.

She lightly patted her sister's shoulder blades and pulled back. "It has been a while. Good to see you."

"You too." Chloe slid her hands to Lauren's sides. Her smile suddenly flattened. She looked down at her hands on Lauren's ribs hidden beneath her oversize shirt. Chloe's eyes met hers, a question written in the green irises.

Their mom cut in. "The restaurant does have 'No Loitering' signs posted."

Chloe shook her head and whispered to Lauren, "Gonna be an interesting trip."

As soon as she dropped her hands and turned back to their parents, Lauren hugged herself, fingertips sneakily feeling the bones her sister must have. They weren't that pronounced. Were they?

"All right, Mom," Chloe said. "If you're that eager, let me show you. Follow me."

Lauren strode after her family. Among the plans she had for the trip, avoiding her sister's touch would need to be top of the list.

Chloe led them to the back edge of the parking lot, where an alleyway cut diagonally through the wedge block and separated the restaurant from the three-story brick building behind it. The brick wore a stark-white layer of paint.

64

"Look up." Chloe pointed toward the top of the building.

Spread across the top two floors was a mural of a young man's face. His dark locks draped on either side of his narrowed eyes. The thin, pointed nose and disproportionately small mustached mouth were the signatures of anime style.

"What am I looking at?" their mom asked.

"It's Ernest Hemingway. See there, to the left of his face?" Chloe pointed to the place where the artist had painted the name of the piece in faint gray letters: *Young Hemingway*.

Their mom tilted her head to the side. "That looks nothing like Hemingway."

"It's him at seventeen," Chloe said. "That's how old he was when he came to Kansas City to work as a reporter. This neighborhood was his beat."

"How neat," their dad said, though his endorsement did nothing to solicit an agreement from his wife.

"One of the librarians told me about it," Chloe added. "Legend has it he kept ties to the city long after he moved away. He wrote part of *For Whom the Bell Tolls* while visiting family here."

"Ahhh," their dad effused.

Their mom crossed her arms.

They stared up at the mural a few moments longer.

"I love his eyes," Chloe said at last. "He looks determined, ready to take on the world."

"He looks angry," Lauren said.

"He looks self-righteous," their mom muttered.

Chloe exchanged a look with their dad. They both laughed.

He wrapped his arm around his wife. "Your ability to see the good in art is inspiring, my love. And, Chloe, I find the mural worth the drive. Thank you for introducing us to it."

No matter how misguided, how wrong, how ill-advised, Chloe never lost his support, nor did their mom. Chloe seemed to take it for granted. Lauren, on the other hand, was so careful not to give either of her parents a reason to rebuff her or coddle her in her missteps. They never had to spend energy worrying about what mess she was getting herself into or how they needed to "find extra grace" for her. Did they appreciate that? Did anyone in her family appreciate how little she asked of them? Did anyone anywhere?

At Chloe's insistence, the three of them lined up in front of the mural for their dad to take a picture.

"Everyone say 'adventure'!" her sister instructed before the snap.

Chloe's was the only bellow that rolled through the alleyway.

15

Both girls dipped inside the restaurant for a restroom break while Grant gathered all the luggage at the back of their daughter's obnoxious yellow vehicle.

Edie stood to the side as he heaved her second suitcase onto the floor of the cargo area.

"You're right, dear," he grunted. "Light as a feather."

"Lucky for you, you won't have to move them in and out of hotels." The reality those words painted cut sharply into the moment. Her being responsible for her own bags meant he would not be there to do it for her. He would not be there to change a flat tire if they should have one, check the fluid levels when they needed to be checked, and know what the fluids were. He would not be there to investigate strange noises in the night or breathe through his nose like a horse as he slept beside her. What if they were in a wreck? What if they got lost? What if they were trapped in their room during a fire?

What if these were the last moments she ever saw him?

Her hands trembled. She gripped the strap of her purse to mask their involuntary movement.

Nine days. They had not been apart for more than a night in thirty-five years. Her friends would talk about their husbands' business trips and how it often felt like a mini vacation with less cooking, far less toothpaste globs in the sink, and better sleep. What a horrible way to live.

After a Jenga-like process, Grant fit all of their suitcases and bags into the cargo area with some room to spare. Beads of sweat glistened on his forehead, stopping where his hairline once was. Despite the changes time had demanded of him, he was as youthfully handsome as the day he'd taken her to the lake near campus for their first date. They'd had a picnic in the tranquil shade, complete with her favorite cookies. He had always made her feel known. The only man ever to do so.

"All set." He shut the liftgate and turned to her. "Got everything?"

Her thumb traced the edge of the purse strap. "Not everything." She could barely hold eye contact. The well of pain in her throat was too much. Thankfully their girls were not there to witness it.

"Edie." He slipped his finger under her chin and gently lifted until her eyes turned up to his. "I'll have my phone at all times. We'll check in regularly." He nodded as he spoke, affirming what he said was gospel solid. When they were dating and had to say goodbye for the evening, he would assure her in a similar way that he would come back—he would always come back.

Her bottom lip quivered, the same way it did all those years ago. She bit the inside to keep it in line, but not soon enough to hide it from him.

"My love." He scooped her against him. She fit in the valley of his chest as if it had been tailored for her. "I'm proud of you for doing this. You'll have an amazing time."

"And you'll have fun being a bachelor again," she said into his shirt, "eating all the things you're not supposed to."

He rubbed her back. "And doing nothing on my honey-do list until the day before you come home."

She pulled in his scent, committed it to memory. "If you don't get rid of that wasp nest on the back patio, you will sleep out there until you do."

"Duly noted." He pulled back far enough to lay a warm kiss on her temple, then he slowly righted. "You and the girls are going to have so much fun."

"Yes." Perhaps if she kept saying it, belief would follow.

"I packed you something in your smaller suitcase."

She dabbed her eyes. "What is it?"

"A journal. For any thoughts that come to mind as you sojourn."

"Won't I be telling you about the trip on the phone?"

"You might have other thoughts you want to capture."

"Like what?"

His hands traveled up her arms and came to rest on her shoulders. His eyes took her in, asked her to come closer. "Seems you may still have a few things to work out with your mother."

The girls' voices carried across the tiny lot. Their privacy quickly evaporated.

"How can I work anything out?" she asked. "She's gone."

His reply started with a gentle smile. "Is she, though?"

Their youngest called out to him, asked him if everything was set. He said it was. Everything that happened next seemed to occur in double time. The last hugs, the double checks, the final goodbyes. Edie went from standing in her husband's arms to sitting in the back passenger seat in the beat of a gnat's wing. And then they were backing out of the spot.

Grant stood at the head of the parking spot, one hand tucked in his front pocket, the other raised in farewell. Chloe rolled down all the windows and encouraged them to wave back.

Edie leaned into the open air. She clung to her husband's gaze, latched on to his smile, and blew him a kiss. She swallowed against the invisible grip around her windpipe. Only a gracious God would bring her back to him.

Above Grant's head, the painted eyes of young Hemingway

followed her. The tenacity in his expression may very well have been the self-grandiosity that imbued his war stories. Or perhaps it was the bud of the machismo he would become known for.

Or perhaps it was something much different, something that made him misunderstood.

Maybe it was the overcompensation of a trembling young man learning to face fear toe-to-toe.

16

The start of something new was the most exciting thing about life. Possibility was unleashed and perspectives were like fresh clay ready to be reshaped by the Potter's hands. The things to see and experience! The people to meet! The eyes to study!

Zeal enveloped Chloe like the light of the late morning reaching through the driver's side window. Based on how her mom and sister stared out their respective windows at the steady retreat of the city, awakening them to adventure would be a task. God bless, they even sat the same, with hands clasped in their laps and gazes stuck on the familiarity they were leaving behind. It was two against one, in no small part thanks to her mom's meddling.

She shook away the creep of resentment. Nothing would ruin this trip.

"I made a playlist!" she announced. "A little soundtrack for our vacay. Want to hear it?" She reached for her phone in the console.

Lauren beat her to it. "Let me. You keep your eyes on the road. I don't want to die five minutes in."

Her sister sounded more like their mom every year. Not that it would be wise to say so aloud.

"It's in my music app," Chloe said. "It's called 'Road Ready.'"

Her sister tapped the screen until she found the playlist. "Does this connect to your car?"

"Goldie's too old for such bells and whistles. Just crank up the volume on my phone."

"You call your car Goldie?"

"Devotedly."

Her sister crinkled her brow in obvious bemusement, then complied with the volume request. The opening riff of a TobyMac song sprang into the cabin. The maxed-out speaker layered the melody with a tinniness, but it didn't matter. The song could still set a good mood, should all three passengers be willing.

Lauren set the phone back in the console. "This sounds familiar."

Chloe grinned. "It's from youth group. Remember?" Though they were in youth group together only for the first part of Chloe's middle school years, and Lauren had stuck mostly with the other upperclassmen in the back of the room where they kept their noses in their phones, they had managed to capture at least a few shared memories. "This was one of Pastor Adam's 'walk-in songs.'"

Her sister blinked. "The songs he had playing when everyone was arriving?"

"Exactly! Remember the dances we used to make up to them?"

Lauren shrugged. "Vaguely, I guess. That was mostly you and your friends." She planted an elbow on the windowsill and rested her chin on her hand.

Lauren usually sidestepped talk of church, but something about her whole demeanor seemed off. Her ribs definitely had not projected as much when they last saw each other at Grandma Moria's funeral.

Chloe stored it all up in her heart.

Up ahead, brake lights brightened. First in the right lane, then steadily across all three. Chloe slowed to a stop. "This doesn't look good."

"Is it an accident?" their mom asked.

"Must be," Lauren answered, turning down the volume on Chloe's phone. "Or construction."

"I'll call your dad." Their mom dug in her purse.

"No need," Chloe said into the rearview mirror. "I can look up the traffic report on my phone."

Their mom placed the call anyway.

As she worried the poor man for no reason, and while he was likely still driving himself, Chloe pointed to her own phone. "Lauren, could you look at my Scout app?" The Scout network of cameras on major Kansas City highways had been a lifesaver more than once.

Her sister retrieved the phone and started to search. A text message popped onto the screen.

"Who's that from?" Chloe asked.

"Sori." Her sister tapped open the message and read, "'Jeremy is loving his time with his aunt.' She sent a picture too." Her sister turned the screen for her to see.

Jeremy was on his babysitter's patio, beach ball near one foot, snout aimed at the camera.

"Handsome as ever," Chloe said.

Another message came through. Lauren read, "'Good trial run for us both.'"

Chloe bit her lip.

"What does that mean?" her sister asked. "Are you giving away Jeremy?"

"No," she said a little too fast. Technically she would be, at least for two years. RISP did not allow pets in staff housing. She pulled forward to even up with the car in front of them, giving herself time to form a reply. "Sori may be doing more dragon-sitting for me in the future."

Truthful, but not wholly revealing. Best of all, it seemed to satisfy her sister. Lauren returned to her search, found the app, and reported the update.

"Accident at 78th Street. Right two lanes closed. Estimated clear time thirty minutes."

Chloe nodded. "Not bad. We'll be out of this before long."

In the back seat, their mom continued her conversation with their dad, trying without much success to relay their location along I-70. Geographical positioning was never her strong suit.

Suddenly Lauren leaned in close. "Chloe," she said in a way that signaled she was about to say something with gravitas. "I just want to ensure you know I plan to pay my own way on this trip. I know you didn't really have a choice in me coming."

"It's okay, Lauren."

"I mean I'll cover my share of hotels and gas too."

"You don't need to. Really. That's all the same whether you're on the trip or not."

Her sister frowned. "You're sure you have the money for this?"

She inched the car forward. "I wouldn't have planned the trip if I didn't, would I?"

By the purse of her sister's lips, the answer was clear. The big sister who had been put in charge of Chloe countless times apparently believed Chloe still needed careful supervision.

"I assure you, Lauren, I have the money for this trip. I am more practical than I seem. Thank you for the offer, though."

Her sister's gaze tarried on her a moment longer. At last, she turned away and stared into the horizon.

Chloe's contention to her dad had been spot-on. She did have a lot to prove.

17

Probability said there was reasonable chance her little sister had neglected to factor in contingencies and extras for the trip. Did she think about tips for housekeeping? Donations for some of the museums they would visit? Had she planned for situations in which credit cards may not work? The latter was a real possibility considering the rural places they would visit.

Lauren waited until I-70 traffic cleared and her sister's concentration was zeroed in on the road ahead as well as singing along with the MercyMe song blasting from her playlist, then she opened her bank app. The balance in her checking account had dwindled significantly over the past month, even with the final payout from Universal, but some things needed to be done, for everyone's sake. In a sequence of taps, she moved $1,000 from her savings to her checking. The next time they were near an ATM, she would get more cash. Just in case.

An older sister must stay one step ahead. Her mom had taught her that, expected it of her from the time Chloe was born. Lauren must lead quietly at all times. Younger sisters didn't know the level of protective thinking that took place on their behalf.

They passed the Kansas Speedway and the last blip of hotels and restaurants, then the metro melted into open prairie. A green mileage sign announced Lawrence to be twenty-two miles down the turnpike. Lawrence, home to legendary University of Kansas Jayhawks basketball and Langston Hughes. As her sister sang and swayed to the song, Lauren reviewed the notes on her phone about the life and work of the man once called the poet laureate of Black America. Poetry might as well have been Greek, for as much as it clicked with Lauren's sensibilities. Unless, of course, Taylor Swift lyrics counted. When it came to Hughes's verse, Lauren needed all the research she could accumulate to unearth the meaning under the layers of rhapsody.

Chloe took the first Lawrence exit off the turnpike, and within minutes, they cruised the city's main strip, Massachusetts Street.

"I love Mass Street." Her sister sighed. "I love Lawrence. It has such a thrum of creativity."

"That's the thrum of liberal policies you feel," their mom said.

"We agreed no politics on this trip," Chloe countered.

"I recall no such conversation."

Chloe looked at her in the rearview mirror. "All the same, we're here to appreciate art, and say what you want about Lawrence, it is a cradle of artists. Painters, photographers, designers, chefs, poets. This is where Hughes got his first nudge of the muse. That says a lot about the brilliance of this city, don't you think?"

"It says something," their mom muttered.

Chloe would have an easier time convincing a dog to meow than to encourage their mom to enjoy time in the city "with far too much illicit activity," as Grandma Moria would say. Many college towns fell into that category. Regardless, it was a reason their parents avoided the municipality so close to Kansas City and were relieved neither daughter chose KU. It had to be hard for their mom to be away from home, let alone in a place she didn't feel at ease.

At the south end of Mass, Chloe found a street-side parking spot, took three attempts to parallel park in it, held up traffic for two of those attempts, then cut the engine with an eager smile on her face. "Our first real stop of the trip. It's exciting, isn't it?"

Lauren turned to their mom, who looked off to the side then opened her door. If Chloe picked up on the tepid reaction, she didn't show it.

The Watkins Museum of History sat on the corner of Mass and 11th. The three-story, red brickwork structure was fashioned in the Richardsonian Romanesque style with rows of arched windows and terra-cotta ornamentation, a stark break from the standard-issue storefronts lining the strip.

They stopped at the bottom of the front steps. The peaked roof pointed toward the limitless blue above.

"Did this used to be a church?" their mom asked.

"It was originally a bank," Lauren recalled from her notes.

Their mom huffed. "Why am I not surprised?"

"Come on, let's go in." Chloe proceeded up the steps.

Inside the front doors, a grand marble staircase climbed to the second-floor exhibit hall. Gold-plated handrails glinted in the light of the intricate chandelier.

"Good morning." A woman in a ponytail and turquoise glasses stepped from behind a desk to their left. "Welcome to the Watkins Museum of History, where admission is always free. Have you been here before?" The name tag on her lapel identified her as Dawn, curator.

"We have not," Chloe said. "But we hear you have a statue of Langston Hughes."

"We do, in fact. We are quite excited that our county's legacy includes such an accomplished man. We have several exhibit panels about Mr. Hughes in our collection, which also includes KU basketball history, if you're interested in that as well."

"Not really," their mom mumbled too softly for their guide to hear.

Lauren bit back a chuckle.

Dawn ushered them to the stairs. "I'll show you where to find the statue."

Their shoes tapped against the smooth stairs, stirring up an echo in the cavernous atrium.

"Are you big fans of Mr. Hughes?" Dawn asked.

"To be honest, we're here to learn more about him," Chloe said.

"I couldn't name a single poem of his," their mom added.

Several titles unfurled from Lauren's research. "'Montage of a Dream Deferred' is one of his most famous," she reported. "Along with 'I, Too' and 'Dreams.'"

Both her mom and sister lifted their eyebrows at her.

Dawn chuckled. "That's exactly right. Well done."

Their mom grinned and nodded. Someone else's praise always brought out hers too. Lauren ensured her notes remained open on her phone, ready, one step ahead.

"You may know this," Dawn said as she led them into the exhibit hall, "but his most anthologized and very first published poem is said to have been inspired by the Kansas River that flows through Lawrence."

"'The Negro Speaks of Rivers,'" Lauren said.

"Right again."

Another nod from her mom.

They wound through displays showcasing Lawrence's history from the frontier days, including the John Brown abolitionist uprising in the lead-up to the Civil War.

In the back of the hall, they came to a space parceled by display boards about the racial history of the area. At the hub was a bronze statue of a young boy.

Dawn held out both hands in presentation. "Here he is."

The boy donned a messenger bag labeled *Saturday Evening Post* and cradled a book etched with "Dr. W. Du Bois."

"This statue was commissioned in the 1970s as a tribute to Mr. Hughes's formative years in Lawrence," the curator explained. "He was born in Joplin, Missouri, but his mother brought him here to live with his grandmother when he was a baby. He moved back in with his mother in his later high school years in Ohio. He published 'The Negro Speaks of Rivers' at nineteen, not too far removed from his Kansas life."

"I take it he delivered newspapers?" Their mom motioned toward the messenger bag.

"He did. And he was influenced by W. E. B. Du Bois, as you can see by the book in his hand. Walt Whitman was another influence. He spent a lot of time at the Carnegie Library at 9th and Vermont, not far from here. The building is a land trust office now. His childhood church is still an operating church, though, and it's about a mile east of here."

Their mom tilted her head to the side. "He was a Christian?"

"It was his family's church, really," Dawn replied. "Hughes himself wasn't particularly religious, though he said the influence of church helped set his moral standards, and you can glimpse that in his writing."

Lauren nodded. Judeo-Christian ethos did have a way of cropping up in one's conscience long after exposure. The TobyMac song on Chloe's playlist resurfaced a long-ago lesson on prayer in Lauren's mind. Something about "powerful and effective." The memory was too blurry for exactness.

"Do you have copies of his work for sale?" Chloe asked.

"We don't, I'm afraid. But there are two bookstores on Mass. One of them should have something for you." The bell above the main entrance chimed. "Sounds like a new visitor. Please excuse me, and please take your time perusing. I'm happy to answer any more questions."

"Thank you so much, Dawn," Chloe said.

When the curator disappeared into the maze of displays, Chloe clapped her hands. "There are actually a lot more places in town with a connection to Hughes. The house he lived in, a plaque outside city hall, and his grandparents' farm, though it's somewhere outside of town and I'm a little fuzzy on exactly where."

"Are you planning to go to all these places?" their mom asked.

"Of course!" Her sister's exuberance clashed against the pucker of their mom's brow.

For all of Chloe's planning, she clearly had not considered the reality of time constraints. Nor her guest of honor's level of endurance. A long day of travel still lay ahead.

Lauren stepped in. "Perhaps this museum, the library, and the church would be sufficient to get the highlights. We do have two more towns on our itinerary today, and the traffic jam put us behind schedule."

At the suggestion, their mom's brow relaxed. Her lips turned upward in an obvious bloom of relief.

Chloe looked between them, tapping the side of her fist to her hip. "I suppose we do have more fun things to do," she acquiesced. "But can we eat lunch here in town? I had a place picked out."

Lauren deferred to their mom, who nodded.

"That would be fine," the eldest Vance said.

"Plenty of time for that," Lauren agreed.

The tension dissipated. Practicality had won again.

Her sister promptly resumed her bouncy encouragement to thrust them all into the world of Langston Hughes, starting with a selfie next to the statue. The others complied.

Lauren filed in on the opposite side of the bronze figure than her sister and mom, a buffer of metal preventing touch. She locked on to the lens of Chloe's camera and kept her gaze sure.

Quiet leaders knew how to take charge and how to keep it— over the situation, over their emotions, and over themselves. If she was helpless to do anything else in the blankness that was her life, she could at least do that for the next nine days. She could keep her family on target, focused on the logical next step, attention directed to the facts and data they were on a mission to acquire. Probability said averted eyes would not notice the thin veil.

18

The day had warmed considerably by the time they drove away from the church, the last of their tour stops. Edie's forehead beaded with sweat in the back seat.

"Anyone hungry?" Chloe asked as she navigated them back to Mass.

"Yes," Edie replied.

"Then to lunch we shall go."

They were soon on Mass, headed north toward the turnpike. Edie fanned herself with the brochure the curator had shoved into her hand on the way out, but the slim breeze wasn't enough.

"Can you crank up the air?" she called to the front.

Chloe's eyes darted to hers in the rearview mirror. "My AC isn't the strongest. I have it set as cool as it will go."

Edie stopped fanning. "Please tell me you're joking."

Her daughter scrunched her shoulders up to her ears and drew out a "Nooooo?"

Fantastic. A busted cooling unit for a June road trip in the Midwest. Clearly no problem there. Edie sighed and lowered her window. Her oldest daughter did the same. The breeze caressed the droplets away.

"Where are we eating lunch?" Lauren asked.

"You'll see." The airiness of Chloe's tone did little to mollify the nagging sense that wherever it was wouldn't be something to write home about.

When her daughter took the first right turn off the bridge spanning the Kansas River and parked next to a muffler shop, the sense became assurance.

"I know we're not eating in that place." Edie gestured to the shop.

"Of course not. We're eating over there."

Both Lauren and Edie followed Chloe's pointed finger to the passenger-side windows and the sharp, grassy rise topped with a walking trail and benches.

"You mean on the levee?" Lauren's nonplussed tone matched Edie's unspoken one.

Chloe used a lavish cadence in her reply, as if reciting Shakespeare. "Yes. By the river that was Hughes's muse."

Shakespeare probably never ate next to the Thames.

"Come on! It'll be fun." Chloe gathered the keys and stepped out before either of them could respond.

"Want me to talk to her?" Lauren offered.

Her husband's words ribboned through her mind. *"Hear her out . . . She is far more capable."*

"It's okay," she told her oldest. "I'm too hungry to turn down food at this point." She pushed open her door.

A cooler, water bottles, and a picnic blanket in tow, the trio hoofed up the incline and onto the trail. The air reeked of fish and mud, churned up by motors of the Bowersock Dam under the bridge they had traversed from downtown.

"Such a beautiful day," her youngest declared.

Edie wrinkled her nose and searched for any sliver of shade. A group of trees down the path a bit afforded some shelter from the sun with their skinny branches. "Let's set up over there," she said.

Chloe spread the blanket over the edge of the trail that was most in the shade. They each chose a corner to sit on, with the cooler in the middle. The river was a raucous mass in front of them. On the opposite shore, a hotel and restaurant rose from the embankment. Both of them offered comparable views of the river. Both of them had air-conditioning.

Chloe opened the cooler and distributed barbecue chicken sandwiches on white bread, snack-size baggies of red grapes, and grape juice boxes. Juice boxes. The kind Edie used to pack for the girls in their school lunches.

Edie set hers on the blanket. "What a lovely lunch."

Her youngest smiled. "Thank you."

Surely that exchange would have warranted a wink of approval from Grant. He had no idea what he was asking of her. She dabbed her temple with the back of her hand, then opened the bag of grapes. They were chilled and crisp, the most pleasing way to enjoy them on a summer day. In that, her youngest daughter had been wise.

Lauren started with the fruit as well, slowly chewing each one.

Chloe, meanwhile, snarfed her sandwich in a manner befitting a wolf. It was like she had forgotten every little thing Edie had taught her.

After a minute or two of eating to the backdrop of rolling water, Chloe laid down her sandwich and wiped her mouth with a napkin. "I just want to say again how much I appreciate you both coming on this trip with me. We're going to see some unique things and, I hope, make memories that will last a lifetime."

Edie picked up her bagged sandwich and gently pulled at the zipper seal. "I hope so too." The memories so far probably wouldn't last until the end of the week.

Several more minutes ensued of quiet eating. Lauren reached the halfway point of her grapes. Chloe finished her entrée and sucked so hard on her straw that the box puckered.

The sauce on Edie's sandwich had made the bread slightly soggy, but the chicken was perfectly moist and flavored. Better than most restaurant versions. Even Grant would have deigned to eat chicken if it tasted like that. She quickly took another bite, a preemptive strike against the ache of the long days ahead without him.

Chloe broke the silence. "I wanted to come to the river to eat because it had such an influence on Hughes. Maybe in his honor we could read one of his poems, like the first one he published, the one the curator mentioned. What was the title of it?"

They both looked at Lauren, who did not fail.

"'The Negro Speaks of Rivers,'" she answered.

Chloe picked up her phone and danced her thumbs across the screen, paused, scrolled. At last she said, "Here it is. I'll read it. You all enjoy."

Edie nibbled her sandwich as Chloe recited the lines. The narrator talked about knowing rivers from ancient times. He cited knowledge of the Euphrates, the streams of the Congo, the flow of the Nile beside the pyramids, all the way to the Mississippi.

What it all meant, who knew? Poetry was not the language of natural conversation.

Edie laid her sandwich aside and washed it down with water from her bottle, leaving the juice box untouched. Women her age had no business drinking out of a straw the width of an eyelash.

When Chloe finished, she sighed as if from contentment. "That is beautiful. Very vivid images. It's incredible how poets and writers can see something so clearly in their minds and, using only strokes of a pen, bring that vision into a form others can enjoy too. What a skill to have. Not unlike drawing."

By the way Chloe peeked at her, it was clear her daughter meant something more. An undercurrent of something bigger to say. Chloe had been drawing since she was a child, insisting the whole time it could be more than a hobby. She had yet to prove it. Baristas weren't known for producing marketable artwork.

"I can see why he was so loved as a poet," Lauren said.

"Me too." Chloe wadded her juice box and stuffed it into her empty sandwich bag. "I will confess, though, I'm not sure what the poem means."

Edie chuckled to herself. Finally something she and her youngest had in common. She used her napkin to shoo away a fly buzzing her sandwich, then dipped the soft paper into the sweat pooling in the notch of her neck.

"I think he's referencing Black history in the world," Lauren said. "He's talking about rivers in the Middle East, Africa, and America, all of which have significance to his culture."

Chloe frowned, glanced at her phone, then back at her sister. "I guess I could see that."

"Hughes was known for his focus on both the plight and rich heritage of Black Americans," Lauren added.

For a moment, the soft rush of water at the dam was the only sound. Then Chloe spoke. "You really did do your research on him."

The oldest shrugged one shoulder. "It's not a bad thing to be knowledgeable about the places you're visiting."

The youngest tilted her head, as if trying to look deeper. "Did you like the poem?"

Lauren glanced toward the water, the source of inspiration for the verses, then replied, "It makes you think."

The kind of answer that satisfies but discourages further demands for insights. The kind Edie had learned to craft in discussions with her mother.

Chloe turned to her. "What did you think of the poem, Mom?"

"I agree with Lauren." She swatted at the persistent fly. The movement, however small, seemed to drum up even more streaks of moisture down the side of her face. "I also think it's too dreaded hot out here."

"Yes, we should get going." Lauren resealed her grapes. "It's almost noon."

"We haven't been here that long," Chloe protested. "Lauren, you've hardly eaten anything."

"I'm not that hungry. Full stomach and hot car isn't the best mix for me anyway."

Chloe twisted her lips and looked down at her phone. Her desire to savor was palpable.

Seeing the response, Lauren paused in her cleanup efforts. She spoke gently. "This has been nice. We've seen parts of Lawrence we probably wouldn't have otherwise, but if we want to have enough time at the OZ Museum in Wamego, we have to keep on schedule."

Such grace, that one. Lauren had been guiding her kid sister since they were little.

The gentle answer unchained Chloe from her wallow. "I suppose you're right."

Once they were in the car again—with Edie in the front passenger seat to be as immersed as possible in the dribble of air from the vents—Chloe blasted her playlist. By the time they merged onto the Kansas Turnpike, the spring had returned to her youngest daughter's movements. Irrepressible, that one.

19

Wamego was a little over an hour's drive, enough time for Lauren to speed-read through her notes about *The Wonderful Wizard of Oz* and its author, L. Frank Baum. While her sister sang to her playlist and endured repeated implorations from their mom to keep her hands on the steering wheel, Lauren filled up on facts about the famed story and its larger-than-life creator. As it turned out, he was as ill-fated as he was artistic. Baum may have had the fantastical skill Chloe lauded, but he didn't have the business prowess to make a viable living off his creation. How would that fact impact her sister's estimation?

With the poor air circulation and climbing temperature over the plains, the back seat became stuffy within minutes, but it didn't matter. Sweat was fat leaving the body. The privacy of the back seat also allowed her to sneak in a workout. As she studied, she clenched her ab muscles and held for a count of ten, a hack she had read about years ago that kept abs firm. One rep was said to be the equivalent of one sit-up. Thousands of miles' worth of upright sit-ups would multiply firmness fast. Bonus: The pain of exertion masked the pain of her mostly empty stomach.

They pulled into Wamego at quarter after one, only a few minutes behind when they should have arrived to give them the maximum opportunity to explore the museum. The town of less than five thousand people carried all the markers of a small community: an abundance of pickups, dusty bumpers, and a Main Street lined with neutral-toned storefronts. Amid the bland shops rose a two-story, emerald-green facade boasting gold letters announcing what resided within: the OZ Museum.

Chloe slid past the museum and into an angled parking spot a block down.

"There's a tour bus outside," their mom groaned. "That means it's probably going to be packed with either high schoolers or old people."

"You never know," Chloe replied. "It might be a busload of European tourists exploring our great land."

It was, in fact, a group of retirees. Many of them wore T-shirts that read "Coffeyville High Reunion Tour." They clogged much of the open space in the gift shop that doubled as the main entrance. Lauren exchanged polite greetings as she wove through the crowds of people and racks. She reached the ticket counter a second behind her sister.

"Three adults, please," Chloe told the attendant.

"Two," Lauren interjected.

Her sister waved her off. "It's ten dollars. It won't break me."

"But we agreed—"

Chloe faced her. "I said I got it, Laur. Enjoy the blessing." She repeated to the man behind the counter, "Three, please."

Their mom glanced at her. Lauren squeezed her lips together. Her sister never stuck to a plan; she favored whatever felt right. That kind of thinking led to trouble. Baum would attest to that if he could. Wherever they went next, Lauren would be sure to be the first to the ticket counter.

The man distributed their tickets and directed them to the exhibit hall entrance, which had been fashioned to resemble the porch of the farmhouse in the movie. Visitors entered through the screen door.

As soon as they stepped through, her sister was in awe. "Wow, look!" she said at nearly every turn, like she was a child again on her first trip to the zoo.

The brightly lit hall featured rich hues of yellows, greens, reds, and blues, mimicking the Technicolor world of Oz in the film. A first-edition copy of the children's book at the heart of the phenomenon was on special display.

Chloe stopped to read the board outside the book's glass case. "Published in 1900. Says it was the first in a series. I never knew it was a series. Did you, Mom?"

Their mom joined her at the board and scanned it for herself. "I did not. Interesting."

Lauren stepped up to their mom's side, more facts at the ready. "The series came after the musical."

Their mom whipped her attention to Lauren. "There was a musical?"

"The musical launched in 1902," she explained. "The success of both the book and musical led Baum to write thirteen sequels."

Their mom shook her head. "I had no idea."

"It must have been quite the success too." Chloe read from the board. "It says, 'The first book sold more than three million copies before it hit public domain in the 1950s.' Well done, Baum!"

And there it was. The moment to reveal the hard truth of a man so admired, a revelation the museum probably didn't permit in its displays. Lauren could choose to keep it quiet, let her sister believe what she wanted, but Chloe needed to know the unabridged version. Hard and happy were both necessary parts of a story.

Lauren clasped her hands at her waist. "Actually, most people don't realize this, but he was forced to file for bankruptcy eleven years after the book was published. He died not long after. He never saw a fortune."

Their mom's lips parted. "You're kidding. How could he have gone bankrupt?"

"Because he shot for the moon with theater production and

the first tries at a movie, and it cost him all he had. He had great ambition and little financial forethought. The only reason the story endured is because someone who was more careful planned the 1939 film."

Their mom tsked and looked at the memorialized book again. "Risk-takers often do end up like that. How sad and unfortunate."

Her sister crinkled her brow as if unsure what to say. Reality hit like that. Some things big sisters couldn't protect against. The inevitable shatter of naivete was one of them.

Small contingents of the Reunion Tour party edged by them. Their mom excused herself and drifted off with the flow of traffic toward a display of Judy Garland memorabilia. For a moment, the sisters were left facing each other. Lauren started to step away, but her sister's voice brought her to a stop.

"Bankrupt or not," Chloe said, "it took courage for Baum to put himself out there like that. To take risks to give others something of value. To create something that resounds with the human experience, which probably required him to tap into his own vulnerability and hurt." She nodded toward the book. "That's why the story endures. Not all success can be measured in dollars."

The words, and the calmness in which they were delivered, struck Lauren still.

Her sister gave one last glance toward the book, then turned to catch up with their mom. Her vibrant red curls gleamed in the overhead lights.

A woman in a Coffeyville shirt stepped into Lauren's line of sight. When their eyes met, the woman arched an eyebrow and nodded in clear agreement.

Heat swelled in Lauren's cheeks.

She hung back long enough for her sister to disappear around the bend.

20

It took everything in Chloe not to peek over her shoulder at her sister as she walked away. Something was definitely amiss. The vast overpreparedness for a trip that was supposed to be pure discovery. The reticence to touch. The thinness. And only eating a handful of grapes for lunch. Details told the story, and there was a story in those details. Whatever it was, she couldn't force it before its time. Light always found what was hidden. Eventually.

She swallowed. That was a certainty she needed to heed more than any of them. September wasn't approaching any slower.

She caught up with her mom in front of a case of screen-worn wardrobe pieces, including a pair of Munchkin shirts and a gingham dress worn by Judy Garland.

A faint smile came to her mom's lips as she tapped the glass in front of the dress. "I had one like that when I was a girl. It was a Halloween costume."

Chloe smiled. "No kidding. Did you have the shoes too?"

"Red ones, yes, but not the sparkly kind. Aunt Gabriella put my hair in braids. She was the Tin Man that year."

Streams of vicarious memories flowed through Chloe's mind. Two little girls giggling as they dressed for a night of celebration and sweets. What fun they must have had. "Did she paint her face silver?" she asked.

Her mom nodded. A twinkle shone in her eyes. "She even figured out a way to paint her hair gray. It took a week of washing for it all to come out."

Chloe chuckled. "You two must have been a sight. I would have loved to have been there. Do you have a picture?"

The brightness in her eyes dulled. "We never took pictures on Halloween." More lay under that statement, but her mom left it at that. Stories from her childhood were rare topics of conversation between them. Especially ones that portrayed her sisterhood.

"I bet Aunt Gab would like this museum," Chloe ventured.

"Gabriella," her mom corrected in predictable fashion. She admired the dress. "I'm sure she would. She loved the movie more than any of us."

No surprise in that. Aunt Gab was the only other person in the family who understood the value of the nonconventional. Her posts about her animal rehabilitation farm—the farm her mom had yet to visit—had exploded in popularity the last couple of years, and it was only an hour north of Omaha, which they would be going through.

An idea stirred to life. It would be risky, but it possessed the potential for greatness. It had the very real potential to change so much for the better. But first she would need to plant a few seeds.

Chloe clasped her hands behind her back. "Mom, did you know Aunt Gab recently acquired a three-legged llama?"

Her mom looked at her sideways. "I don't even want to imagine what that must look like."

"Perhaps you could ask her about it, and you could tell her about this museum."

Her mom scanned the display case one last time, crossed her arms, then replied as she turned away, "I suppose we do have things we need to talk about."

It was an opening. A small one, but an opening. Chloe let the seed germinate as it would and followed after her mom. Lauren loitered several displays back.

Up the main aisle a bit, a group of Coffeyvillers posed with a realistic mannequin of the Wicked Witch. Her glowing crystal ball sat between her and one of her flying monkey minions. She pointed nefariously into the aisle at an imaginary nemesis, which several men in the group pretended to be. Each took his turn standing in the crosshairs of her point and reacting with faux terror or, in one case, a karate stance. Their photographer could barely contain her laughter as she attempted to capture the jocularity on her phone. Their companions egged them on with glee of their own.

Her mom took in the action. She shook her head. "Have you ever seen such juvenile behavior from people who survived the Carter administration?"

"They've earned the right to let loose. If Dad were here, he'd have you posing the same way."

"If your dad were here, I'd remind him there are security cameras recording everything."

More laughter from the group. One of the women finally rounded everyone up and directed them onward "so others can enjoy too." The childlike seniors flowed one by one to the next stop. Except for the karate poser. He noticed the Vance women and waved them forward.

"You all want a picture? Get on up here, and I'll take one for you."

Her mom flashed a congenial smile. "Thank you, but we're—"

"That would be wonderful." Chloe tugged her mom's elbow to coax her to come.

Though her mom complied with being in a picture, she "absolutely" would not fake scream. Lauren looked on from a distance.

In the back of the museum, in a small, mostly enclosed viewing room, the classic movie played on a loop. Chloe ducked into the darkened room and found a spot on a bench in the back. Her mom trailed behind her but stopped in the entrance. On the screen,

Dorothy raced away from her obnoxious neighbor, Miss Gulch, who was after her dog, Toto.

"Let's sit and watch a while, Mom." She patted the bench next to her.

"I've been sitting all morning, Chloe."

"Just for a minute?"

Her mom looked over her shoulder at the exhibit hall.

"You'll get to stay in the air-conditioning that much longer," Chloe pointed out.

That did the trick. Her mom sat next to her and pulled her purse into her lap.

The movie progressed to the moment Dorothy reached home. In a tizzy, she attempted to get Auntie Em, Uncle Henry, and their three hired hands to listen to her stories from the day. Every one of them dismissed her youthful concerns, too busy putting their hands to the daily grind of the farm. "Stop imagining things," her aunt told her. The harder Dorothy tried, the more outright she was ignored.

Throughout the scene, Chloe's mom sat perfectly still, hands crisscrossed over the top of her purse. The light of the screen changed the shadows on her face every few seconds.

So many times as a child, Chloe had run into the middle of her mom's daily business and attempted to share things that mattered so greatly to her, only to have her mom say simply, "That's nice," without even looking at her. Chloe folded her hands and rubbed her fingertips along her knuckles. She prayed again for an inroad through all that stood between her and her mom—for the brains, the courage, the heart to reveal to her mom the biggest news of her life. The biggest risk-taking of her life.

Please, Lord, show me the path.

Suddenly her mom uncrossed her legs and pushed off the bench.

"Where're you going?" Chloe asked.

"The bench hurts my ham bones," her mom said, using Grandma Moria's euphemism for backside. "I have to keep walking. I'll meet you out there." Her mom eased back into the hall, once more too occupied to hear. Some things never changed.

The scenes kept rolling, through Dorothy's decision to run away, through the tornado, and to her arrival in Oz. The land she had dreamed of "over the rainbow" glistened before her in full, breathing color. Her faith had become sight. She had found herself in a place where imagination flowed in loud, beautiful waterfalls. A place where she was not told "you're too much" but rather "you're the missing key."

How? How could Chloe make her mom understand?

"Chloe."

She turned at the sound of Lauren's whisper.

"Mom's ready to go."

"Go? As in leave the museum?"

"We've seen pretty much everything. Come on, she's waiting." Lauren left without any more ado.

Chloe checked her phone. They had been at the museum for barely thirty minutes.

21

The hotel room door clicked shut behind the girls, and Edie exhaled into the cool, dim serenity. Walking, driving, weaving through crowds, and pretending to enjoy it all was finished for the day. Chloe had booked a room for the night in a reasonably starred accommodation in Manhattan, Kansas, up the road a bit from Wamego, and home to Kansas State University. For the first time in many hours, Edie sat on a comfortable surface in an adequate amount of air-conditioning with no expectations from anyone.

Between the unplanned hike up Manhattan's Bluemont Hill in the blazing sun for selfies with the giant whitewashed letters spelling out the city's name on the hillside, and being trapped in a vehicle with the cooling power of a box fan, her hair was flat, her feet screaming, and her shirt soaked at the neckline.

Chloe promised she and Lauren would bring back "delicious grub," but all that sounded good was a shower and the song of Grant's voice in her ear.

Despite the ache in her lower back that demanded to be stretched out on the bed, she held her shoulders back, knees together, feet flat on the floor, as her mother always liked. She tapped Grant's name on her contacts list and raised the phone to her ear.

He answered on the third ring. A microwave beeped in the background.

"Are you eating supper?" she asked.

"I am."

"Is there a single vegetable on your plate?"

"There's tomato in the barbecue sauce."

"Grant Harris, you have to eat something other than red meat."

"You enjoy your time, and I'll enjoy mine." The microwave door shut, followed by the metallic *tink* of silverware on a plate.

She was too tired to press any further.

"Tell me about your day," he said. "What all did you do?"

The list of sites seemed as unimpressive spoken as they did in real life. As she recounted the major points, she peeled off her flats. The pressure on her bunion released, and the glorious freedom made her close her eyes in gratitude. Flats were not meant for walking that much, but walking shoes coordinated with exactly none of her outfits.

"Sounds like a full day," Grant said. His voice was slightly muffled, an indication he was speaking with a full mouth. But only so many battles were worth fighting with energy as depleted as hers.

She wiggled her toes within her no-show bootie socks, loosening the joints after so many hours cramped in one position. "It was an interesting day," she said.

"Mmm."

"What?" she asked. "What's 'mmm'?"

"In Edie-speak, 'interesting' could indeed mean you were intrigued, or, more often, it means you're simply trying to be polite."

"And not succeeding, is that what you're saying?"

"That's what *you're* saying." Muffled sounds of chewing followed his reply.

The list she had recounted included an item or two that stood out. "I did find some things intriguing. Apparently Frank Baum bankrupted himself after he published *The Wonderful Wizard of*

97

Oz. And the ice cream we had at the K-State creamery was some of the best I've ever eaten."

"That's something." More chewing. "Did the girls enjoy themselves today?"

"I think so. Lauren researched all the books and authors, so she came with a whole mental encyclopedia of facts."

"Sounds like her."

"And Chloe . . ." She had lost count of how many times she had to redirect their youngest away from sit-dancing to keep her focus on driving. "Chloe has a good time regardless."

Grant chuckled. "Also sounds like her. Glad everyone had a good day overall. You should write about it in your journal."

She ran her fingers through her limp hair. Reliving the day in written words held little appeal. Still, he had been kind to think of her with the gift of the journal. "Perhaps I should," she said. "But before I do anything else, I'm going to take a shower. I smell like a gym locker."

"Glad I'm not there."

"No. You wouldn't enjoy it." An ache trailed through her chest. If only she could reach through the phone and have him take her hand in his. Before the ache could compound, she implored him to take his pills, promised to call a few more times during the trip, then readied for her shower.

The pair of slippers she kept exclusively for hotel rooms (because hotel floors were dirtier than toilet seats) were stowed in the top outside pocket of her smaller bag. She unzipped the pocket and drove her hand inside. Her fingertips bumped into the rings of a spiral-bound notebook.

"So that's where he stashed it." She slid out the gift from her husband and prepared to lay it aside. The image on the cover, however, made her pause. Splashed across the front in dreamy watercolor were the Austrian hills of *The Sound of Music* fame. Girlhood dreams awoke, the ones of Edie twirling with arms wide and bare feet embraced by the lush grass, singing to the sky that seemed close enough to touch. She used to always talk of someday. When had the hope of someday evaporated?

But Grant had remembered. She smoothed her fingertips down the image to the silver cursive text below: "Whatever is lovely . . . think about such things. Philippians 4:8." The lined pages were clean and tidy, waiting to be filled with "such things" that Grant was so confident would be inspired by the trip. God bless that man.

Her smile faded. What was the point of capturing thoughts about her mother? Her mother wasn't alive to read them. Even if she was, Alzheimer's wouldn't have allowed her to receive them. And even if the disease wasn't a factor, would she have?

Nothing compared to the pain of losing a parent you couldn't reach in the first place.

Edie dug out the slippers and tucked the notebook back in the pocket.

The streams of water from the shower washed the day away. Washed all of it away.

22

Hurry, Lauren!" Her sister's curls swayed as she took off without warning into the first two lanes of McCall Road. "Chloe, no! Stop!"

Her sister scurried on, bent on getting through the gap in oncoming traffic and to the grocery store on the other side. Lauren glanced in both directions of the four-lane thoroughfare, then hustled after her sister. Ballerina flats were not meant for running anywhere, let alone across busy roads.

Chloe reached the other side and turned to cheer her on as if they were in some cross-country race. "You've got this!"

"We couldn't use the crosswalk?" she muttered as the whir of approaching vehicles grew louder. She reached the thin median with plenty of gap remaining, but no sooner had she crossed the painted yellow line than her right shoe flew off behind her. It landed in the lane she had just escaped. Traffic closed in.

"Get it, Lauren! Quickly!"

Scenarios like that were how people died in the movies. They tried to do the thing they were pressured into doing even though they knew it was foolish and risky. Why had she followed Chloe? Why had she allowed Chloe's misjudgment to lead to her own?

She doubled back, snagged her shoe.

"Run!" Chloe shouted. "Now!"

A black truck with extra large tires barreled down on her.

"Run!" Chloe kept shouting.

Her legs jolted into action. She raced half barefoot toward her sister, making it to safety several seconds before the truck rumbled by.

Lauren leaned on her knees, gulping in air.

Her sister clutched her stomach and laughed. "That was a close one."

Lauren cut her eyes to her sister, not that Chloe noticed. She wiped off the sole of her foot and slipped on her shoe. "On the way back to the hotel, we use the crosswalk."

"It's all the way at the end of the block," Chloe protested. "Besides, the cars would have stopped for you. It's the law."

"So is using provided crosswalks." Lauren stamped her foot on the sidewalk to ensure the shoe was on snugly. "Rules exist for a reason."

Her sister's laughter died away, but not her grin. "And I'm sure you can recite the entire traffic code."

"Is that a bad thing?"

Chloe shrugged. "Not necessarily, but it is okay to loosen up and forget it for now. We are on vacation, after all."

The response of someone who didn't have the responsibility of carrying others. Chloe couldn't even admit that what they had done was dangerous, or that she had pushed their mom too hard that day, or that Baum was irresponsible. To Chloe, it was all "adventure."

Lauren sighed. "Let's just get the food." She broke for the store, keeping slightly ahead of her sister the whole way.

They maneuvered through the lot, careful to avoid a few cars reversing from their spots, then stepped through the sliding glass doors. The cavernous store was abuzz with evening shoppers, several of whom wore Kansas State gear or camouflage fatigues from nearby Fort Riley.

Lauren grabbed a cart and headed to the produce section.

"Look, they have ready-made stuff right here." Chloe stopped in front of an open-air cooler positioned conveniently near the entrance. The shelves held wrapped sandwiches, soups, salads, and microwavable entrées.

"Get what you want," she told Chloe as she kept walking. "I'm going to see what else they have."

A minute or so later, Chloe joined her at the organic bagged apples with selections in hand. "Sub for me, salad for Mom." She placed the items in the cart.

"Great." Lauren reached for a bag of apples.

"I have grapes back in the room," her sister said.

"Apples travel better and fill you up more." She examined the apples through the clear plastic wrap.

"I meant for Mom and me," Chloe said. "To go with our mains."

Lauren placed the bag in the cart and kept her attention averted. "Sounds like a good plan."

"Though you're welcome to eat some too. As well as the protein balls I brought for snacks. Peanut butter, oats, honey, and chocolate chips. So good, and they fill you up for sure."

"I'm set, but thanks." Lauren gripped the cart handle and pushed forward. "What else do you need?"

"Chips, probably, and drinks. You?"

"I'm done."

"You're done?" Chloe stopped, forcing her to pause too. "That's all you're getting? Apples?"

"I packed almonds. Plus I still have that sandwich from lunch."

The answer didn't appear to satisfy her sister. Chloe leaned in and whispered, "Is everything okay with you?"

She took a half step away. "Why wouldn't it be?"

"Because you seem off."

"I'm not off, I'm only tired. It's been a long day." A long week, a long month. She turned away from the burrowing stare and wheeled onward. "Let's get the chips so we can get back to the room."

Whatever her sister thought of the brush-off, she let it go.

They traversed into the main section of the store in silence. The same moment they reached the chips aisle, a text message alert brought her sister to another sudden stop. In the middle of the walking path, no less. A man almost bumped into her.

"It's Sori," Chloe announced, thumbs already cranking out a response as the man steered around her. "Jeremy had a great day, she said."

The tapping continued as they arrived in front of the long racks of salty snacks. Her sister giggled at whatever the conversation entailed, too busy to look up and do what she needed to do. Ironic how she did that—not noticing the things she should pay attention to and homing in on the things that were none of her business.

"Sori loves the picture I sent her of Mom and me with the Wicked Witch." More tapping, more smiles, more sharing of her day. Chloe apparently had as much to share with her friend as their mom surely had to tell their dad. Eager recipients waited for them both. The only person whose phone remained tucked away was Lauren. It didn't matter that she kept everyone and everything together, she was still left to fend for herself.

She grabbed a bag of plain ruffled chips on her sister's behalf, then left the aisle. Chloe would catch up eventually.

23

Five in the morning, like clockwork. Months after receiving the nurse's early-morning phone call that had ushered in loss, Edie's body simply couldn't forget. That hour of day, before the world stirred and the sun rose, echoes of the news were at their loudest—news that she was no longer tied to visits to the memory care unit, no longer needed as medical power of attorney, no longer anyone's daughter.

Per the ruthless menopausal curse, she had sweat through her single sheet. Even if she had spooned the air-conditioning register, the midlife maven would have brought her to such a state. She peeled the sheet from her bare legs and sat up. A sliver of brightness from the parking lot security lights wedged itself through the gap in the shades near her bed, giving the right amount of illumination to guide her movements. She tucked her feet into her hotel slippers and scooted to the bathroom, careful not to disturb the girls in the other bed. Both had every available cover pulled up to their chins.

Shutting herself in the bathroom left her momentarily in pitch-black and fumbling for the switch. When she found it and flipped it up, the over-mirror lights buzzed to life. Her outfit for the day hung from the hook on the back of the door, and her makeup and toiletries waited in a tidy arrangement on the counter. With their help, she hid the wet-sheepdog look. Nothing could be done about the bloodshot eyes, though, except let time do its thing.

She paused in front of the mirror one last time, smoothed the loose-fitting blouse down her stomach to gauge how much the pudge poked out. Not too bad. Better than most women her age, anyway.

She cracked open the door before flipping off the light, then waited for her eyes to adjust. Out in the room, she felt her way over to the dresser/entertainment center and patted the top until she found a key card. Her small suitcase was snuggled in the crook of the dresser and wall. She stooped, unzipped the top outside pocket, then pulled out the journal. If nothing else, the journal would give her the appearance of having a reason to be in the hotel common area at an ungodly hour. People generally didn't ask questions of people writing in a journal in the small hours. An old woman sitting in a chair and staring off into space, however, might result in a Silver Alert.

The room door clicked softly behind her.

Down on the first floor, the scent of frying meat wafted through the corridors. A woman with a ponytail and striped apron bustled about the breakfast area, stocking the countertop cooler with individual yogurts and cups of fruit medley. She smiled at Edie and continued with her preparations.

A set of French doors on the far side of the breakfast area led to a small patio at the back of the hotel. Edie pushed through them. The cool predawn wrapped itself around her and eased away the last of the warmth from her night under a hotel sheet. She breathed in the quiet. Forced early mornings did have some redeeming qualities.

She selected the table nearest the doors. The plastic furniture had been molded to resemble their fancier metal cousins and were less than stable, but the chair had a decent comfort to it. She laid the journal on the table. Grant had even thought to stick a pen between the pages.

She drew in another inhale, one that went "down to her knees," as her mother would describe it. "Breathe in deeply, Edith," she would say. "Down to your knees. Mondell women are bigger than emotions."

Edie had been married for a year when Grant convinced her that "bigger than" in Moria Mondell's estimation was synonymous with "scared of." In subsequent years, she'd discovered the need for several other rewrites of lessons she had internalized, intentionally or unintentionally. Some were still making themselves known, often to Grant first. Layers took time to wear away.

Light from the breakfast room spilled onto the journal cover. The watercolor image appeared even softer in that space. Dreamy, in fact, with all the magic her imagination assigned to the real-life inspiration.

Grant knew the wish that had lived in the recesses of her mind all these years. He alone held it in love. He alone received everything she said with love. So why wouldn't any thoughts she rambled onto the page be for him alone too?

She pulled the pen from its storage spot and turned to the first page of the journal. Across the top line, she wrote the date, time, and her current location. Then, starting on the second line, she let out everything she would say to Grant if he were sitting in the wobbly plastic chair across from her.

My long-standing feelings about the town of Lawrence were proven valid.

She wrote about the things he already knew and the things she hadn't gotten to in their phone call the night before. She wrote the what, where, who, and when. Her descriptions included each of the five senses, the way her mother had once pointed out that authors do to immerse their readers into the world they see.

It was no masterpiece, but in his eyes, it would be.

By the time she was done, the rising sun had nearly finished burning away the night. She rested her writing hand on the table, closed her eyes, and willed the day she put the journal back in Grant's hands to come faster.

24

Chloe slowly backed away from the French doors on the edge of the breakfast area. Her mom's closed eyes and open journal in the early touches of sunrise very well may have meant one thing: Her mom enjoyed a morning quiet time too. If so, they did have something in common after all. Chloe grinned.

"I pray you hear his voice," she whispered into the still morning.

A middle-aged couple arrived for the buffet and began filling their plates. More people were sure to follow soon and bring life to the room. She found a table in the corner, out of the way but still within the line of sight of her mom. She arranged her sketchbook, utensil pouch, and phone on the tabletop. Until her mom was finished, she would have her own quiet time, then maybe they would eat breakfast together. Maybe she could make her mom the best cup of coffee the hotel offered, and they could talk about what meditations they each had in their time alone with God. What sweet memories they could make, just the two of them!

She opened her Bible study app to the spot she had left off in the commentary on the book of John, where Jesus meets the shamed woman at the well in the heart of Samaria. As forks rattled and chairs scooted against the tile floor across the room, she read,

Jews and Samaritans despised each other so much that Jews traveling between Judea and Galilee would intentionally, willingly,
go well out of their way via a treacherous route to avoid passing
through Samaria. Not Jesus. He plunged himself, and his disciples,
into the heart of the despised territory filled with despised people to
bring them all face-to-face with a woman even the despised people
reviled. Imagine the questions the disciples must have asked as they
crossed into Samaria. Imagine the doubts they must have expressed,
or how many times they tried to convince Jesus to go a different
route. They couldn't see what he did. They didn't understand that
being about the Father's business often does look incomprehensible
to the world. But how many lives were changed because of Jesus's
"unwise" choice? How many generations of lives?

The last line rang in her soul.

Generations of impact. That was the tagline of RISP, her new
employer.

She needed to be there. She needed to be about the Father's
business there. The certainty was immovable.

She needed to find a way to get her mom to believe it too.

Through the glass panes of the doors, her mom sat with her
chin resting atop her clasped hands, eyes toward the horizon. The
aesthetic was simply too perfect.

She picked a pencil from her pouch and began to sketch. The
square panes of the French doors served as a perfect compositional
grid. She held her pencil on its side, recentering all the momentum
of her movements into her shoulder instead of her wrist. In a series
of oval planes, she built the basic components of her mom's form,
from feet to head. She played with the angles, cutting out lines with
her kneaded eraser as necessary and adding better positioned ones,
until the tilt of the head was right, the diagonals of the arms were
realistic, and the proportions of her body were coherent. Then she
added the profile of her mom's face, the slant of the nose, the ends
of her hair brushing against the sides of her neck. Downward she
moved on the body, to the way her mom held her shoulders. They

were not square as they usually were. They were rounded subtly, bent by an unseen force. What was that force?

Chloe paused and kept her gaze on her mom. By necessity, drawing pulled the artist deeper into any moment than most people ever went. Deeper into the untold. Deeper into the questions that naturally sprang out of what could be found there.

If her mom's shoulders were speaking a story, what must her eyes be saying in that moment?

25

L auren sat at a desk—no, a table. In a room with no decor, with no . . . walls? Where were the walls? Where were the people? She tried to call out. Her throat was locked. Where was she? Why was she alone?

A voice, dim and distant. She turned and turned. Where was it coming from?

There it was again. It said her name.

Where? Where?

"Lau. Ren."

A hand jiggled her shoulder. She flicked her eyes open.

Chloe stood over her in the space between the beds. "Good morning."

Lauren blinked until her eyes adjusted. Was it morning already?

"Breakfast is being served," her sister said. "We didn't want you to miss out."

"We?" Lauren lifted onto her elbows. The other bed was empty. The clock on the nightstand revealed that the new day had already seeped past seven o'clock. She bolted upright and flung off the covers. "You didn't wake me."

"Do you want something to eat?" Chloe asked.

Lauren got to her feet. The room was tundra cold. Goose bumps prickled across her bare arms. "How long have you all been up?"

"For a while."

Her sister was fully dressed and ready. Their mom wouldn't have gone out in public unless she was too. Which meant Lauren was already hours behind. A sloth by comparison, and their mom detested slothfulness. It was on the same level as negligence.

"Why didn't you wake me?" she asked.

"You were sleeping so soundly. Besides, we have plenty of time. The orphan train museum in Concordia doesn't open until ten, and it's only an hour or so away."

Lauren unzipped her suitcase and threw back the lid. One part of her brain said everything was fine, that Chloe was right, she could slow down. The other side screamed the list of things she had to do before she was presentable for the day. "I have to take a shower yet. It's going to take me a while."

"I can make you a plate if you want," her sister said. "Or I have those protein balls I brought."

"I'm good. Thanks." She gathered her outfit for the day and turned for the bathroom.

"What about a cup of coffee? Mom refused my expertise, so I'm standing here with an unfulfilled desire to serve. Use me!"

Lauren flipped on the bathroom light. "I've got to get in the shower." She shut the bathroom door before Chloe could say anything else.

The need to recover lost time weighed heavy on her frame. Within thirty minutes, she was dressed, with makeup applied and Notes app open on the bathroom counter to her research of Joan Lowery Nixon's Orphan Train Adventures series. It had been decades since she'd read the classic children's books. As she reread her logs, she ran her wide-tooth comb through her wet hair. Years of careful curation had allowed her sleek, downy strands to reach the middle of her back. They were as long and flowing as those of the Nixon character Frances Kelly.

Lauren paused mid-stroke, the soft locks draped delicately through the comb. Frances had cut her luscious hair in a desperate attempt to pass as a boy and be adopted with her little brother. She had sacrificed the core of her identity to protect her vulnerable sibling. She had done what she needed to do.

That moment was one of two indelible marks the series had left on a young Lauren. The other one had been seared into her memory a handful of pages prior—when Frances's widowed mother turned her back on Frances's pleas to not give them away. Nixon had taught Lauren that some parents harbored a coldness that could take even the most aware child by surprise. Lauren had vowed then to always—no matter what—keep that coldness away. She would do what she needed to do.

And that Friday in the middle of plainland Kansas, Lauren needed to shake off any possible interpretation that she was in any way a liability.

By the time her family returned to the room, she would have her suitcase packed, her hair dried, and plenty to share about the orphan train history in Nixon's books.

26

The road north out of Manhattan was long and humid. Sweat formed in the most inconvenient places on Edie's body. Meanwhile, her daughter's playlist cycled through two dozen songs, all of which Chloe sang loudly, with interspersions of "Look, a cow!" or "Look how flat!"

Her other daughter watched out her rear passenger window silently, nursing a cup of hotel coffee she had grabbed on their way out the door.

Though Edie tried to keep the growing heat of the day at bay, a rattle in the dashboard resounded louder the higher the AC was set. Chloe had named the rattle Jacob Marley.

Delightful, that yellow beacon of a vehicle.

They reached Concordia, Kansas, by eleven o'clock. Wamego had been a posh metropolis by comparison. This town boasted little to speak of besides a few hotels, a honky-tonk, and train tracks that cut through the north end. At the intersection of those tracks and Washington Street sat the National Orphan Train Museum and Complex.

Chloe pulled into the paved lot and parked in front of a red-brick building that carried the hallmarks of an old train depot.

Two smaller buildings waited to the left. The Xterra was the only car in the lot.

"Complex is a generous word," Edie said.

"I bet there's air-conditioning," Chloe said, pushing open her door.

"One can only hope," she replied.

The signs directed them to the smallest of the three buildings, the welcome center. Inside, a young woman who appeared to be barely out of high school greeted them from a small room to the right of the door.

"Welcome in. My name is Eve. I'm the curator for the museum."

That child was a curator? Either Edie had finally reached the age where everyone under forty looked like middle schoolers or Eve was the Doogie Howser of curators.

The young woman ushered them into the room, which housed a gift shop, then slipped behind the cashier counter. "Are you familiar with the history of the orphan train movement?" she asked.

Both Edie and Chloe turned to Lauren. Lauren at first appeared to be surprised, then said, "I've read the Joan Lowery Nixon books about it."

"Yes, of course." Eve smiled. "Many of our school groups come because of them. Did you read them as a kid?"

Lauren nodded.

"She cried over them," Chloe chimed in.

Her sister shot her a look.

"I can relate," Eve said. "The orphan train movement had a lot of positive to it, but also a lot of grief. Nixon did a pretty good job of representing both, using real history and stories of the riders. Like her characters, many of the riders were children from New York City. Most were true orphans, meaning both parents were deceased, but others were surrendered for one reason or another, usually poverty. New York City was rife with abject poverty and overcrowding during the time of the trains, which ran between 1854 and 1929."

Easterners sending their problems to the Midwest, a story nearly as old as the westward expansion.

"Here I am telling you everything about it and spoiling your museum visit," the curator said. "Would you like to purchase tickets?"

Chloe started to step forward, but Lauren was quick to pull her credit card from her sling bag. "Three adults, please."

Chloe backed away and meandered to a nearby rack of magnets.

"How many children rode the trains?" Edie asked as the curator punched in the total on the cash register.

"We estimate 250,000."

Enough humans to fill dozens of small towns. And they were children. Defenseless children who didn't know where they were going or understand exactly why. Edie adjusted her purse strap over her shoulder and distracted herself with various T-shirts on display.

With tickets secured, they started their tour. Building number two housed a replica of a train car fashioned to resemble the kind the children rode. Hard wooden benches wide enough for two adults lined each side of the "car."

Chloe tested one out. "Wow, these are uncomfortable. Imagine riding on a bench like this for days."

"Imagine sleeping on it," Lauren said. "The Nixon books described the riders doing that."

The books must have been a classroom assignment for Lauren. Edie had certainly never read them to her. Then again, bedtime stories had stopped as soon as the girls were old enough to read on their own.

"What else do the books describe?" Chloe asked.

Lauren stood behind one of the benches on the other side of the car and rested her hands on the back. "The riders were given fresh clothes and shoes to wear for the trip. For many of them, that was the first pair of new clothes they had ever received."

Chloe moaned. "That's sad."

"Even sadder, some of the riders were babies or too young to talk." Lauren pointed to an antique suitcase lying next to the bench. "Some of them didn't have luggage or any personal items with them."

Chloe smoothed the bench seat with her fingertips. "Literally arriving with the shirts on their backs. Those poor kids."

Edie shook her head. "Such a cold thing to do to a child."

Her oldest daughter peeked at her from under lowered lashes. Something was there. A question, a thought. A worry? Before Edie could decide, Lauren drew her hands off the bench and turned toward the exit. "Most of the exhibits are in the depot. Let's go check them out."

"Right behind you." Chloe hopped up and clomped out of the car after her.

For someone who loved the books so much, Lauren didn't act eager to dwell at the complex. Not that anyone could blame her. A certain sorrow beset the place, and Lauren knew the depth of the riders' sorrow better than any of them.

As they crossed the parking lot, Edie shielded her eyes against the bearing down of the summer sun. How many of the riders had done the same thing in that very spot, going from enclosed train car to wide-open Kansas? Faint echoes of little passengers, some too poor for luggage, curled around her. In them, a ring of grief, of bewilderment—of the blunt realization they were no longer anyone's child. She quickened her steps.

The depot building had been completely gutted and replaced with exhibits. End to end, front to back, every space bore homage to the orphan train system. Many exhibits included images of the children themselves.

The gloom sharpened. History was only thoughts until you could look it in the face.

Edie gripped her purse strap with both hands and inched through the displays. She stopped in front of a large picture of a group of riders. They ranged in age from preschool to ten or so.

The boys wore denim and page-boy caps. The girls were in cotton dresses with all or part of their hair pulled back, likely to give their new parents a better look at them.

Chloe came up next to her and skimmed the picture. "Isn't it interesting that none of them looked particularly scared? They're all smiling."

"That's probably because they were told to smile," Edie said. "Every child knows how to make the adult towering over them happy." She let go of her strap and cinched her arms across the pain in her stomach. All that those children had dared to dream of was being wanted. Children did anything to be wanted.

Her daughter leaned closer to the display board next to the photo and read aloud. "'Ethical challenges were levied at the movement, which led to its eventual demise in 1929. However, records indicate that the vast majority of children were placed in loving homes.'"

"Which means a portion were not," Edie said. She tore herself away from the photo. But it did little good. Young eyes stared back at her from every vantage point. Eyes that likely matched a parent's.

Her gaze landed on a photo of a young girl in a white dress with a simple gold cross strung around her neck. The board next to the photo told her story. She was only weeks old when her mother surrendered her to nuns at the New York Foundling Hospital for "inability to care for the child." She was not even two when she was shipped to strangers in Minnesota. Her name was Betty.

The girl was not a true orphan. She had a mother who was alive and two older siblings who, for whatever reason, had not been sent away—they had been the treasures worth keeping. Betty alone was abandoned, an innocent newborn who did not have a choice or a voice. She alone did not know the warmth of her biological mother's kiss.

Did she ever wonder if she was valuable enough to keep around? Did she ever cry for her birth mother to say so?

Off to Edie's left, Lauren stood watching her, eyes moist as if she too heard the entreaty from little Betty's heart. A throb shot through Edie's chest. She turned from the image of the white-dress girl, unable to endure the cry a moment longer.

27

If the museum proved anything, it was the need to value family and home while the opportunity was there, to see both as immense blessings. How had Chloe done at either?

She turned to her sister, who stood in front of a display case of actual suitcases some lucky riders had used to carry all of their worldly possessions. Lauren's attention was fixed on the lonely artifacts, hands tucked in her front pockets. Except for Lauren's college years, the two of them had never lived more than a couple of hours apart. They had always been within visiting distance, but rarely had they taken advantage of it during adulthood. Proximity was a gift that Chloe had underrated without realizing it. Maybe being an ocean apart from her sister would be much harder than it seemed.

She stepped over to Lauren. "How are you liking the museum?"

Her sister glanced at her, then nodded. "It's informative."

Their mom huddled on a bench along the wall, thumbs tapping away on her phone, probably texting their dad instructions of some kind.

"Thanks for paying for us," Chloe said.

"Of course." Her sister tilted her head as if studying a suitcase from a new angle.

"I admit, Laur, I never read the books. I had forgotten all about them, actually, until I was planning this trip. Then I remembered how I found you burrowed in bed with one of the books and a tissue box."

Her sister pinned her with the same sharp expression as back in the welcome center. "If you read them, you'd understand."

The bite nearly set Chloe back on her heels. With all gentleness, she nodded. "I'm sure I would. I've always wondered what it was about those books that hit you so hard. That's the job of art, to make us feel."

Her sister stared at her a beat, brow slightly relaxing. Then she took a step to the side and positioned herself in front of a different suitcase.

Something dug at Lauren. Something she didn't want to carry but didn't want to share. Nothing ate away at joy like hidden pain. Responding to her sister's gnash with anything but invitation would only drive that secret deeper under wraps.

Chloe tucked her hair behind her ear and tried a different path. "I'm struck by how the siblings on the trains were often separated, despite the organizers' best efforts. Can you imagine if you and I were on the train and had been separated? Or Mom and Aunt Gab?"

Both of them turned to the bob-haired woman on the bench.

At that same moment, their mom rose and stuffed her phone into her purse. "I need to find the restroom. Meet me back in the welcome center, girls."

"You're done?" Chloe asked.

Their mom paused long enough to say, "I've seen what I need to." Then she disappeared around the corner.

"That didn't take long," Chloe commented.

"This place obviously upsets her. It's written all over her face."

"She always looks like that. It's hard to tell."

Though she chuckled, her sister cut her eyes to her in silent correction.

Chloe cleared her throat. "I agree, the topic of the museum can be hard to take. But I think it's important to know the history, don't you? Besides, it highlights how important family really is. Which is why—" She checked the spot their mom had last appeared. No sign of her. Nonetheless, she whispered to Lauren, "Which is why I think we should encourage Mom to reconnect with Aunt Gab."

For a moment, her sister was quiet, computations clearly coming together. Then she shook her head. "No, Chloe. Stay out of it."

"Why? Don't you want to see them be closer?"

"It's not our place. They're grown women. They'll be what they want to be to each other."

"But they could be more."

"Not our place," her sister emphasized.

Chloe stepped back. Was that really how Lauren felt? Did she really believe that family bonds were not valuable enough to protect?

"Lauren," she began, "you and I certainly have our differences, but I would never let our connection completely shrivel like theirs has. You're too important to me. Even if I'm on the other side of the world, I'll always want to know what you're up to and that you're okay."

Her sister arched an eyebrow. "Is that why you text me so often now, half a *city* away?"

Chloe dipped her head. It was true. But it was also true that Lauren didn't make much of an effort either. She lifted her chin. "You're right. That should change. We can change it together. Both our connection and Mom and Aunt Gab's. Think about it: We're passing through Nebraska. We could ask Aunt Gab to meet us in—"

"Stop. Whatever you're thinking, stop. You'll make it worse. They can figure things out themselves."

"They could, but it seems they need a bit of kick start, don't you think? We all need a gentle reminder sometimes. Life's too short to spend it on animosity." She smiled at herself for remembering one of Sori's favorite quotes. "That's a Brontë line. Or something like it. I don't remember the exact wording."

"Which Brontë?"

Chloe narrowed her brow. "There's more than one?"

Lauren visibly struggled not to roll her eyes. "I'm going to meet Mom."

"Wait. I'm coming too." She sped up to her sister's side.

They exited the depot building together, into the bright noontime and the pull of the open road. They prepared to leave behind the stories of families torn apart, but they were headed directly into the gaps of their own frayed family ties.

The idea her sister had rejected may very well have been Chloe's best one in a long time.

28

The gentle topographical waves of central Kansas slowly settled into flatter plains along Highway 28. Lauren opened her Maps app and looked up the distance to the National Willa Cather Center in Red Cloud, Nebraska. The fastest route to the small city just across the state line would take them an hour and a half, mostly via backcountry roads. That was long enough to read the full summary of at least *O Pioneers!* online, maybe more.

She switched back to her home screen and to the web search bar. As she lowered her thumb toward it, she paused. Her email app icon hovered near the bar. It was only Friday, and the recruiter had promised to let her know by early the following week if they wanted to move forward. It wouldn't take but a second to check if he had reached out already. She held her breath and tapped the icon.

Nothing. No messages from him or any other company she had applied to.

Before the ache could bloom, she exited her email and searched online for a summary.

To the backdrop of the song thrumming from Chloe's phone, she slipped into the world of Alexandra Bergson and her daring gamble to rescue her family's homestead from the relentless conditions of the untamed Nebraska plains. The strength of Alexandra, her cleverness and wisdom, her steady gain of command over an unpredictable land, puffed Lauren's chest. It tamped down any remnant of ache from the orphan train exhibits and tempered the pangs in her ignored stomach. Alexandra was the kind of woman every girl should aspire to be. Powerful, a leader, immune to others' opinions of her.

Lauren fell so deep into the world of Alexandra, Emil, Carl, Ivar, and the rest of their pioneer community that she didn't lift her head until her sister had pulled into the dirt parking lot of a roadside diner.

"Lunchtime!" Chloe bumped the Xterra along the uneven lot and found a spot along the vinyl-sided building.

Though a few houses peeked through the trees along the edge of the lot and a church rose from across the four-lane highway, open country dominated the area.

"Where are we?" Lauren asked.

"Mankato." Her sister turned off both the engine and her playlist, then pulled the keys from the ignition.

"Apparently this is some kind of hot spot." Their mom motioned toward the diner.

"The online reviews call it 'a favorite Highway 36 stop,'" Chloe said. "They're supposed to have amazing ice cream."

"Highway 36? I thought we were on 28."

Her sister chuckled. "That was, like, fifteen minutes ago, Laur. We've made two turns since then."

"She was reading," their mom defended her. "Lost in a good study, I'm sure. Right, Lauren?"

She smiled, but only to mask the disquiet. How much had she missed? They were both familiar with whatever the eatery was. Had they been discussing it? Discussing something else?

Her sister and mom opened their doors. Lauren unbuckled and followed.

While she and their mom stuck with salads, Chloe opted for

the OZ burger, highly recommended to her by a fellow diner, a young man with a scruffy beard and fluorescent orange work shirt streaked with black stains. Juices ran down Chloe's hands as she ate. The lettuce in Lauren's salad was tasteless, but salad dressing added too many calories.

Her sister insisted on paying for their lunches. Lauren protested, to no avail, then offered to buy their mom ice cream instead, also to no avail. Lauren sucked down the last of her ice-cold water and willed it to freeze the rise of frustration.

At the end of their meal, she escorted their mom out the door as Chloe paid the tab and chatted up the scruffy-bearded young man. Before they could reach the car, Chloe caught up with them, a giant smile on her face.

"Guess what! The guy in there told me about a cool spot close to here that we need to visit. It's not that far out of our way."

Lauren checked her phone. "It's already past one o'clock. The Cather museum closes at five."

"It's only a few minutes out of our way. We have plenty of time."

"What is this 'cool' place?" their mom asked.

"The geographic center of the continental US, outside Lebanon."

Lauren blinked. Her sister seriously wanted to go off plan to see some gimmick?

"It's supposed to be worth the drive," Chloe insisted. "Bruce Springsteen filmed a Super Bowl commercial there."

Their mom huffed. "I wonder if he asked for hazard pay to come to Kansas."

"Please, let's go?" Chloe said. "When are we ever going to be this close again?"

Lauren exchanged a look with their mom. As best she could, she used her gaze to say, *You don't have to go.*

But their mom sighed and gave a single nod that notched away a degree of Lauren's influence. "I hope by 'cool,'" she said, "you also mean air-conditioned."

The geographic center boasted not a smidge of air-conditioning. In fact, besides a chapel about the size of a large toolshed, there were no enclosed buildings at all. The windswept site sat on a triangle of land formed by the convergence of three roads—two paved and one dirt. It offered no restrooms but, oddly, provided a pavilion with picnic tables and several benches under the smattering of shade trees.

"How cute!" Chloe said.

By the way their mom's shoulders slumped, it was clear the feeling was not mutual. No other cars or people were around. Their only company was the heat of the day and the occasional breeze.

Chloe led the way to the chapel. It looked like a country church in miniature, complete with white clapboard sides and a steeple. A gentle-grade sidewalk led up to the open door, above which was a wooden sign that read "U.S. Center Chapel."

"Isn't this cool?" Chloe gushed. "Come on, let's go in."

They entered single file, her sister first and their mom last. Even with only three adults inside, the chapel seemed to strain at its occupancy seams. In ten steps, Lauren would have reached the pulpit. Four one-person pews hugged each wall. Above them, homemade drapes were pinched back from the windows to let in the sun—the sun but not the breeze. The windows remained shut tight.

"It is sweltering in here," their mom said. She fanned herself with her hand and hung close to the door.

Chloe proceeded up the aisle, stepping along the worn path caused by years' worth of foot traffic. Besides the concrete floor, nearly everything in the interior was wood. The pews, the paneled walls, the pulpit. On the wall above the pulpit hung a wood cutout of the contiguous United States painted to resemble the American flag and overlaid with a large wooden cross with a heart in the middle.

Chloe paused at the front row of pews, gaze seemingly fixed on the cross. Slowly she lowered into the pew to her right. A moment later, she bowed her head.

Lauren turned to check on their mom. Sure enough, sweat rivered down the sides of her face. "Why don't you go sit under the pavilion?" she suggested. "Give Chloe a moment in here."

Their mom nodded. "Great idea. Thank you."

Some influence Lauren had retained.

Their mom traversed to the sidewalk and turned left for the pavilion. The light glinted off her blond hair, which increasingly took on a snowy hue. Age made some people more beautiful, and their mom was one of them.

Lauren took note of the time on her phone. In five minutes, if Chloe hadn't moved, she would tell her to move it along, for their mom's sake. In the meantime, she leaned a hip against the side of a pew in the back and crossed her arms. How long had Bruce Springsteen stayed at the chapel? Had he sat in any of the pews? Did he pray? Was he even religious? It was hard to fathom a superstar agreeing to come to such a remote place.

On the seat of the pew, a Bible lay open to the book of Philippians. Someone had underlined a passage. She leaned closer and read silently, *I know what it is to be in need, and I know what it is to have plenty. I have learned the secret of being content in any and every situation, whether well fed or hungry, whether living in plenty or in want. I can do everything through him who gives me strength.*

Whatever the secret was, no one had told her.

She reached down and swatted the Bible closed. She checked the time. Three minutes.

29

Their mom's footfalls had faded into the outside a while ago, but her sister's had not. Why did Lauren stay? Did she feel something too in this little dwelling? Something that drew her back to worship?

Chloe folded her hands tighter in her lap.

You know the reason. Lauren may think she knows the reason. She may think she's staying here for my sake, but show her it's for her own. I pray she turns to you. I pray her knee would bow in humility before you. I pray you will lead her and Mom both in understanding the things of faith the way they understand the things of humans—or at least think they do.

Lauren cleared her throat. "Chloe."

God, whatever is going on with Lauren, please bring it to light. Please open the path for me to help her.

"Time to go. Mom's waiting."

And regardless of what she says, please help me to find a way to connect Mom and Aunt Gab.

She opened her eyes and turned them up to the cross with the heart affixed to its beams. A sweet symbol of the enormity of God's love for the world. "Right behind you, Laur."

Footsteps trailed to the door.

She exhaled slowly, making room for the peace that filled her to the brim. Even if she was the only one who got any meaning out of the unplanned stop, it was worth the extra minutes to visit that site.

Thank you, Lord.

A shrill cry cut through the air.

"Lauren?" Chloe leaped to her feet and dashed outside. To the right of the door, her sister was crumpled on her side between the sidewalk and a wooden park bench. Her phone lay face down in the grass nearby.

"Lauren!" Chloe rushed over and squatted next to her. "Are you okay?"

Her sister bit her lip hard, holding back more cries. She clutched the fingers of her left hand and rocked.

"What happened?" Chloe asked.

"I fell! What does it look like? I hit the stupid bench on the way down."

Their mom arrived, breathless. "What happened?"

"She fell," Chloe repeated. "Must have caught the drop-off of the sidewalk or something." The difference between the edge of the sidewalk and the ground was about an inch. If her sister had been distracted by her phone, she could have easily missed it.

Lauren rolled onto her knees, head bowed, fingers clutched tight.

"You're hurt," Chloe said.

"I'm fine." Lauren grabbed her phone, pushed to her feet, and started to walk back to the car. Dirt and grass stuck to her shirt.

"Let's see your hand, Laur."

Her sister wheeled around and slung a curse that roared across the fields. "I said I'm fine!"

Their mom lurched forward and said through clenched teeth, "Lauren Jillian! We are at a church!"

The redness of her sister's face darkened. Her chest rose and fell with quick, sucking breaths. It wasn't like Lauren to swear. It wasn't like her to unleash such rage. And the pain that pooled on the rims of her eyes comprised more than the physical.

Lauren broke away from them and marched back to the car.

"What in the world possessed her?" their mom wondered aloud.

Embarrassment, undoubtedly. But there had to be more. Chloe lifted her face to the blinding sky. If ever the Lord needed to shine that light on obscure things, the time had come.

30

Her oldest daughter sulked in the back seat. That was just fine by Edie. If Lauren didn't have anything pleasant to say, she might as well keep quiet. If Grant had been there, he would have made her walk for using such atrocious language.

Chloe peeked back at her sister a few times. On the fourth time, Edie leaned toward her and whispered, "Let her be. She needs to chill out."

So did Edie. Of course, that would be harder than it needed to be with the blasted quasi-functioning air-conditioning. At least Chloe didn't attempt to turn on her playlist and blare away the tension. Her youngest could show sense and a level head from time to time. Chloe's reaction to Lauren's outburst had certainly smacked of composure.

Chloe kept her attention on the road ahead. They both would let Lauren be, and the discord among them would smooth eventually. It always did, somehow.

A short time later, they passed a sign welcoming them to Nebraska. The makeup of the land showed exactly zero difference to that of Kansas.

"The welcome sign said Nebraska is home of Arbor Day," Chloe said. "Weird how a state known for corn claims trees instead."

To their left, a paved road looped off the two-lane highway. A row of placards edged the bend.

Chloe looked over her shoulder as they passed. "Rats. I meant to stop there. I think that was the Willa Cather Memorial Prairie historical marker. I can turn around."

"No need."

"But you enjoy Willa Cather. This is a chance to see the view of her beloved land."

"I'm looking at nothing but her beloved land right now."

"If you're sure. It's supposed to be a beautiful spot for pictures."

"I'm sure it is, but . . ." Edie turned partially around. In the back seat, Lauren had her earbuds stuffed in her ears and her attention fully on the view outside her window.

"I understand," Chloe replied.

If Lauren heard any of their conversation, she gave no indication.

Edie settled against her seat back. A mileage sign informed them that Red Cloud waited six miles ahead. The highway curved to the right, then left, then finally stayed straight as an arrow. All around them stretched the wild land that had stolen the show—and some characters' pride—in Cather's epics. The books were among the very few her mother loved that Edie had found pleasure in too. In all their years together, she had never asked if her mother had ever come to those far reaches of the prairie glorified by the author who once found home on its soil. Had her mother ever seen the dips and bends and rises of the land that Cather once compared to the ocean? Had her mother ever been so swept up in Cather's resplendent plains that she wished she was from there too? Cather had used rich, affectionate descriptions for the home she never fully left behind. How blessed the author was to have the language to form such praise.

How blessed to have a home that warranted such praise.

31

wift's *1989* album ended well before they reached Red Cloud, but so long as Lauren kept in her earbuds, the front seat occupants would leave her alone. Her left middle finger throbbed. The top knuckle refused to bend. She kept her finger shielded by her right palm and breathed through the pain.

What a fool. Fool, fool, fool. The pain in her finger was exactly the pain she deserved for letting the veil slip, for using words that stirred up the coldness in her mom that she fought so hard to keep away. She closed her eyes and leaned back. Maybe there was a way for her to get back to Kansas City early, before things got worse.

A few minutes later, her sister's announcement roused her.

"We've arrived."

The city limit was demarked by a carved sign held up by two brick pillars. "Welcome to Red Cloud," it proclaimed, followed by its sole claim to fame: "Childhood Home of Willa Cather." A few paces away, a homemade yard sign added, "Red Cloud FFA welcomes you."

The outskirts comprised a few one-story homes, metal buildings, and pockets of cornfields between trees. Southern Nebraska had a surprising amount of trees considering it lay in the vast prairie. They passed a small city pool, then the pavement abruptly spilled onto brick. Chloe slowed to a crawl to minimize the rumble created by the uneven surface. Ambiance may have been the primary intent for the brick, speed control the added bonus. A block later, downtown began. Two-story storefronts walled in the main strip.

Chloe drove into the second block, then pulled into an angled parking spot along the curb.

"Are we there?" their mom asked.

Her sister jutted her thumb toward the back window. "Behind us."

Both Lauren and their mom turned around. Almost the entire side of the street bore the same red brick, with ornate trim along the roofline. While there was no visible sign for the Willa Cather Center, one of the floor-to-ceiling windows on the first floor contained a black-and-white image of a woman nearly as tall and wide as the door next to it.

"That must be her," their mom said.

"Let's hit it." Chloe grabbed the keys and pushed open her door.

As the others were busy disembarking, Lauren uncovered her left hand for the first time. Her middle finger was noticeably larger and redder than the others. She shook her head. Such a fool.

She got out of the car and gingerly slipped her hands into her front pockets, hiding both from view.

Chloe paid for their admission to the museum before Lauren had a chance to step fully into the building. Just as well. Pulling out her own credit card would have required both of her hands.

The Willa Cather Center was smaller than the National Orphan Train Museum and Complex, but at least it was all in one building. Lauren soon wandered from the others. She followed along the exhibit of a timeline chronicling Cather's life. It ran the length of one wall, tracing her existence from her East Coast birth in 1873 to her move to Nebraska with her family at age nine to her return to the East Coast during young adulthood. Though she lived most of her life elsewhere, the prairie had a clear hold on her creative consciousness, much like it had on Langston Hughes's. Nearly all of her famous work somehow tied back to her formative years among the people and lifestyle of the Cornhusker State.

Also like Hughes, she chafed under the weight of others' views of her. According to the timeline, when Cather was fourteen, she swore she would be nothing like what she was expected to be. She cut her hair like a boy's and vowed to be a surgeon, a profession considered to be for men only. She started to dress like a boy, called herself William Cather Jr., and rode along with country doctors on house visits. She graduated high school at sixteen, and despite being the only student the local paper did not laud as bound for anything of note, she enrolled in the University of Nebraska and began what would blossom into a legendary editing career.

Later in life, when an authority figure told her she wasn't talented enough to write a novel, she wrote it anyway. A year later, she wrote her second book, *O Pioneers!* Five years later, she published *My Ántonia*. Five years later, she won the Pulitzer Prize for *One of Ours*.

If Cather was anything, she was above being defined by others' expectations and opinions—a quality imbued in her character Alexandra. She was not one to be left behind, but someone who blazed her own way and let others decide if they wanted to catch up with *her*.

And Cather started showing that side of herself publicly very early on, with a haircut. Lauren pulled her right hand from her pocket and smoothed her fingertips down her strands.

Cather was the kind of woman every girl should aspire to be.

32

ather's parents lived here the rest of their lives, so she would come back to visit them."

Ten minutes in, and Helen, the demure but talkative docent, still had Chloe and her mom standing near the first exhibit, trapped by sentences that went on for days with few natural breaks. No other guests had come to divert Helen's obvious need for human companionship. Chloe's lower back started to ache from standing in one place, and restlessness began to show in her mom's nonverbal language.

Both of them cast glances into the museum every so often, Chloe usually toward her sister, who had been clever enough to escape right away. Lauren was not clever enough, however, to hide the fact she had an injured hand. She did her best to keep her injury out of sight by tucking her hands into her pockets, but denial did not alter the truth. She was hurt, and she chose pride over help.

Perhaps help needed to barge in like a prairie storm instead of waiting to be summoned. In a circumstance like the one Lauren was in, help went by the name Edie Vance. Lauren could shut Chloe out all day long, but there was no shutting out their mom.

". . . and the family home has been converted into a guesthouse, so you can actually stay there, but even if you're not, you can go by and see it."

At the docent's brief pause for an inhale, Chloe pounced. "Helen, thank you so much for your time and all you've shared with us. We do plan to go see the other sites in town you've mentioned, and we have reservations at the guesthouse, but first we'd love to explore the museum. If you don't mind, we'll excuse ourselves and go do our perusing. We'll let you know if we have any questions." She placed her hand on her mom's back and gently directed her to walk forward—quickly.

"Oh, yes, yes, please, yes, enjoy your visit. I'll be right here if you need anything."

They made it around a display before Helen could start another sentence.

Her mom exhaled. "Thank you for that, Chloe. Bless her heart. I thought we would be standing there all night."

"I have a feeling Helen might have enjoyed us being there all night. Let's catch up with Lauren."

The third member of their party stood toward the back of the museum amid pictures from Willa Cather's life. Lauren had her back to them and her head held slightly to the side.

While they were still a ways off, Chloe pulled at her mom's arm to bring her to a stop. She whispered, "Have you looked at Lauren's hand since she fell?"

Her mom frowned. "No."

"Maybe you should."

"Why? What's wrong with it?"

"Just go look."

The frown on her mom's face tightened. She broke for Lauren. Chloe hung back and let the scene play out as it would.

Her sister turned at their mom's approach and smiled. "You're free."

"Let me see your hand."

"My hand?"

Their mom did not wait another moment. She yanked at Lauren's left arm to try to force her hand out of her pocket.

Lauren winced and stepped away from her grip. "All right," she said. Slowly she lifted her hand from its sheath.

Chloe came closer. Her instincts bore out. Her sister's middle finger was inflamed and discolored.

"Lauren! Why did you not tell me?" Their mom grabbed Lauren's wrist and brought the injury closer to her eyes.

"It's only jammed."

"Or it could be broken. I'm glad Chloe said something. We have to get this checked out."

"No, please. It'll be fine." Lauren attempted to extract her arm but failed.

Their mom turned toward the front and beckoned. "Excuse me, uh . . ."

"Helen," Chloe said.

"Helen!"

Footsteps approached. The docent popped around a display. "Did you need something?"

Their mother held up Lauren's hand. "A doctor."

The woman's eyes widened. "Oh my. Oh my, did that— When did . . ."

"It happened before we got here. Where can we find a doctor?"

"There's a hospital on the northwest side of town. I'll write down the address for you." Helen quick-stepped back to the front.

"Chloe, get the address please. Lauren, come with me." Their mom led Lauren by the arm toward the exit.

As they passed Chloe, her sister glowered at her. But the truth was, Lauren could have saved herself the indignity. A person's greatest need was often the one they refused to acknowledge.

33

Edie folded her hands at her waist as the doctor rolled his stool closer to the exam room counter and tore into the packaging of the splint. Her oldest daughter rested in the bed between them, injured hand lying on the tray table. The broken finger looked even more gross under the fluorescent lights.

Edie could take being next to her mother's bedside; being next to her child's was a different level of anguish. The only time Lauren had been in the ER was for a bout with croup when she was four. That situation had been more serious than a broken finger, but still the guilt raged. Lauren had been in pain and had not said a word. Why? And why hadn't Edie seen it? Chloe had, but not her. Edie had even scolded Lauren. What did that say about her mothering?

Her youngest daughter fiddled with her phone, completely relaxed against the back of her chair by the exam room door, free of remorse or worry.

The doctor threaded the second of two Velcro strips through the eyelet of the padded stainless steel splint, his golden-tone skin a rich contrast to the clinical palette of the room. "You'll need to wear this splint for about four weeks," he told Lauren as he worked. "It's a mild fracture, so it should heal quite quickly. You'll be right as rain before you know it."

Midwestern colloquialisms sounded strange in an Indian accent.

"That's good news, right, Laur?" Chloe said.

Lauren ignored her.

The doctor swiveled on his stool, bringing the splint to the tray table. Blue embroidery across his left lapel identified him as Dr. Deepak Gupta, MD. "Keep the foam dry as best you can. Cover the splint when you shower, such as with a latex glove or a plastic bag." He waved the splint. "Ready for the hard part?"

She nodded.

Edie held her breath, dug her fingernails into the backs of her hands.

With slow movements, Dr. Gupta pulled apart the two metal sides of the splint and positioned them over and under the length of Lauren's finger. Then he pinched the two sides in place and secured the top Velcro strap right over the broken knuckle.

Lauren winced.

"Sorry, I know that's uncomfortable," he said. "The splint needs to be snug but not too tight. It's not too tight?"

"No." Her voice was soft, as if she had suddenly gone shy.

"Good." He smoothed the bottom strap into place, made a few adjustments, then patted the back of her hand. "All over." He swiveled to the counter and began gathering the discarded packaging.

The splint made Lauren's finger three times larger than the others. Chloe lifted her phone and silently urged Lauren to smile for a picture. Lauren clenched her jaw, then buried her injury under the tray table. Physical pain was not the only kind of hurt plaguing her.

Edie's stomach knotted. Grant would tell her it was all okay, that Lauren was okay, but the leap from hearing to believing was too big to make at the moment. What she needed was a distraction.

The doctor tossed the packaging into the nearby receptacle, then settled in at the laptop affixed to a swinging arm hinged on the wall. *Clack, clack, clack.* How curious that someone of his background would end up in the-middle-of-nowhere Nebraska. He appeared to be in his late thirties at most.

She rubbed the back of her left hand with her index finger. "So, Doctor," she began, "how long have you been here?"

Lauren whipped her head up and frowned at Edie.

The doctor's fingers never paused. "I emigrated when I was fifteen."

"Oh, no. I just meant—"

But her daughter shook her head, clearly instructing her to leave it be. All Edie had really tried to ask was how long he had been in Red Cloud specifically.

She cleared her throat and tried a different tack. "Have you always wanted to be a doctor of emergency medicine?"

He switched to the mouse and clicked around the screen. "I'm a doctor of family medicine, actually. But I'm the only doctor for hours, which makes me the ER doctor, the surgeon, the OB, the hospice doctor, and the pediatrician. I also helped deliver a breeched calf once, but mainly in the role of hapless neighbor."

"How exciting," she said.

"That's one word." He switched his attention back to his patient in the bed. "I'm going to start you on a regimen of ibuprofen. It's important for you to stay ahead of the pain. I'll have the nurse bring you a first dose. There's a pharmacy on Webster if you need to pick up more. They'll have latex gloves there too."

Lauren nodded.

"Have you had much to eat in the last hour or so? Your first dose is a large one, and it could upset your stomach if it's empty."

"I have some protein balls in my backpack," Chloe cut in. "I'll make sure she has one."

"Perfect," the doctor said.

Lauren's jaw joint bulged.

Back to the computer he went. Typing and more typing. Surely it was all in English. It had to be, didn't it? She and Grant once watched a documentary on the experience of foreign exchange students and the rigorous preparation they went through to be accepted into an American university. Among the arduous requirements was passing the Test of English as a Foreign Language. For a medical student, the test would be all the more crucial to pass.

Fingertip tracing the back of her hand, she asked, "Do you find English a difficult language to learn?"

The room went still. Three sets of eyes nailed her in place.

Was the question really that out of line?

The doctor resumed his clicks and replied, "I find practicing medicine far more difficult."

Lauren shifted. Chloe bit her lip as if trying to restrain a laugh.

It was a perfectly legitimate, interested question. She crossed her arms as heat spread across her face.

At last, Dr. Gupta locked the computer, stood, and looked down at Lauren. "Be sure to follow up with your doctor when you get home. I'll send the nurse back in with your dose."

Lauren nodded. Chloe said thank you for them all, then the doctor stepped out of the room. Her daughters zeroed in on her.

Edie straightened her arms at her sides. "Was there something wrong with what I asked?"

The laugh finally escaped Chloe's lips. "Not if you're a naturalization officer."

"I was only making conversation. I do not believe I asked anything that was out of bounds."

"If that's true, we need to expose you to more people." Chloe pulled out a storage container from the backpack by her feet and tossed it onto the foot of the bed. "Eat up."

Lauren gave Chloe yet another of those looks and slowly reached for the container with her good hand.

Edie planted her hands on her hips. "There is nothing bad about trying to get to know another human being. Is there?"

Both her daughters looked away.

First her oldest hid an injury from her, now they were both piling on her for a supposed infraction. She couldn't get anything

143

right, in their estimation. She stepped toward the door. "Sorry I embarrass you both so much."

"Mom, where are you going?" Lauren asked.

"To powder my nose."

Chloe held up her hand as she approached the door. "Please don't be mad. I was just giving you a hard time. I don't think the doctor took any offense."

Too little, too late. "I'll be back shortly." She pushed into the hallway.

The restroom was dimly lit and pleasantly cold, the two best qualities a room could have. She lingered in the stall minutes longer than she needed to, well after the burn in her skin subsided. Lord willing, it would stay subdued. Lord willing, something about the trip would be redeemable, because they certainly couldn't brag about a lack of injury, physical or otherwise.

She wiped her brow, gathered her breath, and whispered over herself, "You can do this."

As she rejoined her daughters in the exam room, the nurse handed Chloe a slip of paper with a name and phone number. "This is our group captain. If you do want to join us tomorrow, give him a call."

By the glower on Lauren's face and the glow on Chloe's, whatever her youngest had just arranged would challenge her frail armor of strength.

34

"When are we going to be able to do something as thoroughly Nebraskan again?" her little sister asked their mom as they all proceeded down the main aisle of the pharmacy. "Willa Cather would have done it if it had been a thing back then."

"Chloe, if I never in my life have the chance to bake like a ham in a metal stock tank while floating down a river, I will be none the poorer."

From the exam room to the car to the pharmacy, her sister persisted in getting their mom to agree to accept the nurse's invitation to go with her church group on a tank float, apparently a big thing in Nebraska. The more Chloe persisted, the more their mom replied with some variation of "We are doing no such thing!"

Lauren ducked into the pain relief aisle, attempting to escape the tit for tat. The debate couldn't possibly have stayed relegated to the car and therefore given her a modicum of dignity in public. No, her mom and sister had to hash it out for all of Red Cloud to hear.

The ibuprofen was halfway down the aisle. Lauren quickened her steps, but her family followed her.

"You need to think of your sister," their mom continued. "She must keep the splint dry."

"I know. That's why— Wait, I'll show you." Chloe doubled back and disappeared around the end of the aisle.

"Where is she going?" their mom asked.

Lauren didn't give an answer. They hadn't included her much in the conversation anyway. Three varieties of ibuprofen stood side by side on the middle shelf. She reached for the generic.

"Get the Advil," her mom said.

Lauren paused, hand midair. "The doctor said any ibuprofen is fine."

"Advil works better. I gave it to you for all your fevers and orthodontics adjustments. Trust me. Get the Advil." Her mom grabbed the box of softgels off the shelf and put it in Lauren's palm. Her mom had yet to lose a debate with her, and she clearly wasn't about to start.

Lauren let her full hand fall to her side. She wasn't allowed to even pick out her own medication.

Her sister sprang around the corner with a package of blue latex gloves that were a size too large for Lauren's hand and a roll of medical tape. "Here's what we'll do. We'll stretch the glove over the splint and tape it closed at the wrist. Lauren will have to do this anyway when she showers."

Lauren tightened her grip around the pill box. "A shower is fifteen minutes. A float is all day. I'm not wearing a glove taped to my hand for that long."

"It's not all day," Chloe countered. "It's only for about three hours."

"Three hours," their mom muttered.

"Time well spent." Chloe tucked the package under her arm. "Did I tell you the float is on the *Republican* River? It's practically a flashing neon sign that you were destined to do this, Mom."

"Now you're being absurd. Lauren doesn't want to go, and neither do I."

"But once we've seen all the Cather stuff, what else is there to do?"

"Leave," their mom said.

An accurate answer if ever there was one.

"It's a gentle float on a gentle river with a gentle church group," Chloe pressed.

"And half of Red Cloud," Lauren added. According to the nurse's story, the FFA's annual float brought bigger and bigger crowds every year, and this year was slated to be the biggest turnout yet.

Her sister glossed over the interjection. "Marge said it's not strenuous. In fact, we don't have to row or lift a muscle at all."

Their mom arched an eyebrow. "Marge? You're on a first-name basis with Lauren's nurse?"

"She's really nice. You'll love her."

The hour was getting late, and the conversation kept going in circles. Enough was enough. Lauren cut in. "Mom has made it clear that she doesn't want to go, so let's figure out something else to do."

The day before, their mom had thanked Lauren for course-altering pronouncements, rewarded her for them. In the pharmacy aisle, however, their mom looked at Chloe as if wondering how she would respond.

Chloe stepped closer to their mom, rested a hand on her shoulder. "Think about how proud Dad would be of you if you tried this. Think of how much you'd blow his socks off to say, 'Guess what I did.'"

Instead of immediately shaking off the obvious appeal to her ego, their mom stayed quiet, waiting for more.

"He'll be telling all his buddies," her sister continued. "He'll be showing them the pictures we're about to take, talking about how his wife did something none of theirs ever have. Only three hours for a lifetime of renown." She waggled her eyebrows. "Think about it."

Their mom's gaze drifted off to the side. A million thoughts must have tumbled inside her mind, all of them in a particular direction.

A sudden chill prickled Lauren's skin. She crossed her arms against the cold.

At last their mom sighed. "Your dad would get a kick out of it."

Chloe punched the air above her head in celebration. "I will buy the best waterproof sunscreen this pharmacy has to offer!" Once more, she darted from the aisle and out of sight.

Their mom turned to Lauren. "The glove thing would work to keep your splint dry."

Lauren pulled her arms tighter. "I'm sure it would."

"You're okay with going on this float, then?"

No, it was not okay. Nothing about the last couple of hours was okay. Nothing about their mom turning her back was okay. But she had to remain strong, be the one who boosted others' needs. Leaders made sacrifices, even when they had unmet needs themselves.

"Maybe you and Chloe should do this together, just the two of you," she said.

Their mom shoved her eyebrows together. "Without you?"

"That's why you're on this trip with her, right? To bond?"

"But you'd be by yourself."

And not for the first or the last time. She shrugged. "I'll find something. You all should go. I'll be fine, I promise. I'll probably be too tired after taking these anyway." She lifted the box and rattled the pills.

Though their mom offered a smile, it barely activated the laugh lines on either end of her lips. "You're a trouper, Lauren. Dad would be proud of you too." She turned and followed Chloe, her endorsement of Lauren's resiliency hanging in the air.

Resilient and hurt could be impossible to tell apart.

35

For as proud as her dad would be of her mom for going on the float, he would be prouder of Chloe for getting Edie Vance in the tank. Who knew her persuasion skills possessed such potency?

Apparently Sori did.

"Doesn't surprise me," her friend said when Chloe called to tell her about the major events of the day. "You did convince her to go on a trip you hadn't even planned yet."

Chloe lowered onto the front railing of the guesthouse's wrap-around porch and switched her phone to her other ear. "Suppose you're right. I am killing it, aren't I?"

"Wouldn't go that far, but yes, you can get people to do things they wouldn't necessarily think to do on their own. Like me baby-sitting a bearded dragon."

"If only my superpowers worked on my sister." Lauren had hardly said a word during supper at the local pizza place—or eaten. "I keep thinking there's something going on. I've noticed that she's not—" The last word dried up as the image from the hospital replayed. Lauren had taken her time with the protein ball, one painfully slow chew at a time, as if she had to coach herself through not regretting every morsel. Same with the salad she had picked at like a bird at the restaurant, instead of tearing into the pepperoni pizza like she used to when she was younger.

Lauren deprived herself of even simple joys and increasingly retracted from others, the act of someone in the throes of self-punishment. But why? How many layers exactly were piled upon her sister?

"She's not what?" Sori prodded.

If something was going on, Lauren deserved privacy. Chloe redirected. "She's not the funnest person to go on a road trip with."

Sori guffawed. "I would have predicted you'd say that about your mom."

"I think the trip is growing on my mom. They both like where we're staying tonight. For the most part."

"Where are you staying?"

"The Cather Second Home Guest House. It once belonged to the Cather family. All the rooms have been renovated, and now the Cather Foundation or whatever it's called rents them out to sucker tourists like us."

"Brilliant move."

"Our room is on the second floor and has its own bathroom. My mom's especially happy about that."

"I'd be too."

A breeze kicked across her face. The day slowly drifted into a mild evening. It was only their second night away, only two states from home, yet it seemed much longer and much farther. They had a long way yet to get where they were meant to go.

Chloe tapped her heel against a spindle of the porch railing. "Jeremy doing okay?"

"Hanging in like a boss," her friend replied. "I can tell he misses you, though."

"No, you can't."

"Yeah, not really."

Chloe laughed. "I'm sure he's enjoying his time with you. And if you decide a bearded dragon isn't for you after this week, I can always find someone else to take him. Maybe my aunt."

"The one with the farm?"

"Yes. She lives here in Nebraska. She'd probably enjoy having him, and he'd undoubtedly like life with emus and donkeys."

"I love that for him."

Jeremy in the midst of a weird animal menagerie somehow did make sense. Almost as much sense as her mom and aunt finally removing whatever wedge was stuck between them and suffocating the love out of each. It was no way to live. Too much freedom was sacrificed on the altar of pride. Their greatest need was the one they refused to acknowledge. Maybe if they came face-to-face with it, they couldn't ignore it anymore. And maybe like Lauren, they required a little help to come face-to-face with it.

"Sori," she said, "if my persuasion skills are really that powerful, there is one more thing I need to do today."

Sori's tone resounded suspicion. "Why? What are you plotting?"

She breathed in. "I'm going to make a phone call."

36

Maybe daybreaks in Kansas City were as peaceful and magnificent as they were in rural communities and Edie was too distracted by the duties of existence to notice. But in southern Nebraska, where the pace was simpler and the nights darker, wonder rose with the light that Saturday morning.

She closed the front door of the guesthouse and took her journal to the wicker love seat on the east side of the porch. Her sleeveless top and capris exposed her extremities to the tame air, and she relished it while relishing was still possible. Within hours, she would sweat her life out in a large round trough.

Why did she agree to such things? She sighed and settled onto the cushion of the love seat. Grant had better be proud of her going through with it. Not so proud he'd put it in her bio on the back of her memorial service program, but proud enough that he actually would brag to his buddies about the surprising exploits of his treasured wife.

Grant. Seven more days until she saw him again. Seven more days to chronicle for him in the journal, if for no other reason than to ensure he had all the details correct when he told the story.

She draped her right knee over her left and balanced the open book on top. Taking the pen in hand, she captured everything he should know about the previous day.

we're in the middle of the Great Plains, the vast land Willa Cather gushed about and the orphans of New York were thrust into. Gracious, what a land it is.

She spoke about the heartbreak of the orphan train and the burger at the Mankato diner that he would have downed faster than their youngest had. She relayed their visit to the little chapel of Springsteen fame and the tour of the Cather museum. All the events that led up to but stopped short of the moment Chloe called her attention to the blatant pain she had missed in Lauren.

She paused and lifted her head. Catty-corner to the old Cather home sat the county courthouse. The three-story brownstone grasped at the air of grandeur that courthouses of larger towns boasted. Trying so hard and not quite rising to the standard. Every day of its life, it had tried so hard.

Pen met paper once more.

It's interesting what stands out to you in the places you visit. What's right in front of your face isn't necessarily what you see. When I was sitting under the pavilion at the geographic center of the US, surrounded by the soft silence of open fields, I didn't see the chapel or Chloe's car or any of it. I saw the face of a little orphan girl I read about in the museum. She was a beautiful girl, one that anyone would be glad to call their flesh and blood, angelic in look and stature. Yet her mother disregarded her, and she was made a "foundling."

Did her mother ever dream of her face? Did her mother ever want to cross the massive distance she had put between them? Did she worry about her? Pray for her? Did she ever cry in the lonely hours of the night and ask God to forgive her? Did she ever wish time did not slip like sand through an hourglass?

Pressure built behind her eyes. Before it could turn to more, she shoved the pen into the spine and shut the journal. Enough trouble

153

filled the day without adding that too. She had written more than she had intended, gone further than intended, but she couldn't erase the words. Grant would have so many questions about them. She had plenty of questions of her own about what was inked on the thin blue lines. But they would have to wait for another time.

The sun was fully awake. The day had begun. Her daughter needed her next dose of Advil, and Edie would be there for her with a fresh cup of cold water.

37

Every girl should aspire to be like an Alexandra Bergson, and what did Alexandra do when left to figure things out on her own, despite being saddled with her own hurt and enormous responsibilities? She rose above. She didn't wallow. She found solutions. She found a way forward.

She found *herself*.

Lauren could do that. She could be that, splinted finger and all. And it started with several hours on her own, to do with as she pleased. While her mom and sister were on the float, she could explore and think and breathe. She could begin to define what came next for her. She could reclaim the power within.

She grinned as she pushed open the liftgate of the Xterra. The luggage of all three members of her family waited at her feet on the guesthouse driveway. Her sister was all too glad to give her the keys and stay in the conversation she was having on the porch with another guest about Kansas City barbecue restaurants.

With her good hand, Lauren grabbed the handle of her mom's first suitcase and heaved it into the cargo area. Her splint clicked against the zipper pull as she used both hands to wriggle the bag into the ideal position. The awkward way her left hand functioned with the contraption strapped on her middle finger made showering and dressing a challenge. The middle finger of her off hand had a surprising amount of use. But she was strong, and in this small way of loading bags into the car, she proved to everyone, to herself, that she could overcome adversity.

She loaded her mom's second suitcase and then leaned down for her own. Gravity pulled her hair over her shoulders and into her face. She should have put it up. Her hair tie was buried somewhere in her sling bag in the passenger seat. She'd have to muddle through without it. She attempted to shake her hair away, but the strands were too long to be moved far enough. She set her suitcase onto the cargo floor, then paused to shove her strands back over her shoulders. A few stubborn hairs stuck to her lips. No sooner did she peel them off than her mom parked herself at the passenger taillight and wheeled her smaller bag into the mix.

"Your sister asked me if this is really what I'm going to wear. She said I should be wearing shorts, as if I own any."

Lack of proper attire was one of many things Lauren could have pointed out about the logistics of going on a tank float. She had stayed out of it, though. "You can borrow a pair of mine," she offered.

"I don't wear shorts either, Lauren. At my age, your clothing strategy centers on what must remain covered at all costs. No one needs to see the state of my thighs."

Lauren returned to her suitcase, shimmying it into place next to the others. "I think your capris are fine. It's not like you'll be wading in the river."

"Exactly what I said. How's your finger feeling? Do you need help with these bags?"

"It's feeling better, and no, I've got them covered." Did her mom notice her overcoming adversity? Notice her indomitable strength?

By the way her mom sighed thoughtfully and settled her hands on her hips, it seemed doubtful. "The church people said they'd be here by eleven. God help me, why am I doing this?"

Lauren reached for Chloe's suitcase on the pavement between

them. "Because you promised." She had tried to save her mom from the fate she faced, but her mom had chosen to listen to any voice but hers. Choices had consequences.

"I feel like I should be staying with you," her mom lamented. "Are you sure you'll be okay? I'm not abandoning you, am I?"

She dropped Chloe's suitcase harder than she meant to on the hold floor. Her mom wanted Lauren, of all people, to justify her decision. She picked her words with intention and kept her attention on her task. "I can handle myself for a few hours. I'll be fine."

Her mom was quiet.

Lauren finished arranging her sister's bag and rotated to retrieve the next item.

Her mom pushed her smaller bag forward. Anxiety shaded her expression. "What are you going to do while we're gone?"

Lauren grabbed the handle. "I saw a coffee shop downtown yesterday. I'll probably hang out there."

"Excellent idea. Maybe you could check in with work. Bosses reward that kind of dedication, you know."

Like salt in a wound. Lauren turned away before the grimace could show on her face. "Right," she said and tucked the bag into the side of the hold.

Her sister's call cut through the air. "Mom, they're here!"

With minutes to spare before eleven o'clock, a van from Cornerstone Bible Church came to a stop along the front curb. An eight-foot metal stock tank rode on its side in a trailer attached to the hitch. Red tie-downs held it in place. Chloe ambled down the sidewalk to meet them.

"I guess I better go too," her mom said.

"Guess you better," Lauren said.

Her mom smoothed her hands down her shirtfront and headed toward the delegation gathering in the yard. Lauren shook her head and snagged the handles of Chloe's backpack. With any luck, her sister had taken everything she needed out of it. Lauren wasn't about to double-check. She piled the backpack on top of the foundation of suitcases.

Voices carried across the grass, chief among them a man's, his words clearer than the others'. He introduced himself as Chip, the pastor of Cornerstone, and then his wife as Hattie.

Lauren reached for her own backpack and couldn't stop her gaze from sliding toward the group. Her nurse stood between her sister and Hattie. The white-haired Pastor Chip and another man rounded out the quartet from the church. Like Chloe, the Cornerstone people wore shorts and flip-flops. They each donned a bright-orange shirt. Chip, whose booming voice contrasted with his petite stature, had his back to Lauren. Thick black letters across his shoulder blades blared "Follow Me to Living Water."

One by one, Lauren arranged the luggage into the Xterra. Snatches of conversation floated to her, mentions of "brought lunch for us all," a restroom break halfway through, and "just relax and enjoy the ride." At least one of those things should have given some level of peace to her mom.

Only the cooler remained to be loaded. She started to reach for it, but her sister's call stopped her short. "Bye, Lauren!"

The farewell drew all eyes her way. She gritted her teeth. No attention at all was better than a sympathy acknowledgment. All the same, she waved, smiled, let them know she was fine—strong. Most of the group members returned the farewell, then broke for the van. Her mom, however, remained in place. Despite the space between Lauren and her mom, it was clear the older woman's brow crinkled with worry. That worry wasn't for Lauren, though, and she had attempted enough rescuing.

She leaned toward the cooler's handle. Her hair fell into her face. She swatted it away with as much force as she swatted away the expectations. She was done with them too. Done with everyone thinking they knew exactly what she needed and wanted and deserved. She could make her own choices. She could carve her own way and be rid of the weight of others. Alexandra did it, so did Cather, and so could she.

The sliding door of the van zipped shut. The engine started.

She fit the cooler into place and paused to stretch her back. As the van hummed away, the trailer clanging along behind it, she peeled loose strands of hair off her face and smoothed them back into place. Cather had shed her locks as a stake in the ground. *From this point forward*, her act had declared, *this girl is her own creation.*

Lauren ran her fingers through her own locks. Freedom from the weight had been only one haircut away.

38

Hundreds of people dotted the riverbank next to an old bridge about fifteen minutes west of Red Cloud. The day was ridiculously bright, the air ridiculously fresh, and the smile on Chloe's face ridiculously wide. She didn't try to temper it. One of the most unique experiences of her life was about to unfold, and she would get to share it with her mom.

Better still, one of the most important dinners they would ever have waited in Omaha that evening. Her persuasion skills had worked. Rather, her prayers had. Against the odds, Aunt Gab had agreed to meet them. The divine affirmation put a spring in Chloe's step.

Her mom may not have realized it as they wound through the clusters of people, but the memories they would make that day would be praises that they would raise the rest of their lives. God would make sure of it. Walking in faith was an adventure like none other. If she could get her mom to understand that, Prague would be easier still to understand.

She and her mom shouldered the life jackets Hattie had loaned them. Up ahead, Pastor Chip and Marge's husband, Allen, rolled the upturned tank along the gentle slope to the water. Their wives followed with a chest cooler between them and two life jackets apiece draped over their free arms.

Wild grass brushed against Chloe's bare ankles. Whiffs of conversation greeted her as she strolled by. Men, women, and children all prepared for an afternoon on a nature-made lazy river. Most of the other groups also had metal tanks. Some brought the plastic variety. More than a few individuals opted for pool floats. Laughter flowed through the masses as easily as the smooth current glided between the shores. An Australian cattle dog decked out in its own camouflage life vest wagged a hello to Chloe.

She chuckled and turned to her mom. "Isn't this exciting? I feel so alive right now."

Her mom watched a group of shirtless middle-aged men chug from aluminum cans. "Chloe, half these people are three sheets to the wind," she muttered. Right on cue, one of the men paused to unleash a belch. Her mom shook her head as they passed the gaggle. "This town seemed so civilized yesterday."

"It still is civilized."

"There are far too many American flag tank tops for that to be true."

Chloe came to a stop. "Mom."

The elder Vance halted next to her, brow tight in challenge. "Am I wrong?"

Wrong and blind were often confused. In both cases, details made all the difference.

"Take a closer look around," she told her mom. "Besides those guys, what do you see? What do you hear? What do you notice?"

Her mom scanned the crowd. A child giggled nearby. A man asked his friends if they wanted a bag of chips. Two teen girls batted a beach ball back and forth. The wrinkle between her mom's eyebrows slowly melted.

"These people are enjoying themselves," Chloe said. "It may not be your first choice for fun, but I bet you'll find a way to enjoy yourself too."

Her mom looked out again at the crowd. The life jacket slipped from her shoulder. She pulled it back up. "I suppose there are some redeemable qualities about this situation."

Chloe grinned. "Redeemable is good. We can work with that. I'm sure you've noticed as well how generous and welcoming our hosts are being, yes?"

At the water's edge, the men lowered the tank flat to the ground. The bottom clanged on impact. The wives stepped forward and handed them the cooler to place in the middle of the small benches welded to the inside walls of the tank.

Her mom shifted her grip on the life jacket. "I have. Though I can't help but question what it says about a white-haired pastor when he wears swim trunks with lobsters on them."

"It says he's fun, and we're fortunate to be in his tank."

Her mom arched an eyebrow.

"Trust me, Mom. This tank float is going to be a highlight of the trip. Dad is going to be so proud of you. Envious, and proud."

Another belch resounded behind them. Her mom curled her lip. "I hope you're right."

"I am. You'll see."

Down by the tank, Marge waved to them, urging them onward.

Chloe acknowledged the beckoning, then turned to her mom. "Ready?"

Her mom smoothed her hair behind her ear. "Ready."

Chloe reached out her hand. Her mom looked at it as if unsure what to do. Faith often came like a stranger to those who lacked it. But Chloe had plenty to share. She wriggled her fingers in invitation.

Slowly, her mom met her outstretched hand with her own. The smile returned to Chloe's lips. One assured step at a time, she led her mom into their first major memory of the day.

39

Weightless and free. In more ways than one, Lauren was weightless and free. She tilted her face to the sun over Main Street, sighed into the hug of its warmth, and glided down the sidewalk. What a day. What a stake-in-the-ground day!

The storefront windows caught her reflection, offering back to her confirmation that a new woman had emerged, a butterfly from a cocoon. She lifted her right hand and traced her fingertips through the cropped strands around her ear. The ends prickled her skin in the most satisfying way.

The stylist had been right. The shag-top pixie style accentuated her high cheekbones. They cut shapely lines from the base of her nose upward to the delicate tips of her exposed ears, underscoring her dark eyes that glinted like jewels.

Unfettered confidence burst from every cell in her body. Willa Cather must have known the sensation too as she walked these same streets, under the same sun, enjoying the same distinctive breeze from proverbial gates thrown wide open. A new way forward unfurled, one of her own invention.

A block up from the salon, she arrived at the corner coffee shop she had told her mom she would patronize. The bell above the door announced her entrance. At a table immediately to the right, a man about her age looked up from his laptop. Their gazes touched, and he smiled. She breezed onward, shoulders back. Even her wake had a new talk.

Tall bookcases stretched nearly to the ceiling on both sides of the shop. Every available shelf space held wares for sale and books to borrow. Nestled in between were a few more tables, most of which were occupied, and a mustard-yellow mohair couch.

At the counter in the back of the shop, she ordered her coffee black with a splash of cream, a drink befitting a woman of regality. As she waited for it, she stepped to the nearest bookshelf. Many of the offerings were popular titles of the day, others were classics, including a couple of Cather to keep it authentic. But it was a thin white spine near the end of the third row that caught her. She slipped the book from its spot and held it flat between her hands. *The Bridges of Madison County* by Robert James Waller, the story at the center of their first planned stop in Iowa.

"Drip with cream," the barista called.

Lauren carried the book and her filled mug to the couch. She settled on the cushion nearest the door, where she could rest her mug on the end table to her left. The light above was perfect for reading—and the line of sight perfect for the man's gaze to find her once more.

She turned toward his stare. One side of his mouth tipped up.

She couldn't stop the grin, but she could keep him from seeing the full effect of his attention. Regality came with command, after all. She shifted on the cushion until only the tease of her profile showed in his direction. To solidify the mystique, she raked her hand through the longer locks on top of her head. All of them fell back into place with graceful ease. Weightless and free. She picked up her book, a novella in length, and opened to the first chapter.

Fiction forged what the heart desired. It made the impossible materialize and crowned the forgotten as heroes. It was true for Alexandra Bergson in *O Pioneers!*, and it was true for Francesca

Johnson, the lonely Iowa farm wife searching for her lost vitality. By chapter four, Mrs. Johnson had found the first hints of it in the enigmatic traveling photographer Robert Kincaid, who had ended up in her remote driveway by chance. But that was the thing about fiction: There was no such thing as chance.

As the pages passed and the energy between Francesca and Robert intensified, the presence of the man by the front door continued to pull at Lauren. She refused to yield to it, though she occasionally smoothed the hair around her ear, emphasizing her femininity to both herself and to anyone who happened to watch.

A while later, chair legs scraped against the wood floor. She turned toward the entrance. The man rose from his table. He packed his laptop into his backpack, gathered his mug, and started her way.

She dove her attention back into the printed words before he had an opportunity to look her way. Her pulse quickened.

Footfalls thumped closer, closer, past the couch.

She peeked up.

He stopped at the dish return tub at the end of the counter and set his mug inside. His blond hair feathered back from his face. He was taller and broader in the shoulders than his seated position indicated. He turned his head before his body, and their gazes locked. His blue eyes electrified her.

She tried to refocus on the page, but her chin refused to lower.

He came over to her, one hand holding on to the strap of his backpack.

She held her breath.

"I was curious what you're reading." He indicated the book with his left hand. His ringless left hand.

"It's, uh . . ." She turned the book to show him the cover. Her splint flashed in the process.

He grinned, clearly unfazed by the mark of brokenness. "I've actually heard of that one," he said.

A small, quiet laugh tumbled across her lips. She sat up

straighter, crossed her ankles. The logo on his polo shirt featured an ear of corn over the name Benson Seeds.

"It's set in Iowa, right?" he asked.

"Yes. In the 1960s."

"I'm from Iowa. Headed back there tonight. Maybe I should read the book too sometime. That is, if you'd recommend it."

The old Lauren would have melted in the attention. She would have been willing to pour herself into whatever shape Duncan had wanted. She would have continued to giggle like a shy schoolgirl and hope that his interest would never divert to other girls. But the new Lauren knew her command. All she had to do was possess it.

She steadied her breath, and with it, her voice. "I'd be glad to give you a summary if you want. You can see if there's something there you like." The double meaning not so subtle.

His grin widened. He looked at the couch cushion beside hers, then back to her.

With a simple nod, she granted him permission.

40

The current churned their tank along at a speed that barely outpaced the clouds, and her daughter churned through the third verse of "I Saw the Light" alongside the pastor. God help them all.

The tank drifting next to theirs was also from Cornerstone and happened to have a man who'd brought an acoustic guitar—on a river—and who happened to know the chords for the famous Hank Williams gospel tune. The impromptu concert had attracted an audience. Most of the listeners rode in tanks. One man, the bare-chested one with beer-induced gastrointestinal issues, lazed along in a flamingo floatie. His feet dragged the surface of the murky water. He would be lucky not to end up with ringworm.

"All together now!" the pastor bellowed as the chorus approached for the third and final time.

The makeshift armada erupted into song around her, voices resounding in all directions.

Edie swatted at the millionth gnat to buzz her face and smiled when the pastor's wife glanced her way. Hattie bobbed her head and tapped her foot in time, careful not to shake her phone too much as she recorded. Nurse Marge and her husband sang along as they monitored the tank's progress down the river. The two oar

167

masters had gotten them around several submerged limbs and kept them steady near the center of the river for the past hour and a half.

The refrain reached the home stretch. But toward the end of the final line, Chip shouted, "One more time—'Praise the Lord'!" He raised his hands and conducted the crowd as they uniformly crawled through the words. They held the last note for five beats before he dropped his hand and brought the group sing and the embellished guitar riff to a close.

Cheers and whoops swelled in the air. Chloe's eyes crinkled with laughter. She looked at Edie, eyebrows high as if asking if she got a kick out of it too.

Edie clapped and smiled. She had promised her daughter she would enjoy herself. That was a hard promise to deliver on with minimal shade to ease her burning skin. Despite seventeen layers of sunscreen, the complexion of her arms crept ever closer to the shade of the pastor's lobsters. Meanwhile, sweat trailed down her spine under the girth of the life jacket. Her saturated hair hung limp against her scalp.

They came around a bend. Up ahead, empty tanks dotted the north bank. Their occupants milled about the grass or headed deeper inland, behind a rare grove of trees.

"Looks like we made it to the halfway point," Allen said. "Anyone need a break?"

"Yes," said every woman in the tank simultaneously.

As they passed the grove, a row of six portable toilets came into view, lines already forming outside each one. Allen and Marge piloted them toward the gaggle of empty tanks. They avoided the other vessels with practiced ease, but several yards from the water's edge, the tank lurched to a stop. Edie, sitting on the leading edge, nearly slipped off the bench.

"Sorry, everyone," Allen said. "Sandbar. Might as well get out here. Not going to get much closer."

"Here?" Edie craned her neck over the rim of the tank. The water was too cloudy to judge its depth.

Marge used her oar to measure. "Water's only ankle-deep. Should be fine."

A nurse, of all people, should have understood how many bodily fluids had been secreted in that stream. Edie bit the inside of her lip to keep it from curling.

Pastor Chip clambered out of the tank as if blissfully unaware of the filth. Allen followed and held the tank in place while Chip came up to Chloe.

"Let me help you out." He extended both hands for hers.

Water splashed up Chloe's legs when she landed. "Wow, that's cold!" She laughed. "Feels good, though." She waded to the shore. The water was easily more than ankle-deep. The surface nearly reached Chloe's calves, which was about the height of Edie's capri hems.

Chip turned to Edie, hands extended. "Your turn."

Edie swallowed. "One second." She reached down and folded her capris as high as she could get them. At least her sandals would protect the soles of her feet. Slowly she stood. Allen hung on tight to keep the tank steady. She took the pastor's hands and eased over the side. The chill shocked her system, but it was too refreshing to harbor complete dismay.

"Nice and steady, now." Chip held on to her until she had taken a few steps. Then he let go and rotated back to the vessel to help his wife.

On her second unassisted step, Edie struck what seemed to be a rock. Except it wasn't a rock. It scuttled away, touching her bare ankle in the process. She yelped, reeled, and plopped backside first into the water. Her hands sank into the slimy riverbed. Her legs disappeared under the brown ripples as cold seeped up under her life jacket.

"Mom!" Chloe raced back, her feet sending splatters into Edie's face.

Edie spit away the droplets.

Chip came to her other side. Together the two of them helped her to her feet and guided her onto the shore. Streams poured from her life jacket. All around them, floaters stared at the pathetic swamp rat pulled from the water.

"Are you okay?" Chip asked. "Anything hurt?"

Only her pride. She shook her head.

"You disturbed a turtle," Chloe said. "I saw it break the surface and swim away."

"At least it wasn't a water snake," the pastor said.

Edie whipped her eyes to him. "There are snakes in that river?"

"Don't worry. They're not poisonous."

Pastors were downright unhelpful sometimes. Edie eased her arms from their grips and hugged herself around the stomach. Her toes curled hard against the soles of her sandals.

"Edie, I'm so sorry!" Hattie hurried to her with a full plastic sack and a beach towel. "Did you get hurt?"

"I'm fine," she said. People around them at last started going about their business again. She rubbed her arms.

"Believe it or not, that happens almost every year." Hattie unfolded the towel and draped it over Edie's shoulders. "That's why I bring a spare set of clothes. I've got an extra pair of athletic shorts and a T-shirt you can use. I'll take you to the restroom to get changed."

In any other circumstance, the prospect of changing in a portable toilet, let alone answering the call of nature within one, would be out of the question. But the sooner Edie could get relief, the better, even if it meant she'd come out looking like an undersized NBA player.

"Let me take your life jacket before you go," Chloe said.

As Hattie held the towel off her shoulders, Edie slipped out of the device and handed it to her daughter.

"I'm sorry, Mom," her daughter whispered. Her turned-down mouth testified to her authentic sympathy.

"It's okay." But the truth was, Edie would walk back to Red Cloud that very moment if she could.

Hattie robed her with the towel again, and they walked side by side to the only option for privacy. For many beats, they let the silence linger.

A small group of floaters headed back to their tank noticed the dripping woman wrapped in a towel. One of them mumbled as they passed, "Someone went for a swim."

Edie dropped her gaze to the grass. All the drunk people in that crowd and she was the one who fell in the river. Maybe Red Cloud wasn't that far of a walk.

"We sure enjoy having you and Chloe along on this float," Hattie said. Her tone was cheerful, clearly meant to be a distraction from humiliation. "Was that your other daughter we saw back at the guesthouse?"

Edie pulled the towel tighter around her shoulders. "Yes. My oldest, Lauren."

"Are Lauren and Chloe your only two children?"

"They are. They both live in Kansas City."

They reached the back of the line for one of the portable toilets and joined behind two other women.

"We have two sons," Hattie offered. "The oldest is about Chloe's age. He's married and works in shipping in North Carolina. Our youngest is in Ohio finishing his master's and planning a wedding for next summer."

Both children in or on their way to gainful employment and committed relationships. "How nice," she said.

The restroom door opened. The first woman in line moved forward.

"It must be wonderful having your girls so close," Hattie said. "I sometimes wish our boys lived closer."

The words of her mother unwound from her memory and streamed to her lips. "It's strange to me that staying close to your parents is abnormal these days. Children leaving their parents behind is one of the reasons families are breaking apart. The kids leave their parents to fend for themselves. I don't think that's how

God meant for us to treat our families." Her mother may have said it, but the belief was wholly Edie's. Her sister's departure was proof enough the sentiment was valid. Their family had fractured because of Gabriella's choice.

The pastor's wife switched the plastic bag to her other hand. "I agree it was nicer when families lived closer together and took care of each other. Though I also see our boys living away from us as a family expansion of sorts. We have community now in all three states instead of only one. Plus it gives us a reason to travel."

But wasn't the point for kids to travel to their parents? Shouldn't the kids return the care they'd received all their lives? Shouldn't the parents be the nucleus, not the kids?

A familiar laugh bubbled some distance behind them. It was Chloe, talking to the guitar player from the other tank on her way up to the lines. Chloe could chum it up with anyone, anywhere. In so many ways, the child carried more of Gabriella's genes than she did Edie's. It was mysterious, and terrifying.

"It's hard, isn't it?" Hattie asked.

"What is?"

The woman nodded toward Chloe. "Releasing them to their own lives."

A knot curled in her gut. She fiddled with the hem of the towel. "I'm not sure I'm very good at it."

Hattie met her gaze. A sweet smile came to her lips. "You might surprise yourself."

The genuineness almost made it believable.

41

They stayed until the coffee shop manager politely told them for the second time that the shop closed at three. Neither of them seemed to want to leave the other's company, as if they understood that their time together was limited and precious.

When at last they said goodbye in front of his white truck near the door, she carried the thick memory of his rapt attention and his business card. Gavin Drake, Benson Seeds, Carroll, Iowa. He had offered her his contact information. She did not offer him hers. The dynamic remained in her favor. As it should.

The Xterra waited on the other end of the block in the last angled parking spot. She slid into the driver's seat, the cabin balmy from the sun. The rearview mirror reflected back to her the gleam in her eyes. She ran her fingers through her shortened strands once more, the thrill of it spindling down to her core. Who was that powerful woman in the mirror? She was Lauren Vance.

A white truck rolled past the back window. She turned in her seat as Gavin headed to his next destination and prepared for a week of travel throughout Iowa. Iowa was on tap for her week too. Her sister had planned several stops in the Hawkeye State. What were the chances any of their stops overlapped with his?

Chance didn't exist in the fiction world. Maybe it didn't in the real one either.

A loud chime rang through the car. Then another. Then another. They originated from the cargo area.

Another.

Another.

"What in the world?" She pushed out into the heat once more. Even as she opened the liftgate, two more chimes resounded, all from Chloe's backpack.

She sighed. "Of course she forgot her phone."

The alerts quieted at last. Lauren unzipped the front pocket and took out the device. Ten new-message alerts flooded the lock screen. Most of them were from a 402 area code. She clicked to preview the top message, and a picture expanded. Her sister with her arm around their mom on the bank of a river. She previewed the next message. A group shot of everyone in the float party, cans of soda and white-bread sandwiches in hand. Everyone smiling, having a good time, including her mom. She twisted her lips.

Scrolling through the other messages, she came to one from Sori. Without thinking, she opened the preview.

> Someone ordered 50 protein balls for a bday
> party in 2 wks. Offered $150 when I told them
> it was a missionary fundraiser. Prague, here you
> come!

She read and reread the message. Missionary. Prague. Chloe? That had to be a mistake. Her sister was a churchgoer, no doubt, but missionary seemed like a huge leap. Chloe knew nothing about Central Europe, nor did she speak Czech. And the visa process alone would—

She righted. The earlier text from Sori, the one about the "trial run" with Jeremy. And the trip. The out-of-nowhere, "I want to spend time with you, Mom" trip.

Missionary. Prague. Chloe.

Doing the ill-advised was her sister's signature move.

Lauren huffed. "Mom is going to be furious." No amount of sightseeing was going to lessen that fury, but that was for her sister to learn the hard way. She zipped the phone back in its pocket and shut the liftgate.

Back at the guesthouse, Lauren parked next to the side yard and settled onto the cool grass under a large oak. Replays of Gavin sweetened her wait for her family, who were due any minute.

Sure enough, the church van soon rolled up to the front curb. Her sister disembarked from the back first, followed by their mom, wearing one of the bright-orange T-shirts the church members had come in. A pair of mesh shorts belled around her bird-like legs, coming as low as mid-thigh. Not even God himself would have convinced Edie Vance to wear such an ensemble. Something had gone wrong.

Lauren rose to her feet.

Their mom paused to exchange a few words with the pastor's wife through the open front passenger window. The woman in the van pointed at the plastic bag in their mom's hand, or maybe it was the shorts, then motioned as if swearing off either or both forever. Her mom and sister waved in return.

Lauren hung by the tree trunk as the van pulled away. Her family headed her way, deep in conversation. The closer they got, the clearer their give-and-take became.

". . . and how are we supposed to change, Chloe? We can't get back into the guesthouse." Despite her mom's slender legs, the dimpled skin above her knees jiggled with every step. Her distaste for shorts made more sense.

"We can stop at a gas station and change there," Chloe said. "We'll get fresh clothes from our suitcases."

Their mom lifted an arm and whiffed her skin. "I smell like river."

"I'll get out the perfume too."

Lauren met them on the edge of the tree's ring of shade. "What happened?"

Both women looked up at the sound of her voice. Both came to a dead stop, eyes wide.

"Whoa," her sister said. "Looks like you found something to do, Laur."

The haircut. She had intended to come up with a more ceremonious way of unveiling the new her. She had been too distracted with— Didn't matter. Nothing left to do but own it. She pulled back her shoulders and stepped closer. "I wanted to try something new. Something different."

Chloe nodded. "That's . . . definitely something new."

Lauren smoothed the strands around her right ear, recentering herself on the thrill of choices all her own, the stake in the ground. "I think it accentuates my bone structure," she replied. But her confidence wavered as soon as she met the other set of eyes.

Their mom's lips were cinched into a tight line. The orange shirt sagged on her frame. Orange was a glaring mismatch for her complexion. Their mom reviled mismatches to her complexion. She reviled shorts. She reviled smelling. And she clearly reviled the change Lauren had elected. Her stare was frigid and quiet.

Lauren shifted her weight from one foot to the other.

Finally her mom thrust out her hand. "Give me the keys."

Lauren willed her hand not to shake as she dropped the keys into the outstretched palm.

As her mom tramped away, she muttered under her breath, "This day cannot end soon enough."

Lauren reached her right hand to the back of her neck and rubbed the contracted muscles. The carefully manicured hairline prickled against the side of her pinky. Only hours before, the sensation had infused her chest with pride, had attracted a handsome man's admiration, had forged an unshakable connection between her and strong women of decisiveness. How many of those women had endured the wake of their mother's derision? How many came out unscathed? She had to stand. Somehow, she had to stand.

Chloe cleared her throat. "Now that we're alone, tell me." She drew a circle in the air around Lauren's face. "What's this really about?"

Lauren dropped her hand to her side. "I told you, I wanted a change."

"But why?"

"That is the why."

Her sister frowned. "You don't buy name-brand soda without a coupon. No one who contemplates purchases that closely makes a rash decision like this without a cause."

"Can I not decide to do something and do it?"

"Sure, it's only—"

"You do it all the time."

"Lauren, I'm not saying you can't be spontaneous. I'm saying that this sudden change in combination with other things I've noticed on this trip makes me wonder . . ." She trailed off.

"Wonder what?" Lauren pressed.

Her sister rolled her lips before finishing. "Wonder if something has happened."

The veil nearly ripped out of her grip. She balled her fists, clung tighter, hardened every defense. Her sister's prying would stop then and there. She would make sure of it. "If you want something to worry about, then worry about how you're going to tell Mom about Prague."

Chloe reared back. "What?"

"Don't pretend. You forgot your phone in your backpack. It started going off like crazy. I checked it to make sure nothing was wrong. Sori sent you a message, something about raising money for being a missionary in Prague."

Chloe clamped her mouth shut. A clear signal the secret had been exposed.

"That's why you wanted to do this trip, isn't it?" Lauren said. "You're hoping that you can butter up Mom so that she won't be as livid with you when you tell her about Prague."

Chloe's eyes drifted to the Xterra. Their mom dug through her suitcase for clean clothes that actually fit her frame and complexion. Whatever had happened on the river, it was clearly mortifying. And as long as their mom's anger stayed on Chloe, Lauren actually had a shot of moving unburdened into a revised future.

Lauren leaned toward her. "Yours are the only choices you should be focused on, because you and I both know Mom is not going to sign off on them."

She spun on her heel and marched toward the car. The veil resettled around her, peaceful and secure.

42

Red Cloud had one gas station on the way out of town. Chloe pulled into the spot near the entrance and came around the front of Goldie to escort their mom inside. Lauren beat her to it, stepping in behind their mom like a buffer. Chloe backed off.

Inside the store, Lauren directed their mom to the home goods aisle, where she grabbed a travel pack of baby wipes. "These will help you freshen up until you can shower," she said. "I'll go buy these, then meet you by the restroom."

Their mom watched Lauren head to the cashier, a strange look on her face, as if still trying to process who that person was. Silently, she turned and plodded toward the restroom.

Did their mom see it too? Did she piece together the growing tension in Lauren's demeanor and wonder what was behind it all? Lauren may have found out Chloe's real reason for the trip, but it was only a matter of time before Lauren's revealed itself too, whatever it was.

Until then, Chloe's top priority was to get her mom cleaned up and cooled down, because Omaha awaited.

Fortunately, the hallway to the restroom was near the blast chiller, making the air all the more pleasant to bathe in after long hours in the sun. Unfortunately, the single-person restroom was occupied.

They waited on one side of the hallway. Her mom stood with arms crossed over her change of clothes and eyes pointed to a neon beer sign on the opposite wall. To pass the time, Chloe browsed through her new text messages. Most of them were the pictures and the video Hattie had sent her.

She laughed and angled the screen toward her mom. "Look at these. Aren't they great?" She scrolled down the text chain. "Almost looks like we had a good time."

Her mom nodded, her expression subdued. "Hattie is good people."

She *had* seen the good in the float experience. The "redeemable qualities," as she put it.

Chloe read the remainder of the new messages. Below the texts from Hattie was the one from Sori that Lauren had referenced. It was hard to tell what Lauren would do with the information. She may keep it to herself. But considering the bitter cloud gathering around her, she may not.

Buried at the bottom of the long string of messages, evidently so buried it hadn't been visible to her sister on the lock screen, was an eleventh message. From Aunt Gab.

Let me know when you're about to Lincoln. I'll head to your hotel and bring dinner.

Chloe sent her phone to black, avoiding the risk her mom would notice the name at the top of the message. She worried for nothing, though. Her mom had closed her eyes and swayed gently on her feet like she was absorbing the cool and allowing it to work its magic.

Lauren arrived with the wipes, their mom got her turn in the restroom, and they were back on the road with two iced drinks and one bag of cheddar jalapeño popcorn. They stopped only once more during the three-hour drive, on the west side of Lincoln, where Chloe texted her aunt, avoided a curious peek from her sister, and finished the last of the popcorn.

They arrived at the Sleepy Time Inn off I-80 shortly before seven thirty and rolled their suitcases toward the front entrance. Chloe hurried ahead of her family through the doors. Directly in front of her, in the breakfast room off the side of the lobby, sat Aunt Gab, two grocery bags on the table in front of her. Aunt Gab looked up from her phone and smiled.

Lauren and their mom bustled in behind Chloe and broke to the left for the front desk. The wheels of their bags rumbled on the tile floor.

"I have never wanted a shower so badly in my life," their mom moaned. Neither of them had noticed their guest.

Chloe continued across the lobby, toward the woman who looked every bit the opposite of Edie Vance. Middle-age spread covered by worn khakis and a red Cornhuskers pullover. Graying hair pinned into a slothful ponytail. But that smile on her face! Her smile could lift a boulder.

Aunt Gab laid down her phone and rose from her chair.

"Chloe," Lauren called. "Where are you going?"

Chloe nodded in the direction of the breakfast room. "To say hello." A handful more steps and she was in the warm cushion of her aunt's embrace.

"Hey, chickadee," Aunt Gab said into her hair. "Good to see you again, and under better circumstances."

"You too, Aunt Gab. Thank you for doing this."

Her aunt pulled back and caught her eye. "Suppose we'll know soon if this was a good idea, won't we?"

"Gabriella?"

They turned together. The other Vance women stood several paces off with narrowed brows.

"Hello, Edie." Her aunt used the common name her mom preferred, a direct contrast to her mom's refusal to do the same for Aunt Gab.

"What are you doing here?" Her mom made no move toward the visitor. Lauren stuck close by her side.

"Chloe mentioned you all were coming through town. Figured I'd take the opportunity to see you since funerals and Christmases seem to be our going standard." She waved to Lauren. "Wow, you look different."

Lauren's smile was perfunctory, as was her hello. Quickly she glanced at their mom. Still, neither of them came closer.

"She brought us supper," Chloe said.

"I did. Got some grub on my way down. Thought you all might be hungry." Her aunt looked her mom up and down. "Seems it's been a long day for you."

Her mom lifted her chin under the scrutiny. "It has indeed been a long day, and a very tiring one. I was intending to freshen up once we got here."

"By all means. I can help you take your bags to your room."

"I don't think that's necessary."

Chloe frowned. "Aunt Gab is going to come up to our room anyway. Might as well give her a bag to handle."

Lauren cut in, congenial but firm. "Why don't I take Mom up to the room and get everything settled, then we'll meet you down here for supper. There are more tables and space down here."

"She can come up with us," Chloe insisted.

"No, it's fine." Their aunt waved it off. Then she looked at their mom. "Take all the time you need. I brought cold food anyways. Chloe and I'll visit while you're upstairs."

Chloe opened her mouth to protest, but Aunt Gab shook her head.

"Thank you for understanding, Gabriella." The disliked name once more. Edie Vance wielded rigidity like an art form.

The two of them checked in under Chloe's name and headed up to the room. Meanwhile, Aunt Gab led Chloe to the self-serve coffee bar in the breakfast room for a refreshment of their own.

"Still peas in a pod, those two." Aunt Gab filled a paper cup with steaming coffee and grabbed a handful of sugar packets.

Chloe kept her coffee minimal and the cream plentiful. "Sometimes I wonder if they're the same person."

They sat opposite each other at the table, the grocery bags between them. Chloe parked her bags next to her chair and took a first creamy sip. Not bad for hotel coffee.

Her aunt tore open the first of four sugar packets. "Thanks for inviting me. If nothing else, I truly am happy to see you again."

"Me too."

The first packet empty, her aunt moved to the second. "I'm surprised you all are doing this trip. More specifically, I'm surprised your mom is."

"I convinced her to go."

"You convinced her to do something? What's your secret?"

She shrugged. "Unshakable naivete."

Her aunt chuckled and started on the third and fourth stacked together. "What some call naivete, heaven calls faith." The white crystals dumped from their tiny homes. Once the last ones fell, Aunt Gab swirled the sweetened liquid with a plastic coffee stirrer. "I suppose the more important question for you is, Why are you doing this trip?"

"I wanted some bonding time."

Aunt Gab sipped her coffee and looked over the rim at Chloe. When she finished drinking, she gave a subtle shake of her head. "No one takes Edie Vance on a road trip without a solid reason. Is someone dying or something?"

Aunt Gab saw. She had eyes to see.

Chloe gently swirled her cup on the tabletop in short, tight circles, mixing the cream and coffee deeper together without a stirrer. "I got a job teaching art at a Christian international school. In Prague."

Her aunt grinned. "Wow. Good for you."

An easy, genuine congratulations. Why was it so hard to expect something similar from her mom?

"I take it you're hoping to tell your mom on this trip?"

She nodded.

"How long will you be overseas?"

"It's a two-year commitment."

Aunt Gab whistled. "She's going to hate that."

"I know. I guess that's why I haven't told her yet and I'm doing all this to try to find the courage."

"You've got courage in spades. It's discernment you're seeking." Her aunt took another draw, then asked, "Does Lauren know?"

Chloe let go of her cup and folded her hands. "She accidentally found out today."

"Clock's ticking a little louder now, huh?"

With the dynamic her mom and sister had, delaying was not a luxury. Still, the right moment had to present itself. Like Aunt Gab said, not any moment would do. Discernment was required. The moment had to be intentional, purposeful.

"If you were me, how would you tell her? I mean, how did you tell your mother that you were moving away?"

"You don't want to follow my lead there."

"Why not?"

"I was a very different person back then. I wasn't courageous and careful like you. I barreled my way through those fort gates. I had my reasons for that. Reasons I've never quite known how to express until recently. The animals aren't the only ones rehabbing on the farm, let's say."

Considering the formidable nature of Grandma Moria and her reign, it was no surprise it had taken Aunt Gab so long to unravel from the experience.

"Think you'll express any of those reasons tonight?" Chloe asked.

Her aunt bobbed one shoulder. "We'll see."

"Discernment?"

Aunt Gab tipped her cup in Chloe's direction. "Exactly."

They fell into silence and nursed their drinks.

Her aunt gathered the empty packets in her palm and wadded

them together. "If I were you, I would figure out a way to speak your mom's language when you tell her."

"How do you mean?"

"Every person has a heart's desire, including your mom, believe it or not. You and I, we feel the desire first, like a certainty in our bones, a firm belief that it will come to pass. For others, first and foremost they feel the fear of never getting there. It dominates all their senses, their perspective, everything. Your mom is one of them. So was your grandma. Speak to that fear. Until the fear is quieted, the hope can't be heard."

Quiet the fear. She had tried to do that, encouraging her mom to see the details around them at the river, having her listen to the poetry of a master, asking her to sit and watch the Technicolor dream of a dreamer. But it was all from the vantage point of Chloe's own heart's desire.

What, then, was her mom's desire?

43

Nebraska took the prize for least likable state, by a decided margin. No other state had foisted cruelty after cruelty upon Edie. First, it was a blindness to her oldest daughter's serious malady. Then a dunk in a foul, snake-infested river. To top it off, the ostentatious waltz of Gabriella into the middle of their vacation. Her sister harbored the same expectation that everyone cater to her. Some things never changed.

Even after Edie took a shower, her nose refused to let go of the wretched river odor. She took her time layering herself with lotion, then drying and styling her hair to its normal airiness. A full thirty minutes after she and Lauren had arrived in the room, she dotted foundation over her face and smoothed it in with a brush. The bathroom lighting offered little help for precise tasks like that, not that anyone could expect anything more from a mediocre hotel in Nebraska. Hopefully the bedsheets were washed in bleach.

Lauren appeared in the bathroom doorway. "I could tell them you're not feeling well."

Offers like that proved Lauren was her father's daughter. Lauren looked after her, like he did. In many ways, more so. Edie turned to thank her and was greeted once more by that haircut. Lauren's most beautiful asset, shorn to a minimum, right along with her marriage prospects. Men detested hair above the ears on women, her mother always said. Her mother would have seethed at the appearance of her granddaughter.

Edie turned back to the mirror and continued coaxing the foundation into the web of fine lines. Her voice was tight. "It's fine."

Lauren leaned against the jamb. "Chloe sprung this on you unfairly. You have every right to say no."

The right might have been hers, but exercising it came with the risk that Gabriella would chalk it up to yet another way others had created the fissure in the family, not her. If the evening ended up in shambles—and by all indications, it would—no one could say it was because of Edie not giving due effort.

"We'll go," she said. "It's important to Chloe."

The mirror caught Lauren's downtrodden look before she turned and slipped back into the main area of the room.

Five minutes later, they headed downstairs.

Predictably, the initial conversation over supper dawdled around small talk and the taste of the food. Gabriella's culinary choices amounted to a deconstructed charcuterie board. Prosciutto, salami, mozzarella cubes, crostini, olive tapenade, grapes, cucumbers, and assorted crackers. Her sister's palate had developed over the years, even if her sense of style and proper enunciation had not. Eventually, the discussion moved to the "farm" and Gabriella's recent acquisition of a lame-leg duck.

"Got his little leg caught in a beaver trap," she explained as she smeared tapenade on a poppyseed cracker. "Hobbles around on land, but in the water, you'd never know the difference."

Edie crossed her ankles and nibbled at her cheese cube.

"How many animals does that make for you?" Chloe asked.

Gabriella shoved the whole cracker into her mouth and spoke around the mass as if she had no couth. "Fifteen. Couple horses, waterfowl, cats, pigs, a goat, and sheep. The Des Moines zoo has an ostrich they want to retire. Might take her on."

"Nice." Chloe looked at Edie. She motioned to Gabriella with her head, clearly asking Edie to engage.

No one could say Edie didn't try. She pulled on a congenial smile. "Sounds charming."

On the opposite side of the table, Lauren held impeccable posture while drinking from her water bottle every so often and slowly working through a slice of prosciutto.

"We should come up to your farm sometime," Chloe said. "I've never seen it in person."

"Anytime," Gabriella said. "You're welcome whenever. All of you."

Of course they had to go to her. Not the other way around. One child should never be the nucleus of an entire family.

"Maybe we could swing up there tomorrow," Chloe offered. "Would you like to see Aunt Gab's farm, Mom?"

She drew in her breath. Everyone's gaze swung to her.

Lauren jumped in. "It's out of the way."

The haircut may have taken away important things from Lauren, but not her reliable, even mind.

"We're not on any kind of strict timeline," Chloe argued. "Plus you'd get to pet a three-legged llama and a little duck who could."

Lauren pursed her lips.

It was Edie's turn to step in. "We will have to find another time, Chloe."

Gabriella looked sideways at her and chomped loudly on the last bit of a cracker.

"But it's really not that far off course." Chloe was relentless.

"Another time," Edie repeated, poised and calm. "We certainly appreciate the offer, though, Gabriella."

Her sister noisily swallowed, eyes lingering on her. She wiped her mouth with a napkin, then balled the paper in her hand. "You know, it's funny. The older I get, the less that name seems to fit me."

Edie reached for her water cup and took a sip. "It's the name our mother gave you."

"She did. But I think she'd be the first to agree it's too pretty for someone who looks like me."

"Aunt Gab, don't say that. It's not true!" Chloe looked expectantly at Edie.

Edie lifted her chin. "We determine our appearance by how we want to be seen."

Her sister huffed. "That's what Mother used to say."

"That's right. She did."

Gabriella narrowed her brow. "It wasn't kind when she said it either."

Silence slunk over their table. Lauren abandoned the meat altogether and looked down at her lap. Chloe shifted in her chair. The evening crept closer to ruin.

Into the descent, Chloe chirped, "Mom and I went tanking in Red Cloud."

Gabriella cocked her head. "My sister went tanking? What brought that on?"

"Family," Edie retorted. "I do things for family."

"Is that right?"

"She did great!" Chloe tried again. "Want to see the pictures?"

But Gabriella burrowed into Edie. "Let's just address the elephant, shall we?"

"What elephant?" Edie asked.

"You know which one."

"I don't, in fact."

"Mom," Chloe whispered.

Gabriella crossed her arms on the edge of the table. "You want me to say I wasn't there for Mother."

"You have no idea what I want."

"Then tell us what you want and put us all out of our misery."

Lauren hugged herself. Chloe closed her mouth, clearly no longer eager to show off pictorial evidence of their afternoon.

Ruin encroached, as predictable as stars at midnight. It happened every time. Her sister couldn't stand being confronted with reality.

Edie straightened her posture. "I do agree you weren't there for Mother, just like you're not there now helping me with the estate sale. You have no appreciation for how much responsibility you left on my shoulders."

"I know exactly how much responsibility Mother was. I did it when you went off to college and then got married. Remember that?"

"That's not nearly the same—"

"Right! It wasn't the same. You only think you got the rawer deal. You have no idea."

"Don't start with that comparison nonsense."

"I didn't start it. You did." Gabriella pushed her food aside. "And as far as the estate sale goes, I told you I can't get away from the farm for that long. It was all I could do to find coverage for the week of the funeral. I realize how much work those sales are, which is why I said you can keep all the profits."

Edie scoffed. "That's all it's ever been to you. Money."

A vein bulged down her sister's forehead. "What's that supposed to mean?"

"You know exactly what that means, Gabriella. The only time you deigned to grace Mother with your presence was when you needed money."

"That's not true."

"It's not? So that car you wrecked that you wanted her to replace wasn't about money? Or that rent you needed after that man you ran away with ended up being exactly what Mother warned you he was?"

Gabriella's eyes darted to Chloe. Her curated image was only a mirage, and it was time both girls understood that. Chloe looked between them. Lauren focused on her lap, her mouth a tight line.

"You know what, Edith?" Her sister thrust her napkin onto the table. "You're right. I was young, I was foolish, and I was learning a lot of things the hard way. But at least I learned them. I see you're still in the process."

Before Edie could form a reply, her sister stood, bumping the table. A box of crackers fell face-first on the table.

"I came here because of family. And once again, I'm leaving because of family. Give me a call when you figure out which side of that double-edged sword you're on." Gabriella grabbed her purse from the back of the chair. "Goodbye, girls. I'm sorry about this."

Lauren stayed glued in place. Chloe visibly wrestled with the urge to spring up from her chair and follow.

Gabriella strode through the sliding glass doors. They sealed shut behind her.

Chloe leaned over the table. "Mom . . ."

She shook her head. "Let her." The exact advice her mother had given her all those years ago. *Let her.*

Her daughter bit her lip and watched Gabriella disappear into the Nebraska evening. Thank God it was their last evening in Nebraska. For a good, long, welcome while.

44

Everything had become so complicated. In normal circumstances, Lauren dealt in complexity. She could take it all in, study it from all sides, unwind it bit by bit to simplified terms. But normal circumstances never involved her being behind in her mom's favor while being ahead in a man's. Normal circumstances never saw Chloe making a bigger mess of things yet Lauren still getting looks of disdain. They never saw her trying to shake off an old version of herself who obsessed over the need to be one step ahead.

She pushed herself harder on the treadmill in the tiny fitness room. The inky predawn shrouded the lone window. Her shoes landed with punishing whacks against the churning belt of the machine. The gears chirped as they spun, and the drone of the motor drowned out the sound of her breath in her own ears. Endorphins invigorated her body, still they could not ease the strain of old and new tension.

Her skin recalled its quiver under Gavin's gaze, her mind the way he drank her in from his place on the couch next to her in the coffee shop and the unabated lift of his lips. It wouldn't take much to get back to that enamored gaze. A simple text would do it. Only one question of where in Iowa he was going. The new, powerful Lauren would step onto the throne once more.

But it would take a lot to shed the disappointed glances from her mom. How was it possible to be powerful and weak at the same time?

Her arms pumped in time with her stride. She tucked her hands into tighter fists. The splint forced her middle finger straight out into an inadvertent, shiny obscenity to the world. Maybe she should flash it for real. Maybe that was the answer—to double down. Maybe she needed to step further into mutiny against expectations, including her mom's. The brazenness of New Lauren would usurp the docility of Old Lauren, who was too afraid to tell the world to stay out of her business. No one needed to be in it anyway. Least of all her sister. Chloe's meddling in others' lives was bound to get her burned, if the exposure of her own secrets didn't burn her first.

Lauren pumped the belt speed up a minute per mile faster, pounded out the last stretch of her run. Then, spent and sweaty, she went to take a shower.

Two hours later, they left Nebraska behind. Their mom propped her elbow on the windowsill and rested her lips against her fist. Her stare never ventured from the passing Iowa fields. Chloe had the sense not to play her music. They did not talk about what had happened the night before, or about what was on the agenda for the day. They did not talk.

Shortly after noon, they arrived in Winterset, Iowa, a rare small town with dual claims to fame: John Wayne's birthplace and the setting for the 1990s novel and film phenomenon about a love story amid the historic covered bridges.

"Oprah was here in 1993, after the book came out," the visitors' center attendant, Katherine, informed them. "She filmed an episode of her show at the Cedar Bridge. And of course Meryl Streep and Clint Eastwood spent considerable time here filming. Many of the people in town helped with the movie in some way, including my family and me."

Their mom soon lost interest in the lore, choosing to browse the selection of magnets on a spinning rack nearby. She had yet to look Lauren in the eye that morning.

"How many bridges are there?" her sister asked.

"Six total. If you were to drive to all of them, you're looking at about an eighty-mile trip."

Their mom coughed. The implication was clear. They would not be doing that.

After a needlessly long conversation instigated by Chloe about Katherine's personal favorite bridge and her memories from the days of filming, they left with a marked-up map of the bridge locations, a John Wayne magnet for their dad, and a half dozen snickerdoodles from a local bakery, the latter courtesy of Katherine as "thanks for being so sweet."

Everything remained uncomplicated for her sister.

Outside, the temperature approached the mid-eighties.

"I'm already melting," their mom said as they piled back into the car. "How many of these bridges are we planning to see? Because honestly, they look the same."

The map in their mom's hand served as evidence. The outside panel featured pictures of the six bridges. All of them had the same red tone on the sides with white rail fences at either opening. While there were a few variations of architecture, for the most part, it was the same bridge copied five times.

"How many do you want to see?" Chloe asked.

"One is plenty."

"Only one? We came all this way to see the bridges."

Their mom pinned her with a look. "Chloe Grace, it is hot as the devil, your vehicle has an appalling lack of air-conditioning, and I didn't exactly have a restful evening. Forgive me if I'm not overly eager to look at bridges."

Chloe blinked at the rebuff, then turned to Lauren.

Lauren shrugged. Her sister had put herself in that position.

Finding no help, Chloe lowered her gaze to the plastic container of cookies. The sides popped as she adjusted her grip. "I suppose if that's what you want," she said softly, then looked up at their mom. "Which one should we see, then? Katherine said the Roseman is the most popular because of its appearance in the movie."

"It's also the farthest out," their mom argued. She consulted the map. "Cedar Bridge is on the way back to the interstate."

Lauren cut in. "That one was used on the original book cover." It was a beautiful image that both she and Gavin had admired. Their fingertips had brushed when they exchanged the book. She smiled to herself, the thrill returning.

"Settled, then. Cedar Bridge it is." Their mom refolded the map and began fanning herself with it.

Chloe watched her a beat. "You're absolutely sure you don't want to see more?"

"I could not be more sure. Let's roll."

Me too, Lauren offered silently.

Chloe sighed and handed their mom the cookies. "All right. Tell me what roads to take."

As they drove, Lauren faced her window. Each block of the tiny Iowa town hearkened back to scenes on a page—and a mustard-yellow couch.

Cedar Bridge resided northeast of town, off a two-lane county route. "Park" was a generous term for what surrounded it. A gravel drive led into the park and eventually through the bridge itself. To the right of the drive, a gazebo and picnic tables lazed under the bountiful canopy of trees on a few acres of grass. To the left lay a gravel parking lot with a small cinder-block restroom facility at the far corner. Straight ahead was the bridge.

"I believe this is the only one you can still drive through," Chloe said.

"No thank you," their mom said. "Let's walk it."

Chloe chuckled. "Your sense of adventure has waned since yesterday."

"I cannot fathom why," their mom murmured.

Chloe turned into the lot and found a shady spot to rest the car. They got out and proceeded together to the bridge. Above them, the leaves were still against the serene blue sky, unbothered by any breeze or soaring bird.

The bridge lacked majesty, but something about the understated spot seemed grander than even a skilled writer like Waller, enchanted by its whispers of mystique, could describe. In the book, Robert took photos of Francesca at a bridge, capturing her and studying her long before he realized he loved her. He had been enamored with her beauty, could not take his attention away from her for long. Pinpricks raced across Lauren's skin.

The gravel gave way to the wood planks extending out from the bridge. The white railings opened up like welcoming arms, bidding them forward.

Her mom peered over the railing. "Not much of a creek down there."

"Several of the other bridges have more of a stream under them," Chloe noted. "Katherine gave me information on a paddle trip between them."

"Don't even think about it, Chloe."

Their footfalls turned to faint echoes inside the bridge. The planks under their feet were smooth in the center from the treads of tires but splintered at the edges where little wearing force could reach. The walls wore a crisp coat of white paint, and visitors had filled the blank canvas with messages in pen, marker, and pocketknife tip. Exposed rafters crisscrossed in an even, steady cadence, a testament to the precise craft the builders employed.

"It's amazing how they could construct these with such perfection, isn't it?" Chloe swiveled her head to one of the walls, taking in the messages others had left behind, most professions of love. "Look how many people have come to see this."

In the midst of the crowd of words, thick red letters in the middle of a heart stood out. Lauren stepped over to them.

Our story begins—M + H 11/12/2021

She pressed her fingertips to the tribute.

Her mom and sister continued the length of the bridge, then down the ramp on the other end. Chloe's voice floated over the distance. "Let's go down to the creek."

Lauren strode a few paces after them, then paused. What was the hurry? She was alone in the rousing space, a place where new stories took shape.

The gaps between the wall's slats framed the action of her mom and sister below on the edge of the creek. They were occupied, and Lauren was safely out of sight.

She took out her phone and opened her camera. She leaned against the rail along the wall, angled her camera above her head, and snapped. The Benson Seeds business card slipped easily from its hiding spot in her sling purse. She entered the phone number at the top of a new text message. Then she dropped in the picture along with one simple question for Gavin:

Can you guess where I am?

45

C hest still tight from her sister's rebuttal, Chloe merged back onto I-80 East, heading out of the Des Moines metro and on toward Iowa City. Behind them, likely forever, was Chen's Tacos, an Asian-Mexican fusion joint that earned five stars from locals, tourists, and critics alike. National food shows loved to feature it. It was quirky, delicious, and Instagram worthy.

"But it's in downtown," her sister had said. Lauren might as well have said it was in gang-infested territory for the effect the *D* word had on their mom—and Lauren knew it.

Her sister insisted they find something quick and close to the interstate. Their mom had agreed. As a result, there they were, joining eastbound traffic with food from a gas station. A nice gas station, but still a huge step down from the experience that would have been Chen's Tacos.

Two chicken taquitos from the roller waited for Chloe in their paper serving bag nestled into the console cupholder. She slid one out and bit into the crispy shell. In the passenger seat, her mom twisted the cap of her bottled smoothie. The seal clacked open.

"Are you sure that's enough for you?" Chloe used the taquito as a pointer, motioning toward both the bottle and the banana in her mom's lap.

"More than enough. It's nice to have something cold. I don't think tacos and I would have gotten along today anyway. Not with this heat."

Chloe caught her sister's gaze in the rearview mirror. Lauren lifted an eyebrow in a told-you-so way, then munched on an apple from her stash. Chloe shifted in her seat, focused on the road ahead.

The evening with Aunt Gab would have ended differently too if Lauren had helped her intervene instead of aiding and abetting cynicism. Family bonds should mean more than that. They should be held more precious than that. If Lauren refused to come to the defense of their aunt in the name of family peace, why wouldn't she do the same with Chloe when the time came to tell their mom about Prague? Would Lauren force Chloe's hand and make the confession come sooner than was comfortable? Would she provide their mom an unsolicited risk assessment of living overseas? Would she do both?

Lauren knew the basics about Prague, but she didn't know the why or when or who or how. She hadn't asked questions or expressed any level of curiosity. That alone didn't bode well.

Many miles outside of the city, another set of wind turbines rose like massive white daisies from upticks in the pastureland. Chloe had lost count of how many clusters they had passed. Their blades sliced clockwise through the air in quiet, poetic movements. Much like the covered bridges, they were impressive feats of human ingenuity. If someone stood next to them for a picture, they would be a speck in the frame compared to the towering turbines.

Sori would have jumped at the suggestion to explore back roads until they got as close to a cluster as possible, then leap over the thin wire fences for selfies with the spinning giants. Seymour Bove would have whistled low and slow at their grandeur. Her actual companions, however, didn't bother to look. Her mom broke her stare out her own window only to sip her cold lunch. Meanwhile, her sister replied to yet another text alert. Several had come through since they left the covered bridge.

Both her mom and sister seemed content in their own boxes. They didn't explore more than they had to, didn't notice more than was necessary or form an opinion that fell outside their presumptions. On a road trip aimed at celebrating perspective-shaping books, her mom and sister staunchly remained the main characters in their own stories. What was the point in relishing books if you didn't allow them to lift you out of your silo? What was the point of a road trip if not discovery?

The silence in the car bore down heavier and heavier.

She replaced the taquito in its bag and grabbed her phone. "Anyone care if I listen to a sermon? It is Sunday, after all."

"It doesn't bother me," her mom said before taking a drink.

Chloe leaned toward the rearview mirror. "Lauren?"

Her sister glanced up from her phone. The smile written across her lips faded. "Sure. Fine."

Muscle memory guided Chloe's thumb to find her podcast app. A quick peek and she tapped the podcast of one of her favorite pastors, Dr. Porter Paxton. His fun-to-say name originally drew her in; his teaching kept her there. She tapped the green play button to call up the latest sermon. The violin solo and gentle voice of the host rolled into the cabin at the volume her playlist had been.

"Welcome to another episode of *Mercy Abounds*. Today, Dr. Paxton shares a message on the timing of God's providence."

As the white line stretched beside them and the smaller towns passed, Chloe soaked in the lesson from Joseph's captivity in Egypt and the wait he'd endured for the Lord to rescue him from the slavery his own brothers had sold him into. For years he waited. More than a decade. Falsely accused, falsely imprisoned, unheard, unnoticed.

"But did God notice him?" Dr. Paxton asked. "Yes, he did. Did he remember him? Yes, he did. As Joseph waited for vindication, for redemption from what haunted him, was God there, close to his broken heart? Yes, he was. How many wounds are you carrying with you? How many wrongs are you praying God will make right?

200

Are you waiting and waiting? Though the healing often tarries, we have a promise it will surely come to pass. Habakkuk 2:3 says this: 'For the revelation awaits an appointed time; it speaks of the end and will not prove false. Though it linger, wait for it; it will certainly come and will not delay.' Do you seek healing? Wait for it. It will certainly come."

Chloe took a shuddering breath. Everything was revealed at its appointed time. Including—especially—healing.

She turned toward her mom for the first time since the podcast began.

Her mom had leaned back against the headrest, her face angled down and to the side, the posture of someone asleep. In the back seat, Lauren had her wireless earbuds plugged into her ears and her attention buried once more on her phone screen.

Chloe sighed.

Astounding how much they missed.

46

Eddie had lost track of sleep's company around three o'clock that morning in their Omaha hotel room. It had disappeared right along with all support from the cheap pillows on the bed. Trying to find her way back to it had proven fruitless, until the ride across Iowa. The long hours of being awake, the warmth of the car, the hum of the tires, and the drone of the pastor drew her closer and closer to the fickle companion. One word from the sermon accompanied her on the drift: unnoticed. For years Joseph had been unnoticed.

Unnoticed . . . Unnoticed.

Images slipped around her, of bookshelves and of wingback chairs and of glass hotel doors shutting behind her sister's back. She floated between them. Her feet sought ground in the weird and vague world but found none.

She awoke to a silent engine and her youngest daughter in front of the car, feeding a parking meter. An unsettled sensation crept into her limbs, like she needed to run toward or run away and her brain could not decide which was safer.

Lauren leaned over the center console. "You slept well."

"I guess I did."

Their car sat in the last angled spot before an intersection.

Outside the driver's side window, green street signs atop the stoplight labeled the intersecting streets as Iowa Avenue and Dubuque.

"We're in Iowa City?" she asked.

"We are. Chloe wants to start with the Literary Walk. I'm pulling up the map now." Lauren's thumbs worked the screen of her phone.

A block past the intersection, the gold dome of the old capitol building rose like a demigod from the end of Iowa Avenue. The proud chests of the streetlight poles along the sidewalk held University of Iowa flags aloft.

"I must have been asleep for a while," she said.

"About an hour."

She touched her mouth. Had she been drooling? She pulled down the visor and flipped open the mirror on the back. No signs of dried saliva or red streaks from pressure points, but her hair was slightly flattened on the right side of her head where it had been pressed against the headrest. She attempted to fluff it back to life with her fingers, but much like chasing sleep when it didn't want to be close friends, trying to get her hair to recover from sweat and sleep with only her hand had little effect.

Suddenly Chloe tapped her window. Edie yelped. The unsettledness shot to her stomach and stuck there.

Chloe, all glee and relentlessly voluminous red mane, motioned for her to get out.

"All right, all right." She snapped the visor back into place and leaned forward for her purse on the floorboard. The angle sent blood pounding to her face, arousing a new ache down the center of her forehead. It was going to be another long afternoon. She donned her sunglasses, checked if Lauren was ready, then together they stepped out into the summer afternoon.

"Guess what I found?" Chloe bounded back to the sidewalk and pointed to the first of many bronze relief panels embedded in the concrete. "It's the one for *Field of Dreams*!"

The tour of the Literary Walk had begun before Edie could strap on her purse.

The three of them edged up to the baseball field–shaped panel. A quote from W. P. Kinsella's *Shoeless Joe*, the inspiration for the Kevin Costner movie, arched across the outfield.

Chloe leaned closer and read the line aloud with an air of reverence. "'Three years ago at dusk on a spring evening, when the sky was a robin's-egg blue and the wind as soft as a day-old chick, I was sitting on the verandah of my farm home in eastern Iowa when a voice very clearly said to me, "If you build it, he will come."' Oh, that's so cool!" She took out her phone and searched for the best photo-taking angle.

Farther east on the sidewalk, another panel darkened the concrete, and another one a few paces past it. Edie's sunglasses were insufficient at keeping the brightness of the day subdued. She squinted behind the lenses. "How long is this Literary Walk?" she asked.

Lauren consulted the map on her phone. "It's three blocks along Iowa, both sides. Looks like we're in the middle block."

A walking total of six city blocks. That was a lot, in the heat, on concrete, in full sun. The ache in her head grew.

Chloe squatted next to the home plate of the panel and eased her phone into just the right spot before snapping away. "Think about the greatness that has walked these streets! All these authors who have ties to Iowa or the university's Iowa Writers' Workshop. It's mesmerizing they would all come to this state, of all places."

"There's a panel for John Irving," Lauren offered. "And Flannery O'Connor. You like those writers, don't you, Mom?"

Like and understand were two different things. "Irving is nice," she said.

"Come get in this picture, Mom," Chloe said from the ground. "I'll text it to Dad. Just squat there next to the outfield."

Edie exchanged a look with Lauren, who shrugged one shoulder and slipped off to the side with her phone.

"Dad's going to love it," Chloe assured her.

Fortunately, no other pedestrians were close enough to see. She girded herself and lowered, knees together and angled away from the camera. Squatting in public could still be ladylike.

Chloe repositioned herself farther from the pointed home plate end, then tilted her phone slightly up to bring all of Edie into the frame with the bronze art. "Smile!"

Edie gazed into the camera lens. If only that mechanical eye were really Grant's. If he were there, surely the menacing disquiet within her would settle.

They ventured from panel to panel, intending to cut a clockwise loop down Iowa Avenue and back up the other side. Chloe insisted on reading each author's marker aloud and duly capturing it in pictures. Every minute that passed, Grant's name beat louder in Edie's mind. If only he were there. The tank float would have gone differently. The dinner with Gabriella too. Everything would have.

By the time they reached the final panel on the south side of the avenue, she was a soggy, restless, aching mess. She told her daughters to finish out the last block of the loop without her and ducked inside a coffee shop. Glorious air-conditioning and dim lighting enveloped her. God bless. She basked in the relief, ordered an unsweetened iced tea, then found a table in a quiet corner, far away from the window and the few other patrons. In the comfort of privacy, she called home. Even Grant's "hello" was a salve.

"I was wondering when I'd hear from you again." The television noise in the background faded. He must have been in the living room, probably in his recliner, bowl of chips rebelliously balanced on the arm since she was not there to insist he eat at the table. Her bottom lip quivered.

"How's the trip going?" he asked.

She pulled in a breath and steadied herself against the urge to hitchhike home immediately. "It's okay."

"You sound hesitant."

Another gulp of air, and with the energy it brought, she unspooled the long, frayed thread of events he had missed. "Your oldest broke her finger, then, for reasons I still don't understand, decided to cut off her hair. I fell in a river, and my sister decided to show up for supper last night in Omaha."

A moment of silence.

"A lot to unpack there," he said.

Didn't she know it.

"Let's start with Lauren. She broke her finger? She okay?"

"The pain seems to be more manageable. She's been smiling more today, I've noticed, and the splint hasn't seemed to stop her from staying glued to her phone. She's trying to stay caught up at work, I think."

"Sounds like her. Dare I ask how you fell in a river?"

She recounted the fiasco, from the turtle to the portable toilet. The slimy riverbed still haunted her fingertips.

A grin was evident in his tone. "Someday we're going to laugh about that."

"That's what Chloe said."

"And what's this about Gab coming to dinner?"

"Gabriella," she said. "Apparently Chloe told her we were coming through Omaha."

"I take it that didn't end well?"

"Gabriella walked out, to no one's surprise, except maybe Chloe's. She has stars in her eyes when it comes to her aunt. She finally saw the side all of us have known for a long time."

"Sorry to hear that. Must've been hard for you all."

It would not have been as hard if his hand had been close by for her to hold. The cry for him, for home, rose to her throat. She pushed it down and sipped her tea from its plastic to-go cup. The shock of cold countered the pressure.

"Has the journaling been a help?" he asked.

She pressed the cool cup to her cheek. "I'm not sure I'm the journaling type, dear. Though I do love the cover. I can't believe you remembered about Salzburg. Where did you find it?"

"Chloe found it, actually."

"Chloe?" She set her cup on the table.

"I don't think she knows about Salzburg, but she does know you like *The Sound of Music*. She saw the journal online one day and sent me the buy link. I've had the journal for a while, waiting for the right time to give it to you. For the record, I don't think you should count yourself a non-journaler quite yet. Give it a try. You might surprise yourself."

She blinked. Hattie had used that exact encouragement about motherhood.

"Where did things end with Gabriella?" he asked, switching them back to the previous topic.

She ran her fingers up the side of the cup. "They ended in the same place they were before, with her obsessed with her own life and me left to clean up. She made it clear she had no interest in helping with the estate sale and said I could keep the proceeds. At least she acknowledges she's pinched our mother for enough already." She gripped the cup and swirled the ice. The cubes clacked against each other. Her sister's requests of their mother had finally stopped around the time Chloe was born. Gabriella had lived in Nebraska for two years by that point.

"I've always wondered about that," Grant said. "Did your mother actually give her money?"

"What do you mean? Of course she did."

"That's what I assumed too. But I was just thinking about the time she totaled her car and asked your mother for help. Did your mother give her anything? I don't remember money ever exchanging hands."

Edie started to respond, then stopped. A connecting memory jostled loose from the hidden corners. "That was the year she didn't come down for Christmas."

"Right," he said.

The question loomed larger. She paged back through the stories her mother had told her of Gabriella's requests. Had her mother ever mentioned fulfilling any of them?

"I suppose I never asked," she said at last.

"Makes you wonder, doesn't it?" he asked.

The curiosity was catching. Gabriella claimed Edie only thought she had the rawer deal, that Edie had no idea. Echoes of the pod-cast pastor's word resounded: unnoticed.

Had she missed something?

47

Guess where I am.

The photo that arrived with Gavin's text mimicked Lauren's pose in the bridge. Him, camera above his head, eyes angled up. A large sculpture of an open book stood behind him.

She bit her cheek to hold in the giggle. Her mom and sister were too occupied climbing back into the Xterra to notice anything. An afternoon of texts had culminated in him driving from his hometown of Carroll to Iowa City "just to see you again." A three-hour drive, just to see her. He waited for her summons, ready to report to anyplace she directed, anytime.

She settled into the back seat as her mom jangled her iced tea into the cupholder and her sister fussed with her phone to find directions to their rental for the night. Lauren kept her phone low in her lap and etched out a response.

Seed salesman seems to be a better fit for you than model. Looks like a library?

By the time she buckled her seat belt, a new message had swooped in.

Yep, to both.

She grinned. The picture he'd sent made his eyes seem bluer than they were in the coffee shop. She alone held the power to determine when they saw her again.

Another message from Gavin arrived.

> Library closes at 5 so I hope you tell me soon where to meet you bc I can't hang out here much longer.

He ended the text with a praying hands emoji.

Power elated the soul, enlivened the spirit. She turned to her window and let the grin amplify.

Chloe engaged the engine and started to back out of the parking spot. When she turned to look over her shoulder, she paused on Lauren. "What are you smiling about, Laur?"

She pulled her lips into a neutral position. "Nothing." Quickly she redirected. "Where is our place for tonight?"

Chloe eased onto the street. "Maybe five minutes from here. Corner of Jefferson and Evans."

Translation: They would be staying not far from the city center. Still within walking distance, anyway. Slipping away from her family would be tricky, but if Lauren could lure a man across a state, she could figure out an excuse to dip out for the evening. When her sister's eyes were fully on the road ahead, Lauren shot Gavin a quick assurance.

> I'll send you a time and place shortly.

Keep him waiting. Keep him guessing. Keep him enthralled. And don't let her mom or sister know. On the drive, she searched for restaurants within a mile radius of their rental's location.

They turned onto Jefferson Street and passed through the last of downtown. Jefferson spilled into an older neighborhood. Vinyl-clad houses lined both sides of the street, many with two stories and wooden stairs leading to doors on the top floors. Being a landlord to college students was clearly an income stream for many in the city.

Six blocks down Jefferson, Chloe slowed as they approached the corner with Evans. "Your destination is on the right," her GPS announced.

Chloe pulled into the driveway of the quaint blue-gray ranch with a detached garage. "This is adorable. This whole town is adorable. Don't you love Iowa City?"

Their mom lifted her head off her hand and acknowledged, "Looks like a nice house, Chloe." The exhaustion and festering headache was evident in her tone.

Maybe dipping out wouldn't be that hard after all.

Her sister shifted into park and cut the engine. "I was surprised this place was less than a hundred dollars for the night."

Lauren lowered her phone. "Less than a hundred? For an entire house?"

"That's all they charged me. Two beds, one bath, quiet neighborhood." She laughed and opened her door. "I love this city."

Something was off. No way a college town would rent out an entire house for so little. That misguided confidence of her sister's was bound to sink them all, like it had at dinner with Aunt Gab.

Chloe led them up the front walk. "The hostess's message said to come to the front door for check-in instructions."

Lauren frowned. "Don't they usually send you the instructions?"

No sooner had she said it than the front door swung open. They halted.

A woman in a drab gray dress and a tight bun of faded blond hair came out to the stoop. Her expression was as stern as her inquiries of them. "Who are you? What you want?" Her *w*'s came out as *v*'s.

"So sorry," Chloe said. "Maybe we have the wrong address. We were looking for our rental."

"Yes," the woman said. "Who are you?"

Her sister glanced back at them, then attempted to ingratiate herself with the woman on the stoop. "Hi there. Are you Olga?"

The woman planted her hands on her hips and glowered as if it were the most inept question she had ever heard. "Yes. You?"

"I didn't expect you to be here. Usually we just—"

Olga's brow tightened, clearly impatient with her demand for their identity being ignored a third time. Their mom moved closer to Lauren.

"I'm Chloe Vance," her sister said.

The woman nodded, then jutted her chin toward the side of the house. "Room in garage."

"Room?" Chloe laughed nervously. "No, I rented the house. Two beds and a bath, the description said."

"Yes. Garage."

"I'm sorry," her sister tried again, "there seems to be some confusion."

"No confusion. You stay there. I live here." Olga rammed her finger into the air in the direction of both dwellings. Then she fisted her hand onto her hip once more. "Check in?"

"Um." Chloe turned to Lauren.

The old Lauren would have jumped in, would have rescued her little sister from her own missteps. No more. Lauren shook her head, refusing responsibility. It was all Chloe.

Her sister licked her lips and turned back to Olga. "Yes. We'll check in."

Their mom shot Chloe a withering look.

"Key is in door, around back. Checkout ten a.m. Park over there." The hostess pointed at a small gravel lot across Evans. Then she stalked back into the house and shut the door behind her.

They stood silent on the sidewalk.

After a moment, Chloe cleared her throat. "I'm guessing turndown service is not an option."

"Is staying at a hotel?" their mom asked, a bite coating her question.

"Now we know why it was so cheap," Lauren said. "Were there no pictures of this place on the rental site?"

"Only of the outside."

"For crying out loud, Chloe," their mom said under her breath, proving Lauren didn't need to say anything. Chloe was burying herself.

Not that her sister quit trying to dig out. "You're assuming it's worse than it probably is. Let's at least see it before we make judgments."

It was exactly as bad as the contextual clues had indicated it would be.

As soon as they stepped into the room off the back of the garage, her sister visibly shrunk back. The "two beds" was literal—as in two twin beds, one on either side of the room with fabric shower curtains for partitions. A mini fridge topped by a microwave stood in one corner by the door. A small round table with two wire chairs took up the other corner. Along the far wall, between the "bedrooms," was a door to the bathroom that was clearly once a closet. No television. No Wi-Fi. A single light in the middle of the room. Not exactly the height of hospitality.

"It's cozy," Chloe quipped.

"It's claustrophobic." Their mom shoved her largest rolling bag against the foot of one of the beds. She had only needed to take four steps from the entrance to get there.

"But there's good air-conditioning. Feel it?" Her sister spread her hands, palms up. The gesture matched the wide smile on her face.

Their mom stared her down. "How are we supposed to sleep, Chloe? There's not enough space for three of us."

"No worries. If we pull the curtains out of the way and shove the beds together, it'll be almost like a king size. We used to do it all the time in our dorm rooms. I'll sleep in the middle."

Their mom pursed her lips. The disdain only intensified as her sister waxed poetic about how they could go full-on dorm-room style and order pizza, talk about boys, and play Truth or Dare.

Lauren plopped her suitcase on the end of one of the beds and

213

pulled out a fresh change of clothes and her cosmetics bag. As her sister's convincing waged on, she headed for the bathroom.

The world's slenderest stand-up shower was wedged into one end of the rectangular room, the toilet in the other, with the sink dead center, so close to the door she had to step into the shower to shut it. She ran a cool, wet washcloth over her skin, then changed into the clean outfit and doused herself with body spray. The restaurant she had found wasn't too far away. She could time it so Gavin arrived before her, and she could make an entrance as regal as the one in the Red Cloud coffee shop. Anticipation thrummed through her.

A bit of blush and a refresh of her eye shadow, and she was ready for whatever waited on the other side of a summoning text to Gavin.

Out in the room, her sister had already joined the beds together on one side of the room and used the table and chairs to serve as suitcase holders. Their mom lay on her back on one bed and her sister sat on the end of the other, the last of the protein balls between them.

"We're having appetizers if you want some," Chloe said. "We plan to order chicken and spinach thin crust. Does that sound okay?"

Lauren strode to her suitcase, now on one of the chairs, and laid her clothes inside. "Order what you'd like. I'm going out."

Bedsprings squeaked as their mom shot up. "Out?"

"You're going out now? By yourself?" Chloe asked.

Lauren zipped her bag. "It's not quite five. Plenty of daylight left for exploring."

"But what about supper?" Chloe asked.

"I'll find something." Yes, she would. A very handsome something.

"I don't know that I want you out in a strange city by yourself," their mom said.

Lauren slipped on her sling. "It'll be fine. The scariest thing we've seen today is Olga. I'll be back later."

Their mom stood. "But what are you going to do? Are you taking the car?"

"I'll walk. It's cooling off out there now." She started for the door.

Her mom followed. "Maybe we should go with you."

"No, you're tired. I can tell you're tired. You rest, enjoy your pizza, and I'll see you later."

Worry lines crinkled around her mom's eyes, but it wasn't enough to keep Lauren planted. She turned the knob and said over her shoulder, "I have my phone."

She broke from the cage of a room and into the open evening, breathing deep for the first time all day. She passed around the side of the garage, then paused to send Gavin the text he clamored for.

Wallace Bistro, Linn and Market. Be there in fifteen.

It was a directive, a promise, and an advent of something novels celebrated.

48

Her mom lingered near the door and rubbed her temples. "You okay?" Chloe asked.

"Wonderful."

Clearly untrue. "Want me to order the pizza?"

Her mom sighed and dropped her hands to her sides. "Honestly, Chloe, I just want to medicate and go to bed."

"You don't want any food?"

"I had a couple of those protein things. Besides, my stomach isn't feeling the greatest." She moved to her suitcase propped on the table.

"But we have the whole evening ahead," Chloe said.

"I know. I'm sorry. Maybe you can go on a walk or something too. I just want to be still." Her mom pulled out her pajamas and toiletries bag and headed for the bathroom.

They had so little time together, yet both her mom and sister treated the evening like a lost cause, a throwaway. Chloe brought the container of protein balls to her lap and fitted the lid back on.

At the threshold of the bathroom, her mom paused to take a peek. "Like a clown car," she muttered, then wedged herself inside and closed the door.

Yes, the room was cramped. Yes, a hotel would have been better. Yes, Olga was the scariest person she had met in a long time. But the memories they could have forged together in that room would have lasted them forever. Where her mom and sister saw only uncomfortably close quarters, there was an invitation to draw together. Where they saw lack, there was really a blank canvas, ready to receive whatever their imagination could apply to it. They could have gotten pizzas from two different places and done a taste competition. They could have had a dance-off to Chloe's playlist. They could have played hangman or Pictionary. They could have looked beyond the immediate to find the possibilities. Splendor always unfolded for those patient and trusting enough to wait for it.

The night could have been an unfolding of splendor. So too could the trip, if her family would be patient and trusting enough. So too could what lay ahead the next two years. But if her mom wasn't even mildly receptive to the idea of finding the joy in a cramped room for one night, odds dimmed that she would ever accept Chloe living as a missionary teacher in a foreign country. Would her mom ever understand that great joy existed in sparse circumstances?

The water pipes kicked on. Water splashed in the basin of the shower stall.

Chloe padded to her suitcase and dropped the container next to it. She slid her sketchbook and pencil pouch from the outside pocket. She hadn't done much sketching this trip, and a storehouse of reference photos waited on her phone. She settled cross-legged on the bed and laid the sketchbook on her lap. One photo in particular begged to be studied. She unlocked her phone and found the photo Hattie had taken of Chloe and her mom on the riverbank before the start of the tank float. Her mom had actually smiled in that moment. Whether for the sake of the camera or for the sake of convincing herself she could find a way to enjoy the ride, the lift in those lovely pink lips was forever frozen in time.

Chloe zoomed in until she had the perfect framing, then she opened her sketchbook to the first blank page. She etched wispy ovals and circles, connecting them at angles to form the basic outlines of their bodies.

Were they really so different, she and her mom? They were made by the same Creator with the same materials. They were linked by blood and genes and spirit. There had to be a way to tell her mom the biggest news of her life that would make sense to the woman whose heart was entwined with her own.

She drew guidelines for the faces, started with the noses, then eyes, then ears. She brushed her pencil tip in soft strokes to create her mom's hair. Her dad once told her that her mom's hair was strawberry blond when he met her. Pregnancy had dulled the reddish tint.

The water turned off. A moment later, a loud bang startled her from the page. Her mom mumbled.

"Everything okay?" Chloe called.

"Fine" came the answer, thick with irritation. A while later, her mom emerged from the bathroom. "Thought you were getting food," she said as she slogged to her suitcase.

Chloe closed her sketchbook. "I guess I was hoping the shower would make you hungry. Not really, huh?"

Her mom laid her used outfit and toiletries bag on top of her suitcase. "I took my Tylenol PM before I showered. I just want to crash."

"Even with wet hair?"

"I'm too tired to care about that either." True to her word, she trudged to the other side of the joined beds, the side closest to the bathroom, and pulled back the covers.

Chloe gathered her things and got to her feet. "Maybe I'll go out and find somewhere to sketch. I'll lock the door behind me and take the key. Okay?"

Her mom nodded and cocooned herself with the top sheet. By the time Chloe stowed the sketching supplies in her backpack, soft snores rose from the far side of the bed. She could redeem the evening on her own, regardless if anyone else joined her.

Outside, the sun still hung three-quarters of the way to the horizon. Jefferson Street provided a straight shot back to where campus and downtown comingled, back to where students and literary greats traipsed the same paths. Discovery was the lifeblood of the town. It was worth relishing.

Within ten minutes, she was back to the outer reaches of campus. Houses and businesses, the markers of life as usual, mixed with the halls of learning. Tucked in the northwest corner of Jefferson and Linn was a church bearing the same red brick with terracotta accents as the Watkins Museum in Lawrence. The steeple rose higher above Jefferson than the seven-floor campus building across the street, an appropriate statement of whose wisdom excelled. A row of thin, white-framed windows stood tall and proud along the church's belly.

Chloe stepped into the crosswalk over Linn and approached with her gaze lifted to the cross at the point of the steeple. A calmness seemed to seep between the bricks of the church and welcome her.

The main entrance featured three sets of dark-brown double doors with arched stained-glass windows above and railed steps below. The middle set was the largest, with a placard hanging to its right identifying the sacred house as St. Mary's Catholic Church. The name took her back to a tidbit she had read somewhere in her research of Iowa City's literary history. Flannery O'Connor had worshiped at St. Mary's when she attended the Iowa Writers' Workshop. No wonder she did, if the serenity found within the walls was the same variety that spilled onto the sidewalk.

O'Connor must have found such clarity there, revelations to take back to her writing desk, and details to infuse into the imaginary lives she coaxed out of hiding. What answers she must have uncovered. What solid guidance to hold on to in the collision of faith and creativity. Wisdom was, by far, the most needed muse.

Chloe's fingers itched for a pencil.

Across Jefferson, in the shadow of the seven-story campus hall, a park bench offered an encompassing view of the church's face. She jogged over and settled onto the smooth metal bench. Her eyes traveled up the throat of the church once more.

The cross. The cross needed to be the focal point of her sketch, the place the viewer's eye slid to every time. She started with the church's body, wide across the bottom of the page and narrowing upward. She sliced a slender vertical rectangle through the middle, adding a peak to the top and the rough outline of a cross. The three doorways came next, domed by their windows. With every stroke of her pencil, she sought what O'Connor surely had. The clarity, the guidance, the assurance of the hope she held.

Lord, show me what you see. Awaken my eyes.

The more she sketched, the more she prayed those simple words.

Two young women passed by. Their conversation nudged into her concentration.

"What are you in the mood for?" one asked.

"I've been dying for falafel all week," her friend replied.

Chloe perked up. Her mouth watered at the mention of Mediterranean food.

The girls crossed Jefferson and headed north on Linn.

The sketch could wait. The church wasn't going anywhere either. Chloe took a picture of it from the vantage point of the bench, a reference for later, should she need it. Then she packed up her things, looped her backpack strap over her shoulder, and followed her unwitting guides at a distance.

They walked a couple of blocks to a section of Linn that had been converted to a pedestrian mall. People ate at picnic tables, mingled around food trucks, and danced to a live DJ set up in the middle of the street. Over the crowds, strings of twinkling bulbs crisscrossed between light poles. Underfoot, brightly painted floral stems larger than cars popped against the dull gray pavement. More eateries lined both sides of the street. Whiffs of garlic and sautéed meat emanated from the bistro on the corner.

Iowa City was literally the cutest. She laughed at the unexpected liveliness, on a Sunday evening no less.

Ahead of her, the two girls cut to the right and found a clear path among the crowd, dodging the dancing couples and filled picnic tables, then moved onto the sidewalk. They headed for a narrow orange storefront with an enormous sign over the door: The Pita Shop.

Chloe traced after them, cutting through the revelers. A couple spun too close to the invisible boundary of the dance floor. She attempted to quick-step out of the way but wasn't spry enough. The woman bumped into her. They exchanged apologies, Chloe insisting it was not a big deal. As soon as the woman's partner whisked her away, a gap opened among the throng of dancers. Chloe's gaze caught on the profile of a beautiful brunette. She had short hair, a broad smile, and a familiar face.

She gasped. "Lauren?"

Her sister's cheeks were lifted sky-high. Her brow glistened. She threw her head back with laughter, so far back she seemed on the verge of tipping over. But suddenly she righted. A tall blond man pulled her to his chest.

Chloe froze.

Lauren threw her arms around the neck of the half-hidden man. They moved together in that embrace for several beats. The glee never left her face. She looked up at him through lowered lashes. Then she closed her eyes and tilted her face upward.

Another couple sliced through the scene, blocking what took place between Lauren and the man. Chloe dashed to the slightly higher ground of the sidewalk. She hugged a utility pole and lifted onto her toes. But her sister was lost in the mix. Her sister and the mysterious blond.

Who was he? More importantly, what had gotten into Lauren? Red flags popped up faster than weeds. A knot formed in Chloe's gut. Someone needed to find out what was going on.

And discernment said there was only one person persistent enough for the job.

49

Gavin came around the front of his truck and pulled open
Lauren's door. The cab light danced in his eyes and illumi-
nated his crooked grin. He held out his left hand.

She accepted it and slipped down from the plush leather seat
to the curb of the rental house. For a country man, his truck was
meticulously clean, the way she kept her car. The inside held the
scent of leather and musk. Everything about him carried the scent
of leather and musk.

He guided her to his side, then shut the door. The engine idled.
He placed his hand on the small of her back and led her down the
driveway toward the orb of the security light above the garage bay
door. Their last few moments together. The sweat of the evening
still clung to the nape of her neck.

"Nice place you found here." He nodded toward the house.

She nearly laughed. "Yes. It's cozy." With any luck, Olga was
a sound sleeper.

The soles of his boots scuffed along the pavement. "Any chance
you'll be this way again sometime?"

Leave him wanting, always wanting. "I don't get to Iowa much.
It's a little out of my way."

His eyes drifted to hers. "Maybe I should find a reason to come to Kansas City, then."

She hid her grin. "Maybe."

They reached the ring of the security light. She stopped in the middle and faced him. "Thank you for tonight."

He reached up, ran his thick fingers through the delicate hair along her temple. She braced as his palm cupped the back of her head. "You were worth it."

Her breath caught.

He angled her head upward, slowly leaning in. The warmth of his lips stirred every nerve ending once more. It left her fighting a desire of her own.

When he pulled back, the light glinted in his eyes. "Text me soon, Lauren Vance."

"I'll think about it, Gavin Drake."

He laughed softly, deepening the wrinkles that curved from the ends of his strong nose to the corners of his mouth. He slipped his hand down to hers, the one with the splint, and held it gently. "I'll wait as long as I need to."

A man waiting for her, longing for her, thinking of her. The thrill of it was unlike any sensation.

Gavin walked backward a few steps, grin fully aimed at her, then turned and headed back to his truck. He looked over his shoulder once, winked, then stepped into the shroud of night.

She licked her lips, marveling at the potency she maintained.

While his boots still fell upon the pavement, she headed for the passageway between the house and garage. For all he knew, she was going to the back door of the house. For all he knew, she too would disappear into the night and never actually think of him again.

A truck door closed. She forced herself not to steal one more look. Before her resolve could melt, she ducked behind the house. A moment later, the truck engine hummed away. In the stillness, she proceeded to the back of the garage and the door to their room, afloat from the night that made every happy hour with

Duncan pale by comparison. She turned the corner, smile wide, and came to a halt.

Her sister sat cross-legged in the glow of the porch light by the door.

"What are you doing out here?" Lauren asked.

"Waiting for you."

"What for?"

Her sister rose. "Because we need to talk."

"Now? Here?"

"Yes." Chloe's voice was firmer than usual. She pointed in the direction of the driveway. "Who was that?"

"A friend."

"A friend?" Chloe took a step closer. "A friend you kiss in the middle of a busy street?"

She stiffened. "You followed me?"

"Accidentally. Mom went to bed early, so I went out for food. I didn't know we'd end up in the same area. Who is he? How did you meet him?"

"Stay out of it, Chloe." She brushed past her and tried the door.

"It's locked." Her sister held up the key.

Lauren balled her fists. "Open it."

"Not until you tell me what's going on."

"Nothing is going on."

"Stop with that, Laur. It's obvious something is up with you. The haircut, the eating—or lack of. And now you're sneaking off at night with some guy you clearly don't know well in a city you don't know at all. Don't you realize that's how *Law & Order* episodes start?"

Lauren crossed her arms. "Unlock the door, Chloe. It's late, and I want to go to bed."

"I do too. So let's get it all out in the open."

"I went out with a friend. That's all there is to say."

"Come on, Laur. It's me. Why are you trying to—"

"I told you before, Chloe, you mind your business and I'll mind mine. I'm only on this trip because Mom doesn't trust you. For obvious reasons."

Chloe's lips parted.

The guilt would have panged harder within Lauren had the chance to grab the key from Chloe's hand not presented itself. She swiped it away before her sister could react. "I'm going to bed."

A directive, a promise, and the end of pretending the trip would result in anything good between them.

50

The girls didn't talk much over breakfast at a local diner. They certainly didn't talk to each other. Edie ate her oatmeal and counted on one hand the number of times her girls even made eye contact with each other.

Lauren nibbled on her single slice of unbuttered toast between sips of coffee, mostly keeping her bloodshot eyes turned down to her plate as if dreaming of bed. Chloe chomped through her stack of pancakes with subdued energy, barely delighting in the Iowa Hawkeyes logo emblazoned on the puffy cakes, a novelty she normally would have memorialized on social media.

On the way out to the car, Edie pulled Lauren aside. "Did I miss something last night?"

Lauren glanced toward her sister before answering low. "Nothing worth worrying about."

On the hour-and-a-half drive north to Dyersville, only the buzz of the tires and rattle of the overworked air-conditioning broke up the silence. She nearly asked Chloe to turn on her playlist. If Nebraska was the least likable state, Iowa was the most puzzling. The disquiet that had started the day before still clung to her.

They arrived at the Field of Dreams Movie Site shortly after its nine o'clock opening, when humidity still showed mercy. Ten cars and one tour bus were already parked in the gravel lot at the foot of the iconic farm. The white clapboard house crowned a gentle hill, and from such a perch, it overlooked the surrounding cornfield and the homemade baseball field cut into the side yard. The imagination of W. P. Kinsella splayed out in tangible, lush-green glory, complete with a gift shop in the barn.

The three Vance women met at the front of their car and paused to take in the site together.

"Your dad would be in heaven," Edie said.

"No," Chloe countered, "he'd be in Iowa." Despite the quippy (albeit inevitable) reference to the movie's signature bit of dialogue, Chloe's grin was strained.

"Funny," Edie said.

They proceeded toward the set, Lauren hanging three steps back.

A stone retaining wall encircled the hill on which the house sat, with a white picket fence staked into the top. An ingenious marketing pro had installed a "Field of Dreams" sign at a spot along the fence that maximized the house as a backdrop. What resulted was a must-have photo op. A loosely formed line of visitors waited for their turn.

"Let's get a picture too," Chloe said, though she didn't wait for anyone else to reply before breaking for the end of the line.

Edie and Lauren met up with her behind a middle-aged couple. The man, who couldn't have been much older than Grant, wore a St. Louis Cardinals T-shirt with the name Musial across the back above a number six. He fit in with most of the people who milled about the field and lawn and rows of corn. Youth league to major league, a plethora of teams were represented in the garb. Grant undoubtedly would have donned his prized George Brett jersey.

When the couple's turn came for the photo, the woman turned to Edie with a warm smile and her phone extended. "Could I trouble you?"

"Of course." Edie accepted the device and, following the insistence of Chloe, took several pictures in both landscape and portrait of the couple. The man stood with his arm wrapped around his partner, who rested her hand on his chest and leaned toward him.

"You all look like high school sweethearts!" Chloe cooed.

The familiar ache gathered in the center of Edie's chest. Five more nights until she was back with Grant.

With true Midwestern decorum, the woman returned the favor of Edie's photography assistance by taking pictures of her and the girls on Edie's phone, also in landscape and portrait.

No sooner had the stranger captured the final shot than Chloe turned to Edie. "We also need to get pictures of us playing catch down on the infield. Look, they have extra gloves and balls down by the backstop we can use."

Sure enough, two teen boys rooted through a large blue tub of spare equipment behind the three-panel backstop. An untold number of sweaty, unwashed hands had been shoved into those gloves.

"We can help with that too," the woman offered.

Edie started to reply that she had precisely zero intention of plunging her hand into any disease-riddled abyss, but her youngest spoke first.

"We'd love that! Thank you."

Edie pulled on a polite smile. "Yes, very kind of you."

The group moved forward together. Chloe struck up a conversation with the man about the movie, which quickly evolved into comparing notes about memorable scenes, which led to the man sharing facts about the real baseball players portrayed in the film. The two of them marched to their own pace, ahead of everyone else.

The woman grinned. "I think your daughter reminds him of our niece. We don't get to see her much these days since she and her husband live in Kansas City."

"That's where we're from," Edie said.

"No kidding? We're from the Hannibal, Missouri, area."

"That's where we're headed next!"

"How crazy!" The woman laughed.

Edie joined in and turned to find Lauren. But her oldest daughter had broken away at some point and walked toward the bleachers along the first baseline. Whatever was on Lauren's phone apparently was more interesting.

The woman's voice drew Edie back to the conversation. "I'm Joyce, by the way."

"Edie." She shook her hand. "That's my oldest daughter, Lauren, headed to the bleachers, and that's my youngest, Chloe, with your better half."

"Wes," Joyce said. "When we decided to go to the Wisconsin Dells for vacation, I surprised him with plans to come here on our drive north. It's a little out of our way, but it was worth it to see his face when we pulled up."

"My husband would have been the same way."

Up ahead, Chloe and Wes dug through the tub of dysentery, selecting the gloves that would work.

"How long have you been married?" Edie asked.

"Almost three years. We've known each other since childhood, but the right time didn't come along until later in life."

"Long time to wait."

Joyce watched her husband fit a glove on his hand, punch it like the pros do, and set off to the field with Chloe by his side. "It was worth the wait."

The adoration in her tone flared the longing in Edie's chest. Five more nights.

They stepped past the tub and onto the pebble pathway edging the infield. "Why do you think the right time came along so much later?" Edie asked as they settled in behind the backstop.

"Only God knows. But I suppose sometimes you have work you need to do or roles you need to play before you can step into the place you're meant to be. I'm already seeing how every role I have played has prepared me in some way for my life now. I'm sure you see that taking shape in your girls' lives too."

Out on the field, Chloe's whole face came alive as she caught the first throw from Wes. It was the same look she had when she talked about her barista job or showed off one of her drawings. It was the same one she'd had when they stood under the young Hemingway portrait and on the bank of the Republican River. To Chloe, every role, every opportunity, was a gift to embrace. To Edie, they were scraps—crumbs compared to a feast. What if they were crumbs leading her daughter to the place she was meant to be?

"Maturing can be a funny process," she said and looped her fingers through the wire fencing.

At various spots throughout the field, pairs or groups tossed balls back and forth. Grandfathers, fathers, sons, mothers, daughters. One man practiced grounders with his boy.

"This is quite a place," Joyce said. "Amazing how a decades-old story can still capture the imagination of generations of people. Grown men become little boys again."

The ball snapped against Wes's glove. He chuckled, either at the noise or at the memories it unlocked.

"They look like they're enjoying themselves," Edie agreed. What Chloe brought out in Wes was exactly what Chloe had wanted to bring out in her and Lauren. They were not making it easy on her.

Edie pulled her phone from her purse and documented the game of catch. She captured images of different poses, different moments of play, all of them pointing to the joy written across Chloe's face, the joy her daughter wanted them all to share.

Edie panned to the bleachers. Lauren sat with her feet on the bench below her, elbows on her knees, hands clasped. She stared out into the space beyond the corn. It was hard to pinpoint a moment when Lauren's face had come alive like Chloe's the entire trip.

After a while, the game of catch concluded, and they parted ways with Wes and Joyce, wishing them well on their vacation. As the couple headed for the corn in the outfield, Edie gestured for Chloe to hold out her hands. Her daughter complied, and Edie doused them with sanitizer from her purse.

Chloe rubbed in the cleansing liquid and glanced over at her sister. "I see Lauren's having a blast."

Edie tucked the bottle back in her purse. "Do you think something's bothering her?"

For a moment, Chloe was quiet. Finally she bobbed one shoulder. "I think you should ask her that." She offered nothing further, though she clearly had more to say. "I'm going to the gift shop to get something for Popsie."

Edie stepped aside to allow her to pass. Once again, Chloe noticed things she did not. Lauren obviously did too. Her daughters existed on a plane different from her own, one she couldn't seem to reach. In so many ways, she was still that nine-year-old in the wingback chair of her mother's study, searching for a way in.

The *shiff* of falling sand whispered in the uneasy silence her daughters left behind.

51

- - - - -

Her mom did not, in fact, stay to talk to her sister as Chloe suggested. Instead, she followed Chloe into the air-conditioned gift shop. Lauren stayed on the bleachers, staring into the void and thinking thoughts she refused to share with anyone. Someone needed to get through to Lauren. It was clear, so painfully clear, that her sister wrestled with things bigger than what had come to light so far. Why wouldn't Lauren talk to her? Why wouldn't she trust her? Lauren's biting comebacks the past two days were a defense mechanism, but they wounded nonetheless, and the wounds were still bleeding fresh.

Her mom helped her debate the merits of each T-shirt available in Popsie's size. In the end, Chloe walked out with a heather-gray shirt with the movie site's logo on the front and the famous "Dad, Wanna Have a Catch?" line from the film on the back. Popsie didn't cry often, but that scene got him every time. She also selected for herself a pair of adorable crew socks with baseballs and ears of corn and put them on immediately with her sneakers, much to her mom's chagrin.

They tore Lauren away from her sulking and piled back into Goldie. The same quiet that had sat with them on the ride to Dyersville wedged into the cabin with them on the four-hour drive south into northeast Missouri. Her sister stared out the window, sunglasses hiding her eyes. Her mom attempted to fan away the sweat streaking down her temples with the Winterset map from the day before. The silence was endless and boring.

Just after the state line, Chloe finally broke into the mind-numbing nothingness. "Mom, when's the last time you've seen the Mississippi?"

Her mom shrugged. "It's been years, I'd say."

"You'll get an up-close view tonight on the riverboat dinner cruise."

The fanning paused. "I forgot about that. Another river."

"Yes, but this one has a steak buffet and no direct sunlight."

Lauren spoke in Chloe's direction for the first time all day, her tone possessing teeth as sharp as the night before. "I think what Mom's saying is that she's had enough water adventure for one trip."

Lauren could sulk all she wanted, but she didn't have to dampen the day for everyone else.

Chloe held back any irritation in her own voice and kept her attention on their mom. "I assure you it'll be impossible to fall in the river tonight. At least if you stay in the cabin."

Their mom resumed her fanning. "How comforting."

Before Chloe could reply, Lauren interjected again. "You don't have to go if you don't want to, Mom."

Hours of silence and suddenly her sister talked, only to shade everything Chloe said.

Chloe tightened her grip on the steering wheel. "It's a gorgeous tour with gorgeous food—and nonrefundable."

"Doesn't mean she has to go," Lauren shot back.

Leave it. She would leave it before anything burst out of her mouth that shouldn't. She took a breath and said, "It's up to you, Mom."

All of them left it at that.

They reached their hotel in downtown Hannibal shortly after four in the afternoon.

"A cold shower sounds so good right now," her mom said as they ambled into the lobby.

Cool river air during the cruise would delight the senses as well, but Chloe held on to that particular pitch until a more opportune moment. She had promised her mom it was up to her, and she would keep her word.

The reservationist looked up from behind the chest-high counter as the three of them approached. "Good afternoon. How may I help you?"

Chloe laid one arm on the laminate top. "Reservation for Vance."

"Of course. If I could see an ID, I'll pull your reservation right up. What brings you all to town?"

"Doing the Mark Twain things." Chloe dug in her purse for her wallet as her mom and sister looked on from her left.

"You picked the best hotel for sightseeing. Many of the attractions are on Main Street, which is the next street to the east here." The woman gestured toward the lobby doors. "You'll find Twain's boyhood home, Becky Thatcher's home, and the stairs to the lighthouse all right there. The riverfront is just beyond that. All very walkable."

Chloe slid her driver's license across the counter. "How far is the riverboat landing?"

"It's only a few blocks down. Also very walkable."

Chloe turned to her mom and smiled. "Hear that? Just a short walk."

"Lovely."

On the other side of their mom, Lauren shook her head and turned around to watch the muted television across the lobby playing cable news. Maybe she would opt to stay at the hotel for the cruise.

The reservationist clacked away on her keyboard. After a long moment, she frowned. "It appears we have a slight problem, Miss Vance."

"We do?"

The woman looked up from the screen, brow furrowed. "I'm afraid your reservation was for last night."

Lauren spun around.

Chloe blinked. "What? No, I have the confirmation right here." She took out her phone and opened her email app. At the top of her inbox, in boldface, waited an unread message notifying her that she had been charged a no-show fee. "Oh. I guess it was."

Her sister huffed.

"I'm really sorry," the reservationist said. "Unfortunately, I can't change your previous reservation, but I can make a new one for tonight if you'd like."

"Yes, let's do that," Lauren said, already digging into her sling bag. "You can charge it to me."

"I can handle this," Chloe told her.

Lauren plopped her credit card on the countertop anyway. Her scowl bore into Chloe. "Did you not get the reminder emails from the hotel?"

Chloe tensed under the heat of accusation. "I've been a little occupied the last several days. I haven't been on my phone much." She managed to bite back the "like some people" part.

"Who goes on a multicity trip and doesn't check for confirmations?"

"Girls, please," their mom said.

"It was an honest mistake, Lauren."

"Like it was an honest mistake booking a room in the back of a garage instead of a whole house?"

"Girls." Their mom's plea had little effect.

Chloe's breath quickened. "Getting upset won't help anything."

The spears of her sister's glower dug deeper. "Don't tell me not to be upset. Don't tell me how I should feel about anything. You never think things through."

"What's that supposed to mean?"

"It means I'm sick of getting stuck with your poor choices. I'm sick of riding in that sauna on wheels. I'm sick of doing things that are only fun to you. I'm sick of the fact that the only reason we're doing any of this is because you're too afraid to tell Mom you're moving to Prague!"

Chloe's pulse swelled to a pounding. How dare she! The words rushed out. "And I'm sick of your secrets! How about you tell us about Random Guy last night?"

"GIRLS!" Their mom's command reverberated off the lobby walls.

At last, their attention drew to her.

The reservationist averted her eyes.

Their mom spoke in the measured and firm tone she had used many times when they were little. "I am confident this poor woman does not need to be subjected to any of this. Lauren, take your card and go sit on the couch over there. Chloe, go get the bags out of the car." Her mom turned to the reservationist and pulled out her own ID and payment. "If you would, please, book *three* rooms for tonight."

Chloe reached to stop her. "You're not supposed to be paying for any—"

Her mom stuck a finger straight up in the air.

Chloe recoiled into silence.

"There will be no arguing. There will be no talking. There will be no dinner cruise. There will be nothing but each of us taking a breather for the night. Is that understood?"

"But—"

"No, Chloe. Nothing. All of us need a night off."

She closed her mouth, took a step back, nodded. She would absorb the cost of the nonrefundable cruise as well as the no-show fee and deal with it. She had no other option remaining.

Lauren leaned in to take back her credit card and whispered, "I'm sorry, Mom."

The only response was a glare, then, "Go."

237

52

Lauren pushed past the four-mile mark on the hotel's lone treadmill. The stitch in her side screamed, but she demanded that her body keep pace. Better to take it all out on her body than anyone else. She would hit five miles and hit it in under forty-five minutes or pass out trying.

Move!

Her legs had long gone numb. The pound of her shoes on the belt proved her legs were still attached and functioning. She focused on a spot on the wall in front of her as her mind circled around her mom's look of utter disappointment, of betrayal, at Lauren's plea for forgiveness. *I don't know who you even are anymore*, it said.

Who could disagree? Especially after the email that morning. "We have decided to go a different direction . . ." Besides her name in the salutation, the recruiter didn't bother to personalize the rejection message. No other job openings had come about. No prospects. Her savings would carry her, but for how long? That look of her mom's was bound to come back, worse than before.

Four and two-tenths miles.

Her hot breath scraped against her dry throat. The craving for water burgeoned. She pushed.

Miserable. Disappointing. Unemployed.

All the things people deserved to say she was. All the precise labels that described her. She cranked up the belt speed. Her arms pumped, her calves burned. Stars glinted on the edges of her vision.

Four and nine-tenths.

Dig deep. Push harder. Move.

Five miles even. Final time: 44:52.

Sucking in air, she decreased the speed to a moderate walking pace. Sweat dripped off her jawline onto her shirt. She had done it, but the victory was hollow. She had evaded nothing, beat nothing. All the heavy fear still closed in. What escape was left?

Her legs wobbled as she forced herself to walk the three flights up to her room. Hers was directly across from the other two. She paused outside her mom's room. The strained tone of her mom's voice seeped through the wood. She leaned closer. The words were garbled, except for one: "Grant." Her mom was on the phone with her dad right then, telling him all that had transpired, how embarrassed she was, how mortified by her grown daughters' behavior.

Lauren's chest hitched.

All it would take was a knock on the door. An ask to talk, to tell them both who "Random Guy" was and to promise nothing inappropriate had happened. Her mom would listen to reason. Her mom always listened to her reasoning, trusted her reasoning. It was why she insisted Lauren come on the trip.

She raised her hand, knuckles bent. But reasoning would mean telling her mom what led to the night with Gavin. Her mom knew nothing of Duncan or Universal or the rejection notice in her inbox.

Lauren dropped her hand and stole across the hallway to her own door.

Shame reached its pinnacle when laid bare before a parent.

53

Chloe shed the barrenness of her hotel room and stepped out into the pulse of the river town with a backpack of supplies and an hour to fill before boarding time. She had come to cruise, and cruise she would. She had come to discover, and discover she would. Her sister couldn't control everything.

The museums had closed for the evening, leaving Main Street abuzz with mostly restaurant traffic. No matter. She perused the windows of Twain's boyhood home and the adjacent buildings that included Becky Thatcher's house, the Clemens law offices, and the historic Grant's Drug Store, all buildings that were part of the tour she hoped her mom would be cooled off enough to take the next day. A board fence stretched long and proud along the side yard of the boyhood home, a fictitious version of the fence Tom Sawyer famously bamboozled his buddies into whitewashing. She sat on a bench at the foot of the Twain house and took out her sketchbook. Though the penciled version of the scene seeped onto her page, the proportion of the fence to the house refused to find balance. The angle of the peaked roof was too sharp at first, then too flat. The spot by the fence, where her family should be, empty.

She shut the book and moved on. Maybe the river would offer better inspiration.

The riverfront was a stone's throw due east of the house, at the end of Hill Street, so close that a young Twain could have fallen asleep listening to its dreams. She passed through the levee gates, crossed the railroad tracks, and ventured onto the landing along the vast and unguarded edge of the mighty Mississippi. The air bore the earthy musk of mud and algae. Across the waters, Illinois sprouted lively gaggles of trees that waved gentle hellos to its Show-Me State neighbor. The water frolicked southward, taking with it a brown barge carrying shipping containers stacked like Legos. She stood toe-to-toe with the massive river Twain had loved, smelled, touched, captained, and made into lore. If only she had an ounce of his know-how in bringing others fully into adventure.

Her phone chimed with an incoming call. She dug it out of her purse on the third ring and smiled at the name on the screen.

"Hey, Popsie. How're you?"

"Was calling to ask you that, actually."

She turned from the shore and headed back to a long, narrow park that led to the riverboat dock. "Mom told you, didn't she?"

"Yep."

"She still mad?"

"Yep."

An empty place ripped open within her chest. "I've made a mess of this whole thing. All I wanted was to have a memorable trip with Mom. So far all I've done is give her more reasons to question how I'm still alive at all. Lauren is not helping in the least."

"I've noticed your sister seems quieter these days. She hasn't responded to my text this evening, anyway."

"Probably because she's too busy—" She stopped herself from saying anything more about the man in Iowa City. It all would have been speculation, and unfair. She sighed and finished another way. "Too busy mother-henning me."

Up ahead, a statue of a young Mark Twain at a steamboat

captain's wheel stood on a stone base. He couldn't have been much older than her in the portrayal. Maybe he had been lucky enough to not have an older sibling breathing down his neck.

"You've had several bumps on this trip, haven't you?" her dad asked. "Lauren breaking her finger wasn't great."

"No," she said.

"And the surprise dinner with your aunt was a shock to the system."

She slowed her steps and frowned. "It was."

"The back-of-a-garage room was a bit odd."

She stopped. "Is this supposed to be making me feel better?"

"My point, pumpkin, is criticism is the easy part. Criticism doesn't take much imagination or vision. Do you remember why you're on this trip? Is it really about proving yourself responsible, or something else?"

She switched the phone to her other ear. Above her, the future author stared due north, both hands firm to the wheel, pompadour hair as proud as his posture. The plaque secured into the base described Twain's captain days, when the stories he would one day tell were mere glimmers in a working man's head.

The unfinished sketch of her mom transposed itself onto Twain's brave and expectant face. "I want to see the spark of adventure in Mom's eyes."

"I want that for you too," he said. "I believe you will see it. You dream bigger than all of us put together. For you, failure isn't the end. Failure is the plot of the story you're going to tell someday to inspire someone else."

"You sound so confident."

"I am confident. You know why? Because if you were on this trip alone, even with all the setbacks you've had, you'd keep going, keep driving. Right?"

A breeze kicked strands of hair across her face. She resettled them behind her ear. "Probably."

"Because you're wired to look for the opportunity. Promise me you'll keep looking. Your mom and sister need you to do it more than they realize right now."

She grinned. "Thank you, Popsie."

"For what?"

"For being amazing."

"Now you know where you get it."

She chuckled. "I've always wondered."

At the riverboat dock farther down the landing, the crew set up entrance ropes on the shore leading to the gangplank of the two-story vessel. Boarding time drew closer.

She passed around the statue and continued through the park. "Thanks for checking in on me."

"Always," her dad replied. "And before I forget, I went over to your apartment yesterday afternoon to check on things. Talked with Mr. Bove for a bit. I asked him if he wanted me to pass along a hello."

"Did he?"

"His exact words were, 'Tell her rent is due the day after she gets back.'"

"Such a sentimental guy."

"Very." He paused. "He's rooting for you too."

"I know."

"Because you deserve it."

Her eyes watered. "What am I going to do in Prague without you?"

"You'll do great. And despite what you may believe right now, this trip is going to prove it. Stay unshakable. You'll see."

She blinked away the drops and tilted her face upward. Seeing was all she really wanted. For her, and for them.

54

The midlife maven roused Edie with night sweats at four in the morning. Her new and unhinged companion left her puddled on the bedsheets despite the air-conditioning set to arctic. Sleep had started to slip away anyway. She got up and dipped under the streams of a cool shower that attempted to strip away all the echoes of the restless night and the argument that had kicked it off. No wonder she had felt disquieted for days—revelations were about to hit. Where did they go from there?

Grant had acted neither surprised nor flustered that both their girls had hidden lives that threatened to upturn everything. "Let them tell their stories in their own time," he said. "They're adults."

His lack of urgency infuriated the senses. Their family broke apart bit by bit, and he thought they had time. Did he know how far away Prague was? Did he have any concept how dangerous it was for Lauren to be sneaking off with some guy?

She dried and styled her hair, primed and made up her face. As her watch's minute hand ticked toward five thirty, she completed her ensemble with the gold cross necklace he had given her the day Lauren arrived in the world. She pressed the embellished cross to her chest. The corners of the beams pushed into the flesh above her heart. Not so long ago, a question had dominated pop culture:

"What would Jesus do?" That was only ever half the question for her. The full question was, What would Jesus do, and would Moria Mondell agree? What would Jesus do with daughters who walled off the biggest pieces of their private lives from him? Would her mother nod in concurrence with his choices? Neither of those questions welcomed an immediate answer.

The small breakfast room off the lobby offered little privacy. Worse still, radiant heat from the kitchen suffocated the air. Outside the sliding glass doors of the main entrance, the purplish haze of dawn beckoned her. *Come.* She cradled her journal to her ribs and stepped into the crisp daybreak.

To the left, under a security light affixed to the facade, a simple garden bench stood flush against the exterior wall, accompanied by a wood barrel of red geraniums in desperate need of a gardener's care. She flicked away loose dirt from the bench, then sat with legs crossed at the knees, elbows hugged to her sides, and journal fixed to her lap. In front of her, the town pitched downward toward the shore two blocks away. Beyond, the river rolled and ate away at the earth that tried to contain it. An untold number of granules floundered in its dizzying might. A hush drowned the empty streets. Strange how loud the quiet could be.

She opened the journal to the next blank page and took up her pen. They had made multiple stops since her last entry, only the second of the entire trip. Though there were plenty of details to record, her mind was shackled by the immediate and pressing need.

Dear Grant—
    For the third time this trip, I am on the bank of a river. This one is, by far, the widest and meanest. In this precarious spot, I contemplate how I have become insignificant in the girls' lives. Chloe gleams when playing catch with a complete stranger yet refrains from telling me, her own mother, she is moving to the other side of the world. Lauren, who used to share everything with me, now hides and sneaks. Both

of them wall me out, and despite what you think, time is no friend to the rejected.

She rested her writing hand. Out on the river, the leading edge of a barge came into view from the north. The tips of the wild current were mere licks against its side. That same current once tore at the crude rafts of fictional boys attempting to row to a mid-river island.

She lifted her pen once more.

I have been a mother for thirty-two years, and I am still lost on how to do it with a modicum of wisdom. I am huddled alone on a thin bench in the punishing wake of secrets revealed, and I have no idea how to steer us to the place we need to go. How are we this far in and farther apart from each other than when we started?

Her eyes burned. She dropped the pen on the page and squeezed the bridge of her nose. Grant would not answer her question. Her mother could not. That left only one source.

She bowed her head as light saturated the horizon.

Jesus, she asked, *what would you do?*

55

The plan started to take shape as soon as Lauren kicked away the covers. It solidified the moment she replied to her dad's check-in text from the night before, asking how she was doing.

"Going strong," she texted above a meme of John Cena flexing.

Strong. Bold. Courageous. Those were the things practical people had to be when the need arose. She could be all three. She could. And she could be them even easier from Kansas City.

She walked into the breakfast room and wound through the tables of diners. At a four-person table by the window, her sister slathered butter onto a waffle while their mom sipped from a paper cup and eyed the action over the rim.

Lauren sidled up to the empty chair between them and pinned back her shoulders. "I have a train booked back to Kansas City. It leaves St. Louis at three o'clock."

Chloe paused mid-smear.

Her mom set down the cup and cut her eyes to Lauren. "Why on earth would you do that?"

She steeled herself. "I have responsibilities I need to tend to, and I need to set a doctor's appointment for my finger. It's best if I go home."

"Lauren, you can't be serious." Chloe laid down her knife. "We're only halfway through the trip. You haven't even seen Hannibal yet."

"Like I said, it's for the best."

Her mom jerked her gaze away and pointed it out the window. Chloe looked between them. She softened her tone. "Laur, I'm sorry about yesterday. I was out of line in the things I said. Please, let's reset. We'll sit, have breakfast, and discuss what to do next. Mom was just talking about how she might like to tour the Mark Twain Cave today."

Despite the mention of her desires, their mom cemented her attention on the parking lot outside the glass. Her mouth was a hard, straight line.

"I've already booked my ticket," Lauren replied.

"But to get you to St. Louis in time," Chloe said, "we'd have to cut almost the entire day here in town."

She folded her arms to force her back to keep straight. Her gaze flitted to the woman whose lipstick-ringed coffee cup sat abandoned. "We'd have time to do the cave."

Chloe folded her hands over her plate. "Mom?"

At the nudge, their mom shrugged one shoulder.

"I suppose that's a yes." Chloe looked up at Lauren. "Are you sure you want to go home?"

Their mom's voice was low and austere. "If she wants to go, let her."

The jagged edge of the words sliced into Lauren. Their mom had used them once before recently, about Aunt Gab.

She had to clear her throat before she could speak. "I'll go pack."

They met in the lobby at half past nine. Lauren's phone contained a detailed note of which scenes in *Tom Sawyer* were inspired by the cave, but on the drive to their destination, her mom relied instead on Chloe's knowledge, taking a vicarious tour of the sights Chloe had explored the night before by foot and by riverboat.

Lauren tucked her phone in her sling, closed her eyes, and willed three o'clock to come faster.

Throughout the entire cave tour, Lauren hung close to the front of the pack of tourists, near the tour guide and one step closer to the exit.

56

- - - - -

I s this right?" A note of panic edged into her mom's tone as Chloe came to the four-way stop at Poplar and 16th. The path Chloe took through downtown St. Louis had meandered to that intersection, urged on by the authoritative voice of her phone's GPS. Straight ahead of them rose thick support pillars holding aloft an east-west interstate. Behind it, a second, lower overpass ran parallel, supported by shorter but equally stocky pillars. To the right and left of the intersection lay mostly deserted parking lots guarded by chain-link fences and gangs of weeds that overruled the concrete slabs.

"Turn left on Poplar Street," the GPS voice said, answering the question Chloe had started to ask too. Was it right? Not the directions so much as the very idea of Lauren going through with her plan.

In the back seat, her sister cast a furtive glance through the window. It wasn't too late for Lauren to change her mind. No one would think anything of it. Most of all, it would bring an end to the way their mom rubbed her left fingers between her right ones.

Chloe steered onto Poplar and followed the narrow street. Harsh curbs gave little grace for any vehicle that happened to venture too far to the side. The overpass blocked the sun and threw shadows upon the pavement. The farther they went, the more their mom worked her fingers.

Half a block later, the GPS voice announced, "Your destination is on the right." Chloe turned into a compressed circle drive that wound around all four overpass pillars and ended in the drop-off zone in front of a squat building the color of cement. The shorter of the overpasses practically grazed its roof.

"Arrived," the GPS voice announced. "Gateway Transportation Center." The letters over the double-door entrance confirmed the assertion. Chloe shifted into park.

Her mom clenched her hands together in her lap.

Behind them, Lauren gathered her sling bag and backpack. Did she really not believe there was another way? Did she really have this much pride?

Without a word, her sister pushed out into the torrent of traffic noise. She shut the door behind her.

Their mom shook her head. "What mother leaves her child at a place like this? It's literally under an overpass."

The liftgate opened. Lauren shifted bags around until she could loosen her own.

"She is a grown woman," Chloe said for only her mom to hear.

Suitcase wheels smacked against pavement. The liftgate clamped shut. The force sent a slight jolt through Goldie. Lauren couldn't hear the haunt of desperation in their mom's self-judgment, couldn't see the squeeze of her knuckles. The empty space in Chloe's chest widened.

They joined Lauren on the front walk wedged between two overpass pillars. Her sister positioned the suitcase in front of her, the telescoping handle locked into the highest position.

"Thanks for dropping me off." Lauren's words seemed directed at no one in particular, but she peeked at their mom.

Sunglasses hid their mom's eyes. Her lips were drawn, as tense as her clasped hands at her waist.

"I've texted Dad to ask him to come meet me at Union Station," Lauren added.

"Good," Chloe said. "Glad he'll be there."

"Me too." Lauren jiggled her leg.

A breeze darted under the overpass and trembled the strands of hair around their mom's face.

"I should go." Lauren's eyes swung to her intended recipient once more.

The muscles of their mom's throat constricted. Emotion strained her voice. "Be safe."

An entire motherhood packed into two words. Why couldn't Lauren find a better way?

Her sister took a half step forward, lifted one of her hands. Then she quickly ran her fingers through the hair around her ear, as if that had been her plan all along.

The urge was strong to leap upon her sister and bear-hug her into place.

"I will," Lauren promised. She bid them farewell, lingered a beat, then started toward the double doors. Her suitcase wheels rumbled against the sidewalk behind her.

Their mom unclasped her hands, reached toward Lauren's retreating form, but Lauren was through the doors, taken in by the strange place absent of anyone who knew her or loved her.

Overhead, a semitruck sputtered its air brakes. *Rat-tat-tat-tat* reverberated through the afternoon like a string of exclamation points.

"She can take care of herself," Chloe said.

Her mom clamped her arms one over the other against her belly. "Let's just go." She turned and plodded back to the car.

Chloe had promised her dad to keep looking for opportunity, to keep going despite the setbacks. What would he say now? The spark of adventure in her mom's eyes seemed farther away than ever.

She retraced her steps back to the driver's seat and climbed in. Her mom sat with her elbow propped on the windowsill, sunglasses now off, eyes squeezed shut. She massaged the middle of her forehead with her right hand.

"She will be okay," Chloe said.

"She will be murdered."

The dramatic retort would have been more outlandish had the circumstantial evidence not supported it. Her mom had more imagination than most people appreciated, including Chloe. Her mom *could* see possibilities. She *could* believe in things yet to come. The trick was to funnel that imagination in a good direction. And the best way to do that? Do something that provided a new perspective.

The answer tingled through her. "Mom?"

"Mmm."

"What do you say we spend this extra unexpected time in St. Louis doing something not related to books? Something you've never done before?"

Her mom peeked at her from under her hand. "If it involves a river, I'm a firm no."

Chloe turned the ignition and Goldie rattled to life. "Not a river. More like . . . sky."

57

To will courage to come was to gain courage. Lauren had repeated that mantra on their drive to St. Louis, held fast to it, reached toward the fulfillment of the promise it made, but the moment she stepped through the doors of the dank transportation center, her will waned. Reality descended. She had never taken an overland train in her life. She was alone, among strangers, in a situation she had no experience with. What if something went wrong?

She tightened her grip on her suitcase handle and kept walking. Unlike Kansas City's Union Station, where locals and passengers alike flowed through echoey chambers with gilded ceilings, the Gateway Transportation Center was a single hall with two food booths and a convergence of spiritless rail and bus passengers around a bay of interconnected chairs. Several people attempted to doze, or at least pretended to so they didn't have to stare at the stodgy blankness of the interior. A handful camped on the floor next to the wall, sprawling their jackets or blankets on the tile for cushion. A few families, people in business attire, and fellow single riders all attempted to find ways to tick off the minutes until they were called for their rides. Many passed the time by watching their phone screens. One man watched Lauren. He leaned against the wall on the far side of the chairs, face stubbled, arms slack at his sides, shoulder blades and one shoe sole pressed to the painted surface.

Wherever she moved, his stare followed. A tremor ran through her gut. If she couldn't get away, she at least needed to find a buffer.

In the middle of the chairs, third row in, a man about her dad's age sat alone reading a book with his glasses halfway down his nose. He wore a suit jacket and button-down shirt. She negotiated through the rows, dodging the legs and luggage of other passengers, and secured herself in a seat across the aisle and two down from Business Man, enough distance away for comfort but still in his line of sight.

Even his glasses had frames similar to her dad's.

She walled herself in with her backpack and suitcase around her legs. Though the stubble-faced man was behind her, the back of her head tingled. She was not out of his line of sight either. At least there were barriers between them.

She dug out her phone and shot a text to her dad.

> Train boards in forty minutes. Will text when we are close to Kansas City.

Almost immediately, as if her dad had been holding his phone, three dots appeared from his end. His words followed soon after.

> I will be waiting, maybe with a gourmet cookie for you (and one for me because what your mom doesn't know won't hurt her).

More than two hundred miles away and her dad could still make her grin. He never asked for more than a check-in from her every now and again. That was the best thing about him. He tended his matters and trusted her to tend her own.

Business Man adjusted in his seat, settling into a new posture and exposing the cover of his book, *The Imperfect Life of T. S. Eliot* by Lyndall Gordon. How serendipitous. A note on her phone was dedicated to the city's native son, a preparation that, in the end, had proved wasted. The casebound biography in the man's hands had a doorstop girth to it, appropriate for a poet whose opaque work stumped the most careful of students, Lauren among them. Because poetry.

She opened the note and revisited her bulleted list of Eliot highlights. Born in 1888, a sickly boy, moved to London as a young man, became a British subject, central figure in Modernist poetry, Nobel Prize winner. A list of links to podcast episodes and videos filled the space underneath the list. Perhaps the best way to ignore the clock and the lurker against the wall was to join her fellow Eliot student in deciphering the cryptic poet. She put in her earbuds and tapped the link to a podcast episode about Eliot's classic "The Love Song of J. Alfred Prufrock."

"No greater proof exists that the human heart holds fear and ambition simultaneously than the legendary monologue of J. Alfred Prufrock," the podcast narrator began. "Strap in, listeners, for an exploration of the masterpiece that defines the modern Western experience, even more than one hundred years after the poem's inception."

A prelude of flutes danced through her earbuds. Across the aisle, Business Man turned the page, clearly as thirsty for insight as she was. Whereas his guide was the written word, hers was the spoken teaching of Professor Chan of Yale University's English department.

"Though multilayered and scholastically dense—a signature of Eliot's high-brow writing style—at its heart, this 140-line poem contends with the simplest of human questions: 'Do I dare?' Do I dare ignore the fear and follow ambition to a future that is neither clear nor certain?"

The professor unlocked visions of Prufrock as a young man, stalking through the dreary, urban decay of 1910s London on the eve of World War I.

"Who in that generation could help but wonder if anything

could be great again? Would Prufrock himself ever be great? Pru-frock's laments revealed his gnawing fear he would never live up to his potential, and instead he would see the greatness he longed for last a mere 'flicker' of time. He simultaneously believed he was meant for more but obeyed his crippling fear—of social judgment, of failure—and retreated back to the security of the known and the ordinary. Self-imposed isolation left him rambling through the streets, near people but connected to none."

The resonance rattled through her core. In the middle of strang-ers in a strange and unnerving place, she drew her knees to her chest and tethered them with her arms. She rested her chin in the gap between her knees, ears open, mind wide, chest aching.

"Prufrock knows the torture of unfulfillment. He humorously wishes another existence for himself altogether, one free of the drive for love and achievement he could not seem to bear out. That wish is captured in this famous line: 'I should have been a pair of ragged claws / Scuttling about the floor of the silent sea.'"

Goose bumps prickled her arms. A poet of another century, of another gender, class, and circumstance, understood her far clearer, deeper, truer than anyone ever had.

Including herself.

58

If Jesus had been driven to the Gateway Arch and told by his intrepid redhead that they would hover 630 feet above ground in a claustrophobic viewing chamber, what would he do? Chances seemed solid that he too would regret not putting more caveats on his promise to do anything not involving a river. Alas, Edie's impending fate was the punishment she deserved for not dragging Lauren back into the car when she had the chance. What kind of mother had daughters who only wanted to escape—one on a train, the other to a foreign country? The chasm between them widened every moment that passed, and she was helpless to stop it.

The transparent doors of their compact tram car swung into locked position, trapping them inside. Edie dug her fingertips into her metal seat so hard her pulse hammered against her nails. The back of her head brushed against the rounded ceiling of the tubular vessel that would lift them to the top of the Arch. The stools lacked harnesses of any kind, which meant she and Chloe would tumble around like rocks in a dryer when the pulley ropes snapped and sent them pinging down the inside of the north leg.

"This is going to be so much fun," Chloe chirped. She had said the same thing at least five times since purchasing their passes. She sat on the opposite side of the death pod, hands in a loose fold in her lap and a shine in her expression.

"Thrilling," Edie said through a throat as clenched as her hands.

Despite five stools in the car, arranged in the tightest semicircle known to history, only she and Chloe had been assigned to car number four. At least they did not have to share air or bump knees with perfect strangers, but Lauren should have been with them. Edie should have done better.

Motors kicked on. A steady drone seeped through the thin metal walls. Their car jerked into motion. Edie clamped her arms tight to her sides, pressed her feet staunchly to the floor.

"You okay?" Chloe asked over the buzz.

Nodding would rock the car. Edie clipped her answer to "Fine."

"Mom, your knuckles are white."

Held breath did not produce words.

Chloe chuckled and hobbled, bent at the waist, to the seat next to Edie's. "We are perfectly safe. You heard the tour guide say how many people go to the top each day."

The guide had also evaded Edie's question about how many of those people got stuck.

"Look out the window." Her daughter pointed at the doors. "You can see the emergency steps. Isn't that cool?"

The steady crisscross of staircases and platforms stirred up nausea. Edie averted her gaze to a spot on the floor—the worn floor, in acute need of a sweep and probably bleach.

Chloe wedged her hand between Edie's elbow and ribs, then threaded their arms together. "Here's what we'll do," she said as she placed her phone on her lap. "The tour guide said it was less than five minutes to the top. I'll set the timer on my phone for five minutes. Sometimes it helps to know how close the end is."

The end. It was indeed close. The end for all of them to be together as a family. What would Christmas look like? What would Saturday morning coffee with Lauren be from that point forward?

Would they even be a thing? How did she have so little time left with either of the girls? Why did no one else seem to care?

The black numbers stamped on Chloe's screen ticked down from five minutes.

4:55. 4:54.

The diminishing numbers outroared the falling sand.

Chloe couldn't hear it, though. She chattered on, oblivious. "They say on a clear day like this, you can see up to thirty miles from the top. We'll have to get plenty of pictures."

4:49. 4:48. Minutes, hours, days all passed with insensitive swiftness, too fast for any mother to relish them. Why hadn't she relished them while she could have? Her eyes burned.

"I also hear you can see into Busch Stadium. We'll have to get a picture of that for Popsie."

The late nights of laundry, the early mornings of school lunches, the prom dress shopping, the college visits, the graduation parties. All of it gone, dredged through her fingers before she could close her fist and hang on to them a beat longer. The loss never stopped. It only compounded. And no one else noticed the cost.

Pressure built in her throat, harder and harder, until the question gnashed free in the middle of Chloe's prattle. "Why Prague?" she asked. "Why do you want to move so far away?"

The question knocked Chloe from the false high. A wrinkle formed on her brow.

4:27. 4:26.

Chloe pivoted on her seat. Her knees pressed against Edie's. "It's not the distance that attracts me, Mom. It's the purpose. I'm sorry I wasn't the one to bring it out into the open to you. I should have told you much sooner." She squeezed her arm. "The full truth is, I have an incredible opportunity to be an art instructor for elementary students at an international school. The students are mostly children of missionaries. I've been praying for years for God to show me what to do with this love of creating. He's taking me to one of the most incredible cities for art and history and culture, and I get to serve his people there. I couldn't ask for a better job. It far surpasses anything I could have come up with on my own."

There it was. That gleam. It filled Chloe's face once more, larger than ever. Not a mere hint or an echo or a note, but the full thing, radiant and pure.

Edie's stomach knotted. Letting Lauren go on a train to the other side of Missouri was hard enough. How could she let Chloe go to the other side of the world?

"How will you live?" she asked. "Prague is expensive, and teachers don't make much."

"I get a stipend for housing, and the rest of my income comes from the support I raise."

Edie blinked. "Support you raise? You mean *you* will be a missionary too?"

"Kind of. Not in the truest sense of the word, but similar in principle."

Her daughter was going from broke barista to even broker missionary-teacher. In a foreign country. That she had never been to. Edie leaned her head against the curved ceiling and closed her eyes.

"I can get a part-time job in a coffee shop if I need to," Chloe continued. "I checked—they do drink coffee over there. The good news is, I've saved enough so far to cover a good portion of my first year."

Edie righted. "What do you mean *first* year?"

Chloe bit her lip before replying. "It's a minimum two-year commitment."

2:38. 2:37.

Her head pounded. "Dad knows about this, doesn't he? That's why you two conspired to get me to go on this trip."

"It wasn't a conspiracy. I wanted to make memories with you, to have an adventure together."

Edie extracted her arm from Chloe's and shoved herself against the wall.

"I know this doesn't make complete sense to you, Mom, and I know how scary this sounds hearing it for the first time. I have fears of my own. It may not seem like it, but I do." She leaned closer. "I have so many questions about what is waiting for me in Prague. There's a lot I don't know yet, a lot I need to figure out. But I do know this is something I'm supposed to do. I feel the certainty of it in my bones."

Edie clamped her arms over her stomach.

2:05. 2:04.

"I also know that if I go overseas without your blessing, it will break my heart."

The last words landed as the buzz of the motors lessened. The tram slowed. They approached the end.

Edie shook her head. "I can't talk about this right now."

Her daughter dipped her head and pulled away. "Okay."

Grant had known the full details of Chloe's plans the whole time. He had known and hadn't told her. Did Lauren know too? Her whole family had constructed walls without her noticing.

With time left on Chloe's clock, the doors swung open. Edie stepped out first and followed the crowd up a set of stairs to the viewing deck that sloped across the tip of the Arch. Chloe at least kept her promise and let Edie be.

Narrow windows lined the cramped deck. Fellow riders leaned their upper bodies on the slanted sills to get better views. Most gravitated to the west side for the eyeful of downtown and the peek into the baseball stadium. Edie chose the Illinois side.

Farmland stretched for miles, pointing evermore eastward toward the place where the sun rises, and onward to the city that waited to engulf her daughter. Her chin trembled.

How could she give her blessing to Chloe's plans? How could she willingly step into such loss? She couldn't protect Chloe in Prague, couldn't help her find her way or learn the language. On top of that, she would have even less to relate to Chloe about, even less life experience through which she could guide her child. The option to explore never materialized for people like Edie, people who listened to the no of others, people who believed that "you have responsibilities here" was argument enough to stick close to home.

A burn kindled in her chest. Gabriella had chosen not to listen. What if Edie hadn't either? What if she had chosen instead to believe the certainty that once existed in her own bones? What if she had followed that nudge all those years ago to explore the city that had long captured her imagination?

It was a special kind of pain to have someone in your life to whom you gave everything they asked for yet who refused to believe your dreams were worth the space they filled in your heart. She blinked away the tears.

Did she really want to be that source of pain for her child?

On the other side of the deck, Chloe rested on the sill and captured the downtown sights on her phone. A small sign above the window implored visitors to post the pictures they took with the hashtag #seedifferently. That was what Jesus would do—see differently. He would be different. He would choose differently.

She inhaled against the clench in her throat, then she took the first step toward Chloe.

Her daughter didn't notice her approach. Edie came to her side. Leaning in far enough for their conversation to be private from the squash of other visitors, she said, "Salzburg."

Chloe looked up. "What?"

A family with two preschoolers slipped past. Edie moved closer to Chloe. "I have always wanted to go to Austria, and maybe Switzerland."

"You mean, like *The Sound of Music*?"

She nodded. "I never went because someone important to me didn't think it was a good idea."

Chloe slowly lowered her phone and pulled herself upright. By her expression, it was clear she understood who that someone was. "Maybe you could go now," she offered. "Use the money from the estate sale."

Edie huffed. "Wouldn't that be ironic."

A grin slipped onto Chloe's lips. "I believe authors call it poetic justice."

Words formed at the back of Edie's tongue, explanations of why she needed time to think and sit with the idea of Prague, but a chime from Chloe's phone cut into the moment. Her daughter turned the device over to read the new text, and her face soon pinched into a frown.

"What is it?" Edie asked.

"It's Lauren. She texted both of us."

Edie dug for her phone. "Why? What's going on?"

"Apparently her train's been canceled."

59

The Xterra was impossible to miss turning into the circle drive of the transportation center. The bright yellow struck a dissonant chord as it invaded the drab underbelly of the interstate.

Lauren rose from the bench outside the main entrance. She kept her suitcase knitted to her side as she stepped out from the cover of the entrance's awning. Her legs were like lead. Every reason she had used to escape lay broken at her feet. Every plan B had come undone—airfare too expensive, rideshares out of the question, Business Man disappearing before she could ask for advice. The harder she had tried to break free, the stiffer the headwinds became, buffeting her back to the white-hot bull's-eye of shame.

The Xterra neared the pickup zone. Lauren maneuvered toward the curb, wheeling around the other passengers who waited for their own alternate plans to materialize. To her left, Stubble Face leaned against a pillar, taking a drag on his cigarette. His eyes grazed hers, but he had stopped being a threat as soon as she resigned herself to texting her family. Let him stare all he wanted. His thoughts toward her were not the ones that mattered anymore.

The brakes squealed softly as Chloe brought the car to a stop just ahead of Lauren. A portion of their mom's face reflected in the outside mirror. Lauren's fingers numbed as she moved toward it.

Chloe came around to the back and opened the liftgate. "Hey, Laur. Sorry about your train. That was unexpected."

Lauren approached her rescuer with caution, gauging. Heroic acts had a way of going to people's heads. "Yes, it was." She stepped off the curb and lifted her suitcase to the empty place among the luggage.

"We got here as fast as we could. We were at the top of the Arch when we got your text."

"Top of the Arch?" She wriggled the bag into place and stepped back. "Mom went to the top?"

"Sure did. White knuckles the whole way, but she did it!" Gratification shimmered in Chloe's smile.

Somehow, her sister had gotten back on the good side of their mom, despite everything, despite reason after reason for distrust and ire to magnify. The scale of significance leaned ever more in Chloe's favor. How in the world was that possible?

Chloe shut the liftgate and brushed her hands together. "Glad you weren't on the train when it experienced mechanical issues. You really would have been in a mess."

Lauren was in a mess either way. She nodded all the same and reported to her post in the back seat.

Their mom twisted around to see her. "You did tell Dad about the train, didn't you?"

"I did."

Chloe climbed in and shut her door.

"Was he glad you're staying?" their mom asked.

"He didn't say," Lauren replied.

Chloe turned the ignition and looked at her front-seat passenger. "We're happy she's staying, though, aren't we?"

Their mom smiled briefly. "I'm happy you're safe."

A noncommittal answer. Lauren strapped herself in and hugged her backpack to her chest.

As they pulled onto the street headed back to the four-way stop, Chloe called over her shoulder, "What will happen to all your responsibilities back home? Can you do any from the road?"

"Maybe." The simpler the answer, the better.

"You can certainly make a doctor's appointment from the road," Chloe said.

"Sure." She hunkered lower in her seat.

Her family left the conversation at that. Chloe made a right at the four-way stop, pulled them out from under the shadow of the overpass and into the light, and the trip resumed.

For the ensuing afternoon hours, Lauren remained quiet as her sister routed them to the city's various literary landmarks. For as many as there were, St. Louis didn't do much to capitalize on them. The Eugene Field House Museum was closed for construction. Maya Angelou's birthplace, Kate Chopin's final residence, and T. S. Eliot's boyhood home all had been preserved, but none welcomed the public. Chloe insisted on pictures in front of them anyway. Lauren and their mom obliged, always with a hedge of space between them. Several times, their mom glanced at Lauren with a certain brightness in her eyes. Most of those times, though, Chloe was standing right next to Lauren.

Late in the afternoon, they arrived at their final stop, "Writer's Corner," the nickname for the quaint intersection of Euclid and McPherson in the Central West End. Each of the four corners of the crossroads featured a bust of an icon who once lived in the neighborhood: Chopin, Eliot, William S. Burroughs, and Tennessee Williams. Requisite pictures were obtained in a matter of minutes, ending with Eliot on the southwest corner. His bust stood near the open entrance of a small bookstore reminiscent of the kind seen in movies. Its wares overflowed onto tables and carts set up on the sidewalk for passersby to peruse, and peruse Chloe did, occasionally pulling a book from the piles and telling their mom, "Look at this one." Their mom complied every single time, and when Chloe breezed toward the door with a winsome "Let's go inside," their mom traced after her.

At the door, though, their mom paused and looked back at Lauren. "Are you coming?"

Lauren feigned interest in a tattered collection of Chopin stories in the used-book bin and replied, "Right behind you."

When next Lauren lifted her head, the doorway was empty. She slipped over to the bust of Eliot. The sculptor had depicted the poet in his later years, head balding and under-eyes puffy, but his chin was lifted with defiant pride of achievement. She adopted a similar pose and snapped a selfie of the two of them. It was the only moment in St. Louis she saved to her phone.

Their mom contracted the yawns in the midst of their browsing. Chloe suggested getting a pizza and taking it to their rental for a movie night. No one argued.

The rental, a modern condo a walkable distance from the store, shattered the two-night streak of lodging debacles.

"Chloe, it's gorgeous," their mom marveled from the threshold. High-end appliances, two (actual) bedrooms, two designer sofas perpendicular to each other around a coffee table and fur rug, large plasma television affixed above a sleek gas fireplace, and glossy hardwoods throughout.

"You know the best part?" Chloe asked, setting the pizza box on the breakfast bar. "This building is where Tennessee Williams lived as a boy. Legend has it the setting for *The Glass Menagerie* is modeled after this building."

Their mom laughed and pulled her suitcase to a stop against the wall near the hallway. "Look at you, so full of fun facts."

Lauren padded off to the side. Her own research had not uncovered that fact about Williams, or much of anything about him.

Her sister opened cabinets until she found plates, then she began stacking tableware next to the pizza box.

Their mom ran her fingertips over the back of one of the couches. "This place looks expensive, though. How much is this costing you?"

"Don't worry about it," Chloe said. "It's a treat night!"

"Even so, it seems like too much for someone preparing to be a teacher."

Lauren righted. "Teacher?"

Their mom frowned and looked between them. "I thought you knew about the art teacher job."

"I . . ." Lauren turned to Chloe.

Her sister tossed a stack of napkins on the bar. "We haven't had a chance to talk about the details of what I'll be doing in Prague." With a glance, her sister made it clear that Lauren had missed more than she knew.

They spent the evening nibbling pizza on the couches and streaming the 1987 film version of *The Glass Menagerie*. Halfway through the five-minute opening monologue of Tom, their mom swallowed a bite of pizza and lamented, "I don't get this movie." By the twenty-minute mark, she was snoozing against the back of the couch, her plate of half-eaten pizza neglected on her lap.

Chloe scooted across the couch she shared with their mom and gently moved the plate to the coffee table. "She's really glad you're back, you know."

From her spot on the other couch, Lauren chewed. Muted-tone scenes flickered on the screen.

"For what it's worth," her sister said, moving back to her place, "I am too."

Their gazes locked.

Lauren was the first to break the connection. She dropped her slice onto her plate. "Sounds like you got your big secret out in the open. How'd she take it?"

Chloe shrugged. "We were in the middle of talking about it when we got your text."

A soft snore emanated from the woman between them.

They ate and watched, guarded. On the screen, Tom's unmarried sister chafed under her mom's scrutiny about her prospects, a tale that would endure for as long as mothers had daughters.

Chloe peeked at her. "I want to assure you, in case you're wondering, mine was the only secret we discussed while you were gone."

Lauren crossed her ankles and drew them flush to the skirt of the couch. "I appreciate that." She may have been stuck in the center of shame, but at least she maintained control over how far back the veil moved to reveal what she kept hidden, including Gavin.

"Want me to tell you more about Prague?" Chloe asked.

"Maybe later." Lauren picked up her plate and took another unwanted bite. The pizza was cold and the movie stilted, but both helped secure the veil in place.

Chloe acquiesced. Several minutes later, though, she turned from the screen. "Lauren."

"What?"

Her sister sighed. "I wish we talked."

That was the difference between them. Her little sister didn't know when to accept that things might never be as great as she imagined they could be. Some things weren't meant to be great, no matter the level of aspiration poured into them.

Some things were at their best on the floor of the silent sea.

60

The blunt edges of morning rays stopped shy of Chloe's seat at the breakfast bar. She laid her phone on the marble and swiped through the pictures from yesterday afternoon's tour of St. Louis author sites. One unmistakable thing came through in those images: Lauren's eyes never quite met the camera. They instead targeted spots off to the side or below the lens, as if Lauren wanted to avoid all variety of eye-to-eye contact.

What was her sister so afraid of? Why was there such a chasm between her and the rest of the world?

Water kicked on in the hall bathroom. Moments before, Lauren had tucked herself inside, with only a nod to Chloe on her path from the bedroom. Chloe had given her the room for the night, opting to sleep on the sofa, which turned out to be as cloud soft as it was showroom worthy.

Chloe selected an organic granola bar from the basket of goodies the hostess had left for them on the bar and flipped through the last of the previous day's photos. Lauren's expression in every way carried some variation of sullen with a weak mask of happy. Her eyes begged to tell a story, but she kept them restrained.

The door to the second bedroom opened. Her mom trundled

out, hair crumpled to her head and pajama shirt askew on her frame. "How did I get in there?" She pointed to the bedroom.

"Lauren and I took you in there last night. Don't you remember? We helped you change. You were very specific about your sleepwear."

Her mom shrugged and shuffled to the single-serve coffee maker. "I was out of it, I guess."

"You slept well. It's nearly eight o'clock."

"It is?" Her mom caught the time on the microwave, then raked her fingers through her disheveled hair. She loaded a coffee pod into the machine and placed a mug underneath. "I haven't slept that well in ages. Your dad would be shocked."

"I'm sure he'd be as happy as we are you got the sleep you needed."

Her mom glanced up on the "we." She pressed the brew button, and the machine whirred to life. "Is Lauren doing okay this morning? I hear a shower going."

"I think so, but she isn't talking much to me."

"That makes two of us." Steaming coffee gurgled into the mug, releasing a rich, earthy aroma. Her mom watched until the stream finally ended. "I am glad she stayed, and I hope I showed that well enough. It's easier on a mother's heart when she knows her girls are safe."

Lauren's presence, though good, had stopped all talk between Chloe and her mom of Prague and Austria and dreams. Having both girls together again may have eased their mom's heart, but it crimped Chloe's.

Her mom tossed the expended pod in the trash and gathered her mug. "I better get moving too. What time do we need to leave for Mansfield?"

"Not too early. Maybe ten or so. That would give us the afternoon to spend at the Laura Ingalls Wilder farm."

Her mom drew in a first sip, then nodded. "You girls loved those books when you were little. We used to have the full box set."

Chloe grinned. "Reading the Little House books is a rite of passage for every Midwestern girl."

Her mom leaned against the counter and took another sip. "I remember that time Dad and I came home from a dinner party and found you two asleep on the floor. You said you were camping out like the Ingalls family on the wagon trail."

"That night Lauren babysat for me? I remember that too. We ate apples and beef jerky for supper and pretended the jerky was salt pork. Neither of us had a clue what salt pork was, but we figured jerky was close."

Her mom harrumphed. "Yes, that was an interesting choice. You were, what, six or seven?"

"Had to have been seven because you didn't let Lauren babysit until she was thirteen."

Middle school Lauren was old enough to be solely responsible but young enough to hold the joy of play. The salt pork had been her idea, and the campout. Middle school Lauren was Chloe's favorite version.

Her mom shuffled across the tile floor back to her room. "I'm going to go make myself presentable. I promise to be ready within an hour." The bedroom door shut behind her.

Chloe took a bite of her granola bar. In the hallway bathroom, the water streams continued to fall.

Would Lauren remember that night too, when Chloe's bunk beds became the covered wagon, her stuffed dog the Ingallses' beloved Jack, and the glow-in-the-dark stickers on her bedroom ceiling the mantle of stars over the whispering prairie? Could she still hear the giggles and feel the tingle of imagination as things that weren't became things that were? How they lay on the floor of the bedroom, shoulder to shoulder, unworried about tomorrow, secure in the care of those who were bigger, fully trusting that the unfolding of their lives would contain beauty unimaginable? If only she could get Lauren to speak the language of play and wonder again.

Her phone screen lit up with a new text message from Sori. It contained a picture of Jeremy munching on a kale leaf and a simple caption.

> Someone loves the Wednesday morning farmers' market.

She chuckled and tapped the phone icon next to Sori's name. "Surprised you're up," she said when her friend answered.

"It's my day off, and I relish every minute I can. How's the trip? Tell your mom yet? Please say no because I bet Seymour ten bucks you'd wait until the last day."

"I'm not sure if I should be offended or tickled, but pay up. I told her yesterday."

Sori faux groaned. "Good for you, though. How'd she take it?"

"She didn't disown me, so I'm cautiously optimistic."

"Sounds about right. Good luck."

"Thank you."

"Random question for you, Chloe. Does your sister still work at Universal?"

"Far as I know. Why?"

"Because I heard that maybe she doesn't."

Chloe sat back on her stool. "From who?"

"I went out with my cousin last night, and we happened to meet a guy who works in IT at Universal. I asked him if he knew Lauren, and he got all weird about it. When I pressed him, he claimed she had been let go."

Chloe swung her head toward the bathroom door. "Let go? As in fired?"

"Something about violation of electronic usage policy."

"What does that mean?"

"No idea. But it makes me glad I don't have a corporate job."

The water shut off in the bathroom. Shower curtain rings jangled against their bar.

The drastic haircut, the uncharacteristic risk-taking with Random Guy, the last-minute availability to go on the trip, the bitterness. The hiding. All of the clues pulled into one unified revelation.

"I hope I didn't overstep," Sori said.

"No, not at all. Thanks for telling me."

"Are you going to bring it up with your sister?"

Chloe pushed the last of the granola bar away. "I don't know."

"If you do, please tell her how sorry I am about her job."

"Of course. Thank you, Sori."

After promising to connect later, they ended the call. Chloe's phone reverted back to a picture of Lauren outside T. S. Eliot's boyhood home with her finger splint glinting at her side and her eyes averted. Her sister was broken in more ways than one, and the thing she needed most, she rejected. She needed someone who could help her find rest from it all.

This trip was supposed to be a way for Chloe to make inroads with her mom and reach further toward her dream without guilt. It was becoming clear that her real heart's desire was not Prague; it was much closer to home. It involved the two women she loved most aching for fulfillment of their own yet refusing it because of pride.

She closed her eyes.

Lord, I don't know what to do with all this. How do you sway stone hearts?

61

The St. Louis metro dropped farther behind their car, and late-morning traffic thinned around them on the southwest-bound lanes of I-44. Lauren's reflection flashed in Edie's outside mirror. Her daughter kept her sunglasses on and rested her head against the back of the seat. The majority of Edie's interaction with her so far that morning had centered on mere small talk. *How did you sleep? Are you hungry? Ready to leave?* Though Lauren would answer every question Edie posed, she always found a reason to break away shortly after.

The sting grew worse each time.

From the moment Lauren had slipped into the back seat at the transportation center, Edie had tried her best to show her there were no hard feelings about her sneaking out to meet a man and hiding the truth about it, only sheer relief that both of her girls were safe. Lauren was an adult, after all. Yet she stood farther off than ever.

Edie cleared her throat and turned toward the back seat. "Do you have any interesting facts about the Little House books you can share with us, Lauren?"

Lauren shrugged. "Probably on my phone, but I'm nursing a headache. Sorry."

Chloe flicked her eyes to the rearview mirror, then to Edie.

For the rest of the morning, neither of them could engage Lauren beyond that. A lunch break at a diner in Rolla did little to change the pattern. Lauren picked at her salad and bowl of cottage cheese and offered no input on their plans for the afternoon in Mansfield.

On the way back to the car after lunch, Chloe leaned close to Edie and whispered, "She'll come around. She just needs space to work things out on her own."

Edie smoothed the cross pendant to her chest. Jesus would love Lauren the way she needed to be loved. If only stepping back didn't demand so much faith that it was not the same as abandoning.

Mansfield was a speck in the northern swath of the Missouri Ozarks, hilly, rocky, wooded, and nothing like the undulating prairielands depicted in the Little House books. But there was a placidity to the town, as well as to the forty-acre farm a stone's throw from the city limit. Rocky Ridge Farm, as the author's golden-years home was called, curled inside a ring of woods. Its rambling farmhouse rested upon a grassy peak.

Upon arriving at the Laura Ingalls Wilder Historic Home and Museum, guests were directed to a grand visitors' center fashioned to look like a hay barn. Beds of wildflowers and tallgrass skirted its exterior, giving it the utmost prairie look. The inside of the center possessed deliciously thick air-conditioning and a small theater dedicated to a short film about the author's life, from her early years in the "big woods" of Wisconsin, to the Kansas plains, to her retirement years in Mansfield, where she was laid to rest in a local cemetery.

The next stop was the Wilders' farmhouse, where a docent guided the Vances and six other people through every room on the first floor, starting with the kitchen.

"Notice how low the countertops are," the woman said. "Laura was under five foot, and this kitchen was custom-designed to fit her

277

stature and needs. Her husband, Almanzo, did much of the home construction, building one room at a time as finances allowed."

The knock-out cubby for the refrigerator existed because of Almanzo's ingenuity. As did the screened front porch and the foot box under his wife's writing desk in the small office off the bedroom. Mrs. Wilder's humble fold-top desk befitted the farmhouse and its unpretentious owner. Pigeon-hole slots housed supplies preserved for more than half a century—a bottle of glue, a wooden ruler, a tape dispenser, a glass canister of Carter's ink. Under protective glass on the desktop lay an envelope addressed to Laura from her publisher.

Chloe ran her hand across the author's favorite blue shawl slung over the back of the simple wood chair. The gleam returned to her face. "Amazing to think the scenes we remember so well first came to the page right here at this small desk, in this small room. The creativity is so alive, I can practically touch it."

No doubt she could. Edie smiled and turned toward Lauren. But her oldest was already filing out of the room along with the others.

In the parlor, the docent stood near the fireplace and delivered a soliloquy about the uniqueness of each feature of the room, like the hand-hewn stone of the chimney and the walk-in library Almanzo had installed for Laura on one end.

"And this photograph here on the mantel"—the docent pointed to the eight-by-ten framed picture—"is of the couple in 1942. It was one of their favorite pictures. Notice Laura's girlish grin. She certainly never fell out of love with Manly, as she called him."

Edie stepped closer to the picture. Despite age having sagged his face, Almanzo retained the strapping posture of his youth. His thick hands, the source of tilled ground and comfortable houses, hung at his sides. With his gaze aimed firmly at the camera, his entire demeanor displayed readiness to defend or serve. His classy white shirt and dark slacks complemented his wife's tasteful floral dress adorned with a sash tied into a bow in front.

It was not hard to imagine a crackling fire warming the room, Laura with a bit of needlepoint and Almanzo reading from the paper. They were cocooned together in a place of their own making, where the world's worries blew away with the Ozark wind.

Edie folded her hands at her waist, and her thumb found the inside of her wedding band. Grant, with hands that stilled nerves and held fast. They had built a life together, a family, and a home. Had it been enough to keep all four of them always, always, turning back for each other?

"This picture," the docent continued, "was taken about ten years after Laura published her first book. Did you know it was their daughter, Rose Wilder Lane, who first encouraged her mother to write the books? Many people don't remember that Rose was an accomplished author in her own right, a world-traveling contemporary of Ayn Rand and Sinclair Lewis, and at one time one of the highest-paid women writers in America. At Rose's insistence, and some say under her coaching, Laura penned the first of what became the serial phenomenon—at the age of sixty-four. Can you imagine branching off into something completely new in your sixties? Especially something that revised your entire life?"

The crowd chuckled.

Edie rubbed the back of her ring. Her gaze drifted toward the plucky redhead whose imagination may have outshone Mrs. Wilder's, and whose belief in Edie's daydreams of Austria was sure, even at Edie's age.

But Chloe didn't notice the attention. She was too busy studying her sister, who stared out the front window as if counting the minutes until she could leave.

62

By the time they arrived in Branson, Missouri, the entertainment capital of the mid-South, Lauren's total upright sit-up count topped 925. The accomplishment meant nothing to anyone else, nor would she reveal it to anyone else, but she held her chin in contented Eliot pride and dabbed the beads of sweat from her forehead. No one needed to recognize her accomplishments anyway. She could find her own way to be perfectly, wonderfully, wholly content.

For an early supper, Chloe picked a popular restaurant with a thirty-minute wait at four thirty on a Wednesday and artery-hardening Southern food, including pancakes so large they could be flipped with a shovel.

Chloe's eyes lit up when she saw the image of them on the menu. "Let's split those, Laur!"

"I'm not a huge fan of pancakes," she replied.

"Since when?"

"Since I was a kid."

"We're in Branson. What better place to be a kid again?"

Their mom cut in. "I will share them with you."

Chloe's eyes widened. "You will?"

"Mom, are you sure?" Lauren asked. "That's a massive amount of sugar and gluten. You don't eat like that."

Their mom shut her menu and sat back. "I've been good all trip. I've been good all my life, in fact. Let's eat pancakes."

Chloe laughed. "Attagirl, Mom!"

Yet again, Chloe's influence won out, and Lauren's counsel meant little. Lauren leaned against the wall of the booth and let them order their overindulgence without further comment from her. She ate her plain chicken breast and salad and waited for her unheeded caution to prove warranted.

Their mom moaned the whole way to the hotel.

Lauren and Chloe helped her to the room and sat her on the edge of the bed nearest the bathroom.

"I never want to eat again," their mom groaned.

"Want me to find you some Tums?" Lauren asked as Chloe bent down to peel off their mom's shoes.

"I took some already, from my purse." Free from her shoes, their mom settled onto the pillows and waved them away. "You all go do something. Let me writhe in private."

"What if you get sick?" Lauren said.

"All the better not to witness it," her sister mumbled as she stood.

Lauren cut her eyes to her.

"I'm fine. Go." Their mom waved again, then curled onto her side.

For the second night in a row, the sisters were left on their own. The difference was, Lauren didn't have to stay cooped up in the same room. She could break away, find her own style of peace. First, she would need to evade her sister.

"What do you say, Laur?" Chloe asked. "Want to go to the strip? The night is young."

"You can. I'm going to stick close in case Mom needs something." Lauren squeezed past her sister, took their mom's phone from her purse, then laid it and the remote on the bed next to the patient. "I'll be downstairs, Mom. If you need something, text or call, okay?"

A moan stood in for an acceptance.

"We could go to the pool," Chloe offered. "That used to be our favorite part of hotels."

Lauren shook her head. "I need to try to stay caught up on some things like I planned. I'm going to find a quiet place." She slipped a key card into her sling and headed for the door. Her sister didn't try to stop her.

Down in the lobby, a large family camped among the circle of couches with takeout food and a card game. The scent of General Tso's chicken and their raucous laughter filled the room. Lauren zipped by and out to the patio area on the other side of the front drive.

Branson boasted more dramatic Ozark hills than Mansfield, one of which held their hotel aloft over a thickly wooded valley. The stone patio sat near a precipice, providing a panoramic view of the treetops and the sun that slowly knelt to kiss them. Lauren lowered into a rocking chair at the side of the patio, facing the serene valley. The soft evening welcomed her there, a bubble of quiet amid the rush of Branson.

The Wi-Fi signal reached the patio. She checked her email for any job alerts. Nothing. She opened her job search app, entered various keyword combinations to garner any results she may have missed before, but they were all the same fruitless leads. Her bank app, though, did have an update: Rent had been withdrawn. Utilities came next. Her balance dwindled, and the reserves along with it. Two more nights of hotels remained, multiple tanks of gas, at least seven meals. The trip had left her with a broken finger, medical bills from said broken finger, unwanted Amtrak credit, and several hundred hard-earned dollars less. And for what? For her mom to disregard her as easily as Duncan had and her sister to pry into her business. Gavin was the one bright thing, but even that she couldn't openly enjoy without inviting Chloe's intrusion. She left him tucked away for another day and lowered her phone to her lap.

The rolling waves of trees in their bright summer green would soon absorb the shadows of dusk and lose their luster. A midnight pall would descend upon the deepest sections of the ravine.

The valley of the shadow of death.

Psalm 23 was etched in her memory after all those years of Sunday school and youth group. The famous passage painted the Lord as a shepherd who rescued and calmed his sheep in all terrain. No one ever explained how the sheep became trapped in the valley of death to begin with. Was it the natural course of living in a harsh world, or was it from their own foolish mistakes? If the latter, wouldn't they deserve to stay there?

She closed her eyes, leaned her head against the back of the rocker. What shepherd came for a fool?

"Hey, Laur!"

She flung open her eyes and straightened.

"Sorry, didn't mean to scare you." Chloe plopped in the rocker next to Lauren's and laid her sketchbook on her lap. Folded bills peeked out of her fist. "You'll never guess what happened."

So much for peace. Lauren hid her phone under her thigh. "What?"

"Did you see that family in the lobby? The one with the blond-haired woman who looks like Aunt Gab?"

"I barely saw them, Chloe." Though none of them had looked anything like their aunt.

"Anyway, I chatted with them for a bit, and get this—they paid me thirty dollars to sketch them playing their game." She held up the bills. "Took me all of twenty minutes."

Lauren furrowed her brow. "Strangers paid you to draw them?"

"Yep!"

"Why?"

Her sister shoved the money into her pocket. "Because it's better than a photograph and more unique than those ridiculous caricatures. At least that's what the Aunt Gab-ish lady said."

Thirty dollars for twenty minutes' worth of work equated to 75 percent of Lauren's hourly pretax rate at Universal. Of course her sister would catch such a break. Chloe never tried hard at anything.

"Guess you're thirty dollars richer for Prague," she said.

Chloe chuckled. "I suppose so. Maybe I can teach the kids how to sketch strangers." She peeked at Lauren. "That's what I'll be doing, by the way—teaching elementary art at a small school for expats' kids."

Another detail fell into place about her soon-to-be life abroad. It was still hard to imagine her little sister going through with it. The dream and the reality were often vastly different things.

"I thought you were going to be a missionary," Lauren said.

"I am, in a way. It's a Christian school, and I have to raise my own support, which is why I've been selling those protein balls on the side. They've been doing really well, by the way. I hope to take a few art classes myself at one of the design schools in Prague and maybe explore Europe during breaks. It's an experience of a lifetime."

"Sounds like it." It also sounded far and above Chloe's feasible budget. Lauren folded her hands and let her attention fall to the horizon.

"You don't think I'll do well, do you?" her sister asked.

"I don't know what to think."

Chloe leaned forward, caught her eye. "Yes, you do."

Lauren pursed her lips, tried to hold it all back, but the urge to speak was too strong. "What if something goes wrong? You have no savings to fall back on, no family nearby, you don't know the language or the culture. God forbid you get seriously ill or injured." She thrust her left hand in the air as evidence. "It does happen."

"But aside from those things, I could do well, right?" Her sister grinned, obviously trying to lighten the mood.

Chloe would always be a kid at all the wrong times. Lauren shook her head and resumed her study of the day's fade.

They sat in silence for a moment.

Chloe smoothed the cover of her sketchbook. "Laur, I'm curious. If you could do anything, anything at all, what would you do?"

"What does that have to do with anything?"

"Because I'm curious."

She shook her head. "I don't think like that, Chloe."

"Why not?"

"Because it's pointless. Not everything works out the way you want it to."

Her sister's response came soft but firm. "Nothing works out if you don't try."

Lauren sighed and pushed out of her rocker. "Maybe in your world." She started for the door or anywhere else besides where Chloe was.

But there was more that needed to be said, more her little sister needed to hear that apparently no one—not friends, not their dad, not even their mom—was willing to tell her. Lauren turned around.

"I think in terms of what is realistic, Chloe. You think in terms of what feels good. Case in point, you can make thirty bucks off simple sketches, yet you're spending energy and money on protein balls. Do you realize how big your profit margins would be selling prints compared to treats?"

Chloe blinked. "That's actually a good idea."

"Exactly my point. You think on the surface, not four or five steps deep, and it's going to burn you. And what you don't seem to appreciate is that when you're halfway around the world, we won't be there to save you."

"Save me?" Chloe stood. "I don't need you all to save me, Lauren."

"Yes, you do. You've needed it every day of your life. You've needed it nearly every day of this trip. And it's usually me rescuing you. I can't be your net forever. I certainly didn't choose to be it in the first place."

Chloe's lips parted. But the stun was short-lived. With slow movements, she tucked the sketchbook under her arm, then took a step closer. Her gaze never lost its connection to Lauren's. "I didn't choose that for you either, nor would I. I know I've had some missteps, and I fully expect I'll have more. But the truth is, I trust God with all that I hold dear, including my dreams. If I succeed, great. If I don't, I'm not afraid, even though it definitely doesn't 'feel good.' You know why I'm not afraid? Because it means he is leading me to something worthier. *He* is my net, my hope, my rock. He's my courage to be still. And no matter what—whatever happens between you and me, no matter how badly you try to convince me otherwise—I will always want you to know that kind of courage too. It's the sweetest freedom there is. If only you would open your eyes." She slipped between the rockers. "Excuse me. I'm going to go check on Mom."

Chloe's footfalls traced to the entrance, their cadence as even as the phantom refrain of her profession.

He's my
Courage
To be
Still

Declared like one led out of the valley by a shepherd.

63

Chloe shaped a wide berth between herself and Lauren that night. She wedged herself into the narrow space that remained between her mom and the edge of her bed and feigned sleep when Lauren snuck into the darkened room well after sunset. She fell asleep to the replay of the scene on the patio. Had Lauren heard a word of it? Actually *heard*?

When her morning alarm chimed on Thursday, Lauren's bed lay empty. The missing key card said why.

Lauren showed up an hour later as Chloe and their mom prepared to head downstairs for breakfast. Sweat dripped off her sister's chin. Her feet plodded in exhaustion.

"Want something to eat?" their mom asked.

Lauren tossed her key card on the entertainment center and grabbed fresh clothes from her bag. "I'll be down later." Not once did she look at either of them. She shut herself in the bathroom.

Their mom turned to Chloe. "She's been running too much."

"Yes," Chloe agreed. But that was what scared people do. They ran. They pretended they needed no one and no one needed them. They carried their secrets in stone hearts, crippled by the weight of their own making, and called it a secure anchor.

Chloe shut the door behind them and took their mom to the breakfast room.

The Shepherd of the Hills park opened at nine o'clock. Chloe pulled into the parking lot at quarter after. Though built around the historic farm that inspired Harold Bell Wright's 1907 novel of the same name, the park was Branson in miniature. A "village" of shops and eateries doubled as the welcome center. Behind it, built into the side of a hill, was an open-air theater where stage productions of the book took place. To the west of that stretched the farm itself, and westward still, an adventure park that attracted adrenaline junkies to its massive stone observation tower, zip lines, ropes course, and mountain coaster. Of all the guests in line, the Vances were the only ones who signed up for a tour of the farm, the core reason the place existed.

Their guide, Tad, a gangly man with a white cowboy hat and a bluegrassy drawl, lavished them with historical knowledge about the area and farm as he led them between the weathered log and wood-slat buildings. Each had been preserved in its early-1900s state as much as possible, the way Wright would have known it.

"Not too many people in these parts back then," Tad said. "That was when roads were only footpaths through the brush and the railroad hadn't come this far south in Missouri. To a man like Wright, who wandered down here from Kansas City much like y'all, this was a foreign yet fascinatin' place."

Lauren stayed several steps behind, right hand wrapped around her left elbow. In the couple of moments when her gaze brushed against Chloe's, she tucked her lower lip inward and quickly looked away.

The pinnacle stop on the farm was a ramshackle log cabin perched on a majestic ridge, far more rustic and homegrown than the Wilders' farmhouse. Thick, squared timbers were held together by a grayish plaster. A stone chimney crested the peak of the wood shingle roof, which jutted out over a front porch. Somehow, it had survived more than one hundred years of elements. A humble, stalwart relic that defied probability.

Tad gathered them in the yard on the west side of the cabin, close enough to the enormous stone tower marking the boundary of the adventure park that Chloe could wave to the people waiting to go up. He pointed at the grizzled dwelling. "This cabin belonged to John and Anna Ross, who hosted Wright on his visits to the Ozarks. Yes, this is the original cabin in its original spot, and this view is why the good writer loved their farm so much." He spread his arm toward the southern horizon, where the windbreak of trees in front of the cabin opened up to reveal a miles-long vista of the rambling Ozarks.

"Wow," Chloe breathed.

Tad nodded. "Probably close to Wright's exact words, young lady. This is called Inspiration Point. The author liked to bring his desk out to this spot and sit under a tent to write. *The Shepherd of the Hills* was born right in this yard."

"You said he visited before the roads and trains were established," their mom said. "What made him want to travel to a place like this anyway, so far from civilization?"

"Healing, actually." Tad settled his hands on his hips and recounted the story of a sickly young man whose duties as a pastor in the city exacerbated his symptoms. His physician prescribed going to a milder climate at least twice a year, so the young pastor ventured south, met the Rosses, and enmeshed himself into their foreign yet fascinating way of life.

"The fresh air and warmer temperatures helped ease his achin' lungs," Tad said. "He especially needed the slower, peaceful pace. He loved to walk the trails around this area, several of which still exist today. If you go back up the road a piece, there's a trailhead for the Dewey Bald, a place which plays a significant role in the book."

Lauren stood a couple of feet away from the group, nearest to Chloe. She surveyed the dips and rises in the ground. Her chest expanded as she took in a deep breath, as if settling her own aching lungs.

"Turns out," Tad continued, "his adoration of this area sparked others to find what he did. The book introduced people to the Ozarks, a place many of them had never heard of, let alone visited. When the book was published, it was a huge bestseller, eventually sellin' more than a million copies, and readers were so smitten with the wild he described that they, too, began wanderin' this way. They'd come in droves."

"Wait." Their mom held up a hand. "Are you saying the novel started tourism to Branson?"

"Yes, ma'am. Had a lot to do with it. You have to remember, that was when cities were explodin' and factories and industry really started changin' the country. People wanted to step back, to take that breath."

"Still do." Lauren's reply was so soft, so closed, neither their mom nor Tad seemed to hear it. A white butterfly meandered through the air in front of her. Her gaze moved from the hollow to the tiny, winged creature.

How many times must Wright have done the same thing, allowed himself to be taken in by the quiet, hidden scenes of creation? He had accepted the invitation to step away from the rush and demands and had chosen to abide in wonder. To him, nature wasn't the god. He did not ascribe to such a shallow view of a profound display. Nature was a pulsating testimony of the Creator. It touted his love of beauty, his benevolent tilt toward the insignificant and defenseless, and his intricate order that gave butterflies lift and made hills trundle. Creation invited the suffering soul to believe that if God could provide a home for swooping swallows and teach the grotesque spider to catch its food with delicate artistry, he could also hold every moment of a human life. He could ignite dreams in the heart that pointed to his will.

Lord, does she see it?

Tad ushered them to the front door of the cabin, promising

290

peeks at the author's desk and the humble lifestyle of his hosts. Their mom followed on his heels. Chloe hung back a moment, waiting for Lauren. When her sister tore her attention from the white flutter, they both fell in behind their mom, Chloe a step or two ahead of Lauren.

As they passed the front porch, her sister suddenly stopped. Chloe paused as well. She turned around. "What is it?"

Lauren was fixated on a pole supporting the porch roof. Her line of sight led to a lizard clinging to the splintered wood. Its slender, dark body was not much longer than a cell phone, with pale yellow stripes from nose to tail. The clomps of Tad's boots on the porch sent the reptile skittering up the pole, though he didn't get far. One hind foot appeared to be gnarled at a gruesome angle, no more useful than if it hadn't been there at all.

Their mom noticed their gawking and came toward them. "What are you staring at?"

The lizard struggled to hobble around the pole, away from the noise.

"It's a lizard," Chloe said.

"A li—" Their mom clutched her arms to her stomach and bolted behind Tad.

With obvious familiarity with wildlife, the tour guide tiptoed to the railing and peered around the pole. "Look what you found. That there's a prairie racerunner. They're all over around here. They're harmless. Won't bother you, but won't befriend you either." He turned to their mom. "Wanna see?"

"I prefer to go inside, thank you." Her feet already edged toward the screen door.

He looked over his shoulder at the girls, gave them a wink, then escorted their mom inside. His voice soon wafted through the screen, carrying insights about the desk and other furnishings.

The girls stayed near the lizard frozen to his perch.

"He's hurt," Lauren whispered.

"He is," Chloe said. Worse, the little guy could not stay where he was, exposed to predators and unable to run. She stepped forward, slowly reached out with her right hand.

"What are you doing?" her sister asked. "Don't touch him."

"He just needs a little help. I'll be gentle."

Her hand moved closer, four inches away, then two. The racerunner lurched, but that back foot dragged like dead weight. In a smooth, quick movement, Chloe pinched the slim body and peeled it from the pole.

"I'm not going to hurt you," she cooed to the creature. She placed him in her left palm, which she kept flat and firm for his spindly feet. "There you are. You're safe."

Her sister took a hesitant step forward, hands folded at chest level. "What are you going to do with him?"

"I'm going to get him to a more secure spot. But first, I'm going to let you pet him." She moved carefully toward her sister.

"What?" Lauren twisted her clasped hands away.

"It's okay, Laur. He's calm, and he knows you mean well. Take your first two fingers and lightly trace them down his back."

"I'm not . . . I don't . . ."

"He won't bite. I promise." She brought the critter closer to her sister, an arm's length away. "Try it."

Little by little, her sister untwisted.

"Go on," Chloe urged.

Lauren extended her right hand, farther, farther, until her two front fingers grazed the lizard's back. She jerked away, laughed nervously, then tried again. Her touch lingered a little longer. "He's bumpier than I thought he'd be."

Chloe grinned.

Her sister traced the lizard's spine a third time, an ease in her movements.

"Let's get him to safety," Chloe said.

Together, they crouched near a small gap in the porch skirting. Chloe lowered the injured reptile to the grass, elevating the heel of her hand to signal permission to flee.

The lizard hobbled down and into the shadow of the floor-boards.

"The Ross cabin is a sanctuary once more," Chloe said.

Her sister's eyes found hers. The faint wrinkles at the edges were relaxed, lids open wider than normal, pupils larger to better capture the wonder. She radiated an openness not of her own making.

The promise of a coming answer to prayer grew stronger.

64

Before Lauren could finish her lunch at the farm's on-site restaurant, her sister insisted they go to the Dewey Bald trail that Tad had mentioned. Having scarfed her burger, Chloe extolled the virtues of the trail, including how it would "put them in the shoes of the characters." And it was free of charge.

The more Chloe shared, the more she lit up. "There's also an observation tower at the peak. We could climb it."

"I'm not sure where you are getting the 'we,'" their mom said.

In the end, though, Chloe wore her down. She consented to walking the trail despite the compounding heat of the afternoon. Chloe had a way of breaking through.

Fortunately, the trail from the parking lot to the tower was both paved and shaded. It traced back and forth in mild-grade inclines and sharp switchbacks on the western face of the hill.

Chloe broke ahead of them. "This is going to be so much fun!"

"She said the same thing about the Arch," their mom murmured to Lauren as they walked side by side. "I nearly died for a mediocre view."

Lauren nodded. "She likes to hype things up."

It was the longest answer she had given her mom since they'd picked her up at the transportation center. They fell in step with each other. Her mom stayed close to her side, making no attempt to break away or cast disappointed looks her way. But the peace was tenuous, as if allowed to exist only because Chloe wasn't there to disrupt it.

Questions lingered between Lauren and her mom. Heavy questions, and heavier secrets.

After a moment, her mom turned to her. "Do you know about Chloe's job in Prague?"

She nodded.

"What do you think?"

Lauren shrugged. "Sounds like something Chloe would do."

Up ahead, her sister paused to point her phone camera toward streaks of sunlight cutting through the leafy limbs.

"It's funny," her mom said. "If you would have asked me before this trip whether I thought Chloe would make it in Prague, I would have given an easy no. But now? Now I can't help but think there's more resilience in her than I appreciated."

Her mom's eyes cut to her.

Lauren crossed her arms. The about-face cut deep.

Resilience was often accompanied by courage. Where one appeared, the other wasn't too far away. Courage was what Chloe had wished for Lauren, because she didn't believe Lauren had enough of her own. Did their mom believe that too?

A half mile in, they reached the bare peak and followed a bend in the path around a final grove. Chloe was the first to see the tower.

"Oh, wow!" Her exclamation echoed in the glade.

Lauren and their mom came around the curve—and stopped cold.

The metal tower reached forty feet in the air, taller than most of the surrounding trees. Steep staircases zigzagged between six wood-plank platforms, leading to the larger, L-shaped deck on top. The guardrails were as thin as a fire escape's.

Their mom's eyes widened. "Absolutely not!"

"It's perfectly safe, Mom," Chloe said, already headed for the structure.

"Chloe Grace, you stay off that thing. I do not want to be on the news."

Her sister proceeded anyway, saying over her shoulder, "If it wasn't safe, the Department of Conservation wouldn't let anyone on it."

"For all we know, they condemned this tower three months ago and someone stole the warning sign." Their mom stepped forward. "Chloe!"

But she was already nearing the first flight of steps.

Courage. That was what her mom admired about Chloe. But courage took many forms. Some were quieter than others, like the form of an older sibling who did what older siblings were expected to do. Maybe her mom needed to see it to know it.

Lauren lifted her sling bag off her shoulder and handed it to their mom. "I'll go with her." Similar assurances had crossed her lips countless times in her life. *I'll watch out for her . . . I'll make sure she doesn't get herself into too much trouble.* Had anyone noticed the courage that required?

Her mom clutched the sling. "Yes. Please."

Lauren held up her chin in the manner of a gruff, immortalized T. S. Eliot and jogged toward the steps. "Chloe, hold on!"

The instruction brought her little sister to a halt. Chloe smiled as Lauren hustled toward her. "You're coming!"

"And I'm going first." Lauren reached the entrance and ran up the initial flight of stairs. The tower jangled with her movement.

The noise, and noticeable sway, intensified when her sister clambered up behind her, laughing. "I can't wait to see the view from the top!"

Lauren followed the first platform around to the next flight. She grabbed the handrails on either side of the narrow stairs and used the leverage to propel herself up faster. Her knees pumped. Each footfall rattled the wood treads against their metal frames.

She reached the second platform. Though the splint on her finger clinked against the handrails, the pain of the fracture no longer bothered her. The higher they climbed, the more her grip on the handrails tightened. The boards underfoot were well weathered, held down by rusted nails. Gaps between them allowed a view straight down to the hard-packed glade. She counted the steps as she took them, toward the next platform, the next rise. Forward, onward, no going back. Courage.

Fourth platform. Her heart pounded. Amazing how strong and weak the same heart could be. Strong to the task she undertook but weak to the callousness of the man who'd disregarded her when she needed him the most. Would Gavin do the same? He waited for her, waited for her text. But he waited for the version of herself she had let him see. If he knew her for who she really was, would he retreat too?

Fifth platform. Her palms sweat. Her lungs labored at third-mile intensity. She could prove her mettle against a treadmill timer but not in a job application. Why? What had she done wrong? The longer her inbox sat empty, the louder the degradation banged on the closet door. What happened when the trip ended and she lost her cover? She could not hedge her mom forever, nor could she stop the look of disapproval from showing up again—soon.

Sixth platform. Money. What would she do for money? She would be no better than her sister halfway across the world and broke, with no one to save her.

"Almost there!" Chloe cheered.

One final staircase, one final push. She gripped the rails, propelled up. Her feet planted on the deck. They had arrived.

The earth fell away. Miles upon miles of openness unfolded on all sides. Waves of emerald and jade with glints of gold rolled under a dome of piercing blue flecked by pearly clouds.

"Look at that!" Chloe breathed.

Lauren's legs trembled. Her throat burned. She pushed to

the southern railing and held herself upright by the top bar. Chloe joined her. They stood on the edge of the sky as specks upon glory.

"It's beautiful," her sister said.

Even Harold Bell Wright never knew such a view. For all the inspiration he'd absorbed in those hills, never did he gain such a clear, wide visage of what was behind, beside, and before. But where was Lauren's inspiration? No answers floated on the wind like they had for Wright.

Chloe had asked her what she would do if she could do anything. What Lauren couldn't admit to her, neither on the hotel patio nor there on the tower, was she would find someone who knew the answers she couldn't grasp. She would ask them to take over. Because she was tired. Tired of fighting, of trying to stay ahead, of guarding. She was so tired, with no one to save her.

Her knees wobbled. She clung to the metal, clung with what strength remained in her broken hand. But it wasn't enough. It never had been.

She sank to the deck. The exhaustion poured out in reverberating sobs.

"Laur?"

She could hold on to nothing. Every small gain, every big win, could be swept away in a moment. She couldn't predict when or how or from what direction, but the sweep would come, and there was no defense against it.

Chloe's arms wrapped around her. Lauren tried to wriggle away, but her sister held firm. "I got you."

How did Chloe escape such fear? How did she live blithe and confident?

If Lauren could do anything, she would win what her sister had.

Their mom's voice cut through the distance. "What's going on up there? What's wrong?"

"We're okay," Chloe called back. She cupped Lauren's head and nestled it against her shoulder. "We're okay, Laur." She didn't ask why Lauren was crying. Maybe she didn't need to know. Maybe she already knew.

Clangs of boards on metal rose from below. The tower vibrated.

"Mom?" Chloe shouted. "Is that you?"

A mumbled lament.

Chloe loosened her grip and twisted in an effort to peer down through the gaps in the deck boards. "What are you doing?"

"At the moment, trying not to plummet to my death." A moan, then more clangs.

Lauren lifted her head, tears clouding her eyes. They both searched the gaps.

"You don't have to come up," Chloe said. "We're fine."

"Too late." Their mom punctuated her words with a whimper. The clangs came at slower intervals.

"I should go to her," Chloe said.

Lauren wiped her cheeks and nodded.

Her sister stood and started for the stairs. "Hang on, Mom. I'm coming!"

"Stop moving, Chloe! You're shaking the tower!"

"But—"

"Stay still!"

Chloe froze halfway across the deck, then looked back at Lauren.

The lump in her throat refused to quiet. She hugged her knees to her chest. Their mom had never seen her in a weeping disarray. Neither had Chloe. No going back. No hiding.

Minutes later, when their mom reached the final flight, tears still ran down Lauren's neck. What she wouldn't give for their mom to go back down the tower.

As promised, Chloe had not moved. "Almost here, Mom."

A blond head rose into view. The hair was slick with sweat, the face ashen, the eyes squeezed shut.

"A little farther," Chloe coaxed.

Their mom clung to the inner handrail with both forearms. She rose two more steps, dared to peek, and regretted it instantly. She moaned and dropped to all fours.

"Let me help you." Chloe started forward.

"No!"

Chloe stopped.

Lauren sniffed, wiped her neck and face with her shirtsleeve. But there was no point. She was still a mess, and their mom would see.

Thump, thump, thump. Their mom crested the final step onto the deck. Her purse and Lauren's sling dragged against the boards. Though her arms visibly shook and her breath came in heaves, she crawled forward, eyes closed.

Chloe knelt and stretched out her hands. "I'm right here, Mom. Keep coming."

Lauren balled tighter.

Following the voice, their mom inched toward Chloe. When she was close enough, Chloe reached for her and gathered her into an embrace. "You made it!"

Their mom dug her fingers into Chloe's shirt, breath coming in bursts.

"Want to stand up and see the view?" Chloe asked.

"Didn't . . . come for . . . view." She opened her eyes, gaze fixing on Lauren. "Came for . . . you."

Lauren blinked. "Me?"

"You . . . needed . . . help."

Heat streamed through her. Not from shame or summer or sweat. From the answer to the question she didn't yet have the words to ask. Her unformed plea for grace, met before it was uttered. Their mom, in the face of her own overwhelming fear, only wanted to chase Lauren's away.

Chloe looked between them, smiled.

Forget the wet face. Forget the indignity. Lauren lifted onto her hands and knees. The wood scraped against her palms, beat against her knees, but she reached her family, and she enfolded herself into their arms.

They stayed huddled for several minutes there on the edge of the sky, where they were specks upon glory.

"Imagine what Popsie would think of this," Chloe whispered.

The laughter started with Lauren. It soon spread to the other two.

Before they made their way down, Chloe took a selfie of them sitting on the deck forty feet above the earth, "to prove it to him." The picture, though, would be evidence for them all.

65

Sweet slumber still held the girls in the other bed when Edie slipped out of the room with her journal. Outside the hotel's main entrance, the predawn chill caressed her cheeks. She crossed to the patio, which was bathed in the gentle illumination of string lights. The sky retained its midnight robe speckled with stars. Beyond the cloaked valley, a red light pulsated atop a tower. Chloe had claimed it was the stone tower at the Shepherd of the Hills farm, the one five times larger and sturdier than the Dewey Bald travesty.

Before they had even reached the ground from the rickety tower, Chloe had texted their selfie to the family group chat. Not that Edie noticed until well afterward. She had been too busy sliding down the steps on her backside with Lauren as her guide. In the caption, Chloe told Grant that Edie "was a beast." The phrase was a compliment, Chloe assured her. The younger generation became more enigmatic every day.

At least Grant was comprehensible with his GIF of an opossum giving a thumbs-up. "Can't wait to hear the whole story," he added to the image.

One more sleep before she was back to him and they all would return to their respective corners of Kansas City. No more rattly sputter of the car air-conditioning or Chloe's energetic singing to her playlist, or traipsing through the heat or "fun" opportunities on rivers and tall structures.

But the "no more" included an imposing question: What then? Was what happened on the tower a product of momentary rhapsody, or was it a marker for what was ahead? Would they, no matter what circumstance befell any of them, always turn back for each other?

Edie settled into one of the rocking chairs. She crossed her legs, positioned the book on her top knee, and began what would be her final entry.

Dear Grant—

The whole time I stood by and watched our girls climb that death trap of a tower yesterday, the only thing I could envision was the entire thing collapsing like a sandcastle and taking them from me. I have been so afraid of them wandering off on their own, foolish enough to believe it couldn't happen by force and leave me with no opportunity to tell them how much they amaze me.

Because they do, Grant. They amaze me, and I have passed up far too many chances to tell them.

She wrote of Chloe having grace under fire, from the way she handled changes to plans with unbreakable hope to the way she kept assuring her that Lauren would come around. It was a character quality that had long lived in their youngest, one that situational need had made shine. Living abroad would require such character, in large amounts.

Lauren, meanwhile, clearly conceals an entire part of her life, and I wish I could somehow convince her—through words, through action—that she doesn't have to hide. I wish I could convince her that while I may miss details, I will always come *for her. Her tears were why I scaled a tower. She needed help. She needed her mom, though she wouldn't ask.*

Even now, the haunting cries of her daughter tore at her. Her child, in pain. She paused to drink of the cool air. The blast stemmed the clench of her throat.

I had let Lauren feel alone too many times. I wasn't going to do it again. I will never do it again. Mothers should always reach for their children first.

On the black canvas of the wee hours, the memory of her mother's study etched itself. Her mom behind the mahogany desk, clacking away at her typewriter or making tight red swirls on the stack of student papers. Edie's young heart had sought nothing more than to beat under the admiring gaze of the woman who hunched over other people's needs. Edie's middle-aged heart, despite knowing better, despite knowing it was too late, craved her mother looking at her from across the room and seeing the version of Edie Mondell Vance that was, not the version her mother invented.

I believed a lot of things growing up. I believed that the world was unwieldy and the only way to stand against it was to do what was expected of me. I believed I had to validate the space I took up. Unless I was doing something others deemed worthwhile, then I wasn't doing anything of value. I don't want these same lies to ensnare our girls, Grant.

I love my mother, and I will always want her approval. A daughter cannot completely relieve herself of either inclination. But it makes more sense to me now why Gabriella drew a different boundary between where our mother ended and Gabriella began. I wish I understood better how my sister did it.

One of many questions she wanted to ask Gabriella about her relationship with their mother—and with Edie.

Though her entry veered to topics of oversize pancakes and their planned stops in Oklahoma that day, one more update regarding her sister returned to her pen. She added it as a PS to the entry.

Chloe asked if she could send the picture of us on the tower to Gabriella. I said yes.

66

Unhiding was a funny thing. It could cause a heart to release its pain in torrents of tears, but not in words. Words were much harder.

Multiple times as they gathered their belongings in the hotel room, Lauren came close to stopping her mom and sister mid-pack and disclosing everything. Duncan, Universal, finances, rejection, Gavin. Every reason that had devolved her to a sodden mess on top of the tower. They clearly knew something had driven her to her knees, though neither had pressed her to say what.

And she couldn't. As if the language simply didn't exist.

Truth grew heavier the longer it was withheld.

They grabbed breakfast to go and had loaded into the Xterra by eight o'clock. Missouri blurred into northwest Arkansas, which eventually flattened into eastern Oklahoma. Her sister bought them snacks along the way, sang too loudly to her playlist, and taught their mom a sequence of dance moves that a semi in a neighboring lane mistook for a request to honk. The air horn blast flung their mom against her seat with a yelp. Chloe laughed so hard she cried.

Lauren leaned toward the merriment, giggled along with them, almost reached out, but the weight on her shoulders pulled her backward. If she couldn't say what she needed to, then she might as well not say anything.

Shortly before noon, they arrived in Sallisaw. The small town, situated within the overlap of the state of Oklahoma and the Cherokee Nation, possessed a certain level of fame as the beleaguered town in John Steinbeck's Great Depression novel, *The Grapes of Wrath*. The book painted Sallisaw as a glum, dust-covered place. The lively town center and handful of chain motels spun a different yarn.

For lunch Chloe chose a diner called Bettie Mae Moon's, "Home of Blue-Ribbon Biscuits" and, based on the crowded parking lot, the choice of many locals. They took the last open booth by the front windows. Lauren snuggled up to the glass and lowered behind her menu. Her sister, never short on words or the courage to say them, struck up a conversation about biscuits with the elderly man at the table across the aisle. By the time the Vances' orders headed to the kitchen, the two strangers had advanced to exchanging life stories.

"I must have looked at that *Grapes of Wrath* print in the library coffee shop a hundred times," Chloe told him. "I figured if we were doing a bookish road trip, we had to include the Joads' hometown."

The man tsked. "Unfortunately, you won't find much about the book round here."

"The librarian told me the same thing," Chloe said. "Why is that? It's such an important book."

"The way Steinbeck portrayed us." He pushed his red OU Sooners cap back on his head, showing more of his thin, snow-white hair. "My father lived in Sallisaw during the dust bowl, and he said Steinbeck never came here for research. He went to California to talk to migrants there, but everything he wrote about Oklahoma and its people was pure imagination."

Their mom leaned forward. "There's no marker or memorial of any kind?"

The man shook his head.

The contrast to Wright was stark. Wright, who had not only visited his setting but lived in it, was embraced by the locals and his work revered. Laura Ingalls Wilder, same. Willa Cather, Mark Twain, and Langston Hughes, same.

Lauren sipped the coffee the server had brought upon her request and kept the mug elevated near her mouth. At least it was busy doing something.

The man scratched his cheek and continued. "The young people organized some kind of event several years ago. It made the papers and all that, but nothing's stuck. They don't understand why the book upset the old folks the way it did. But listen, if it's memorials you want, head out to Sequoyah's Cabin. That's really where you want to go."

He went on to tell them that Sequoyah, a Cherokee leader, built the cabin himself and in it developed an alphabet for his nation, bringing their oral traditions and storytelling to the page.

Chloe brightened. "Sounds fascinating!"

"It does, actually," their mom said.

Lauren nodded and took another sip.

"Cabin's just north of town." He gestured in the general direction. "Take 59 north to 101, you'll be there in a jiff."

A "jiff" turned out to be about twenty minutes deep into the Oklahoma plains, to a ten-acre park walled in by mature trees. A larger, climate-controlled museum encased the 1800s one-room cabin. Once inside the museum, her mom and sister dove into the exhibits. Lauren trudged behind, stuck in the tension between following them and quick-stepping back outside into the open afternoon. Had it not been for one mesmerizing display board, she would have opted for the latter.

The board listed all eighty-six characters of the Cherokee syllabary. According to the introduction above the list, Sequoyah invested more than ten years developing the system of characters that represented syllables of the language. A man who could not read or write himself unlocked his nation's ability to express themselves in new, life-changing ways.

He had literally given people words.

Lauren chewed her lower lip.

Without warning, Chloe appeared at her side. "Did you know Sequoyah the man was the namesake for the tree? Spelled differently, but the same root. Pun intended." She handed Lauren a sheet of paper. "Found this in the kids' section in the corner. To help you learn Cherokee."

Basic English terms and expressions ran the length of the page along with their Cherokee translations, both in syllabary and phonetic spellings.

"You'll be going home bilingual," Chloe added.

If only. Lauren had a hard enough time finding the right utterances in one language.

Chloe looked behind her. Their mom ambled around the corner of the cabin, attention engrossed in the displays lining the wall. "So." Chloe turned back to Lauren. "About yesterday."

Lauren dipped her head, fiddled with the sheet. "I'm sure that was weird for you."

"Not weird so much as . . . heartbreaking." She stepped closer and lowered her voice. "You don't have to talk if you're not ready, but I hope you know I will always prefer your smile over your tears."

Her feet begged to move, to run, to flee. But her center pleaded to stay, to speak, to reach. To step once more into the open arms extended to her in love.

The board before them showed the building blocks of language, the glue of community. What were they, really? Simple noises that carried layers of meaning. They didn't have to be eloquent or perfect. They only needed to be put to breath, one syllable at a time.

She could do it. She needed to do it.

She filled her lungs, closed her eyes. The first string of overdue words unspooled. "Have you ever made a mistake?" Eight syllables.

Her sister guffawed. "Some believe I invented the concept."

Inhale. Five more syllables. "I made a big one."

The string unwound further, syllable after syllable, about Duncan, Universal, the rejection letter from the recruiter. Until all the revelations lay in a jumble between them.

Lauren opened her eyes. The board had not changed, nor the day, nor the paper in her hand. But her sister. Her sister's knitted brow conveyed that everything had changed. They had changed.

"You are so strong, Laur. You know that?"

The response, gentle and pure, stole her breath. Then, just as quickly, it invited her to take her fill of peace.

Chloe laid her hand on Lauren's shoulder. "Here's how I see it. Universal lost more than they know, you wouldn't have been happy at that other job anyway, and Duncan needs a good throat punch."

A sensation spread across Lauren's shoulders. It seeped down her back and radiated into her chest. It was the tingle of lightness. Her mom had come for her, chased away her fear—and so had her sister.

"You are going to come out on top of this," Chloe said, attention never leaving her for a moment. "There is no way you won't."

The sensation spread upward, all the way to Lauren's lips. She allowed it to lift the corners high.

Her sister echoed the smile threefold.

This—this was a step toward the sweet freedom her sister heralded.

On the sheet in Lauren's hand, one Cherokee phrase stood out from the others. She lifted the paper and pointed to it for her sister to see.

Wado.

Thank you.

Chloe chuckled. Taking Lauren's cue, she scanned the list herself. She found a response and placed her fingertip below it.

Gvgeyui.

I love you.

Their gazes met. Lauren's pain to Chloe's grace. Her thirst to Chloe's refreshment. Weariness to rest. Sister to sister.

They had set eyes upon each other countless times in their lives. But that was the first time either of them saw the other.

67

Chloe drove slower than normal on the highway to Tulsa, a subtle allowance for her sister to have unrushed time with their mom. Lauren laid out the hidden things in the clean light of day, starting with her firing. At first, their mom's mouth hung open. As Lauren proceeded through each turn in the story, their mom's lips drew closer together until they were clamped shut, and she homed in on the road ahead. Her eyes, the windows to her honest thoughts, were shielded by sunglasses.

To her credit, Lauren kept speaking, though her voice weakened. "I don't know if I'll ever see Gavin again," she said over the rattle in the dashboard. "But right now, I'm focused on finding a job."

Their mom propped her elbow on the windowsill and touched her index finger to her lips. Several beats passed.

"Mom?" Lauren said.

"I just need time to think," their mom replied from behind her hand.

Chloe caught her sister's attention in the mirror. Fear edged into Lauren's expression. Chloe nodded, a silent assurance that Lauren had done the right thing.

Her sister twisted her mouth and looked at her lap.

During the rest of the drive to Tulsa, Chloe skipped any song on her playlist that didn't extol the Lord's grace.

Unlike Sallisaw, the second-largest city in Oklahoma celebrated the novel and its movie version set within its boundaries. Several filming locations for *The Outsiders* had been preserved around the Tulsa metro for the delight of those who loved the young adult classic, including the DX gas station where two characters worked, the park where the rumble between the Greasers and Socs happened, and the drive-in theater that served as a backdrop to a key scene.

The pinnacle was The Outsiders House Museum, a white bungalow situated in a blue-collar neighborhood on the rim of the city's central hub. Lauren's demeanor brightened as they walked up to the front gate of the chain-link fence. Her head lifted and stayed there. The movie had meant so much more to her than anyone else in their family.

"Everything looks like it did on the screen." Lauren pointed to a sharp dip in the top bar of the fence. "Look! Even the dent is the same."

She passed through the gate first. The sidewalk cut through a short yard plagued by bald spots burned by the summer heat. The front porch boasted a set of metal chairs and a glider freckled with rust. The paint on the siding flaked off in places, and what remained intact had a faded appearance.

Lauren looked back at them from the top of the steps. "It's so close to how it was in the movie, it's like walking on the set."

The shine of wonder in her sister's expression put a bounce in Chloe's step too. Middle school Lauren was surfacing again.

The front door opened, and a man with graying dark hair slicked into a ponytail sauntered out. He wore a museum staff name tag on his black T-shirt, which bore "Stay Gold" in large, bold letters across the front, a nod to the novel's famous line.

"Afternoon," he said. "Here for the tour?"

"We are," Lauren replied.

Her delight did not fade the entire tour.

Chloe took pictures of her in every room, each of which contained framed photos of how the room appeared in the movie for the sake of comparison. In the living room, Lauren sat on the floor where the character Two-Bit had watched cartoons while eating chocolate cake off a tray and drinking a beer. The museum staff had re-created the tray of snacks as a prop for fans to use. In the kitchen, Lauren posed next to the stove where the Curtis brothers had prepared breakfast. In Ponyboy's bedroom, she sat at the desk where the youngest brother and narrator of the story wrote his essay about his exploits with his buddy Johnny. Lauren never tried to hide the splint on her finger, as if she had forgotten about it.

At some point, their mom wandered away unannounced.

"I'll go find her," Chloe said to her sister. She left Lauren with the tour guide and retraced their path through the house. After several minutes of no luck, she stepped out onto the porch.

Her mom sat in the glider, back straight, sunglasses on, and gaze cast toward the distance.

Chloe shut the door behind her. "Not like you to be out here in the heat."

"I needed to sit for a minute, and I wasn't sure we were allowed to be on any of the furniture."

Chloe crossed the concrete porch, then lowered onto the glider next to her mom. "Lauren's having the time of her life in there. Remember how she used to watch the movie on repeat? I think she has it memorized. I feel like *I* have it memorized."

Her mom nodded. "I remember. Though, for all those times she watched it, I am having trouble remembering it accurately. It's about a group of teen boys, right?"

"Three orphaned brothers and their friends. The Greasers. Darry is the oldest, trying to keep the gang together."

Dropping her chin, her mom folded her hands in her lap. "Does he succeed?"

"Depends on how you look at it."

Her mom tapped the pads of her thumbs together. The question clearly came from a deeper place. A more personal place.

Chloe softened her voice. "He did the best he could. That much I remember. And he was loved for it."

Tap, tap. The sheen of her nail polish twinkled with the movement.

Maybe the message got through. Maybe it didn't. Directness was the only way to make sure. Chloe shifted slightly in her seat to better face her mom. "Lauren wants to know you're on her side. Your disappointment hurts more than the mistake."

Her mom tucked her thumbs together. "That's my regret."

"What is?"

The answer came out strained. "That you girls ever knew such hurt." Her throat bobbed. "No one should question if they are worthy."

Chloe took one of her mom's hands in both of hers. "You're right. No one should. Including you."

Her mom shook the entreaty away. Her chin trembled. "I'm terrified of you going to Prague. But what scares me more"—she pulled in a shuddering breath—"is you never coming back to me because you found something better."

"But I am coming back to you. What makes you think I wouldn't?"

A tear trailed down her mom's cheek. "I don't have family that does."

The answer, and the experience that wrought it, seared into her. Grandma Moria, her long-gone grandfather, Aunt Gab. All had left her mom behind in their own way. The impact shaded everything her mom understood about family, about herself.

Chloe squeezed her mom's hand and scooted closer. "I love you. Lauren loves you. We always will. You are worth coming back to, Mom."

Her mom's face wrenched. She turned away as another tear cascaded.

Chloe leaned in, spoke directly into the anguish. "You know what makes you a good mom? You fought to shield us from the worst pain you had to suffer. You found a loyal man to anchor our family. You invested your life in us. You push us to be our best. You overdo it from time to time, but I realize now it's because you want us to have all the love and attention you were deprived of. I'm sorry I haven't appreciated that."

Drops fell from her mom's jawline—that regal jawline so easy to draw.

Chloe held on tight. "I believe you are worth coming back to, Mom." She nodded toward the living room windows behind them, and the young woman beyond the panes. "So does Lauren. Please never doubt that."

Of all the unsaid things she'd needed to tell her mom on their trip, that part, as it turned out, was the most important.

Her mom slowly turned to her as more release streamed down her cheeks. A small smile strained against the tremble of her chin. "Thank you," she whispered.

Even if Chloe settled on the far side of the sea or made her bed in the deep, she would never stop wanting to be as close as that to her mom.

When the tears finally settled, her mom pulled her hand away to swing her sunglasses to the top of her head. She wiped her lower lashes. "I saw a gift shop around back. Do you think Lauren would like one of those 'Stay Gold' shirts?"

Chloe nodded. "I have no doubt."

"Good. It's about time I return to air-conditioning anyway."

They giggled. Soft wings fanned from her mom's eyes, the effect of unadulterated joy and security. The warmth of it enveloped Chloe.

Her mom patted Chloe's leg, then stood. "See you in a bit." She soon disappeared around the side of the house on her way to the detached garage that had been converted into a gift shop.

Lauren's laughter floated through the windowpanes, followed by her amused voice. The smile lingered on Chloe's lips.

Lauren had not been pretending she didn't need anyone. She truly had believed it, much like their mom had believed she wasn't worth the effort. God had helped them see. He had taken each of them by the hand and shepherded them toward where they were meant to be and what they were meant to find. Whatever was around the bend could look different than any of them imagined. But it would be good. It would be better. It would be best.

Chloe retrieved her phone and swiped through the pictures she had taken of Lauren in the house. The triumph in her sister's expression complemented the release that had flavored their mom's reaction moments prior. To watch someone live their heart's deepest, purest desire was an inexpressible fulfillment. Those were the images—the victories—to treasure.

68

The gates to the Admiral Twin Drive-In opened an hour before the Friday night showtime, the House Museum tour guide told them, and the lot filled quickly. "But it's a must-visit for *Outsiders* fans," he added, which sealed the deal for Edie's oldest daughter.

Temperatures hung in the mid-nineties, firmly in makeup-melting range. Dusk would wane the brutality only a little. Regardless, Edie insisted they go.

"It's our last night," she told Lauren. "Let's do what you want to do."

Chloe not only agreed, she hatched a plan to make the night "the funnest one yet." When they checked into their hotel and dropped off their bags, Chloe pulled Lauren aside, whispered the details of the plan, and off they went. The girls shooed Edie off the bed and gathered all eight pillows, both comforters, and the spare blanket in the closet.

"What are you doing with those?" Edie asked.

"You'll see!" Chloe gestured for Lauren to head for the door.

They looked both ways in the hallway, then snuck toward the side exit, precocious titters accompanying their stealth. Edie was forbidden from peeking.

They arrived at the drive-in with thirty minutes to spare before showtime. The iconic double-sided screen tower stood between two lots, one to the west and one to the east. Each screen showed a different double feature. They opted for the west screen, scheduled to show an action-hero movie paired with a World War II love story.

Chloe found a parking spot toward the middle of the lot and backed in so the rear of the car faced the screen. "This is going to be so much fun!"

Her daughter's favorite expression held more promise than ever.

Chloe lowered all four windows and turned off the car. "Snack procurement time. Anyone want to go with me to the concession stand? It's all on me."

"I'll go," Lauren said and opened her door.

Chloe looked at Edie. "Coming?"

"I'm going to check in with your dad for a minute. Please bring me the largest chilled water you can find."

"Will do, and here." She tossed Edie the keys. "You should check out the back. I think you're going to like it."

Both girls headed off to the concession stand at the base of the screen tower.

Edie pushed out into the hot evening. Around her, fellow patrons set up lawn chairs and arranged the backs of trucks and minivans. The parking lot contained no trees or communal shade of any kind. Everyone created their own with umbrellas or raised liftgates. Surely that was what Chloe had in mind too. On the screen, ads for concessions and local businesses began to play.

Twenty-five minutes until showtime.

Edie walked around to the back of the car and unlocked the liftgate. The door eased upward and unveiled the girls' handiwork. They had created a cushiony carpet out of folded comforters. Stacked against the back of the bench seat were five of the bed pillows. Three pillows rested closer to the edge of the cargo area like ottomans. The opened windows allowed for a cross breeze to freshen the blissfully shaded suite.

She chuckled. The setup was reminiscent of the "campout" the girls had created on Chloe's bedroom floor all those years prior. She smoothed the comforter as the memories took her back to another, simpler era, when time with the girls at home seemed to be nowhere close to running out. How fast it had all gone.

Her eyes watered. She blinked against the rush and called Grant.

"Our girls are adults," she said when he answered.

"Yes, my love. They are. Have been for a while."

He didn't quite understand, and she didn't quite have the words to explain. Her voice strained. "Grant, they are amazing, breathtaking adults."

"Agreed." He paused. "Everything okay? You sound sad."

Tightness grew in her throat. She swallowed it down. "I started this trip thinking I knew the girls, maybe even had the audacity to think I knew them better than they knew themselves. But the truth was, Lauren has felt alone for so long my heart hurts to think about it, and Chloe has felt belittled far more than I ever cared to admit. Two wounds I never wanted any of my children to sustain. Not after—" The clench cut off her words.

Grant, in his usual ways, filled in her gap. "I know," he said softly.

She couldn't reach that little girl she once was. She couldn't do a thing to change her mother's choices. She couldn't take back any words or choices of her own as a mother, and there were far too many to count. But she could use the rough beginning to craft a better ending.

She could start right then.

"Let's have the girls stay for supper tomorrow," she said.

"I like that idea," Grant said.

"And let's plan a farewell party for Chloe."

"I like that idea even better."

She bit her lip. "And let's plan a trip or two together."

"Of course. Anywhere in particular?"

Previews began to roll. Twenty minutes until showtime.

"Salzburg is not so far from Prague," she said.

"It's really not."

"But first, perhaps we could go to a little place I heard about. A farm with a menagerie of animals and a slightly eccentric owner."

"Well, now," he said, his smile evident. "That's the best idea of them all."

They had so much to rewrite, all of them, together. And what could emerge would indeed be the best of all.

They talked a few minutes longer. Though she didn't steal Lauren's chance to tell him herself about all that had happened, she did tell him virtually everything else, as their wedding vows had dictated. When their goodbye was imminent, the ache that usually pooled in her chest remained only a pinch.

Fifteen minutes until showtime.

The girls arrived with bottled water, packages of candy, a bag of popcorn, and a few hot dogs. Chloe handed her a contraption and said, "Look what I found! For your personal cooling needs."

Edie laughed as she took the mist bottle topped by a battery-operated fan. "This is perfect." Chloe had painstakingly slipped bits of crushed ice into the reservoir along with cold water.

Edie sat between her girls in the homemade suite, pillow tucked under her knees and personal mister aimed at her neck. The girls divvied up the snacks, each woman able to pick the sweet treats and savory items she most desired. Chloe passed up a hot dog in favor of the giant pickle she pulled from her pocket, much to the facetious disgust of her sister.

Ten minutes to showtime.

Three grown women in the back of an Xterra made for little room to wiggle. They were snuggled as close as bedtime stories once brought them. A gust of wind would not move them. The rage of a river's current could not break them apart.

It was hard to release one's children to their own lives. That

321

was true. But it was also true that releasing them was easier when they knew what was worth returning to.

Five minutes.

Chloe tore into a bag of candy vines, ripping too hard and spilling some onto her lap. The girls bit off the ends of two vines and used them as straws. They lobbed popcorn kernels at each other's open mouths.

One minute.

There would be goodbyes ahead. Hard goodbyes. Sad goodbyes. But there would be far more hellos—on video chats, on calls, over coffee, in airports, at holidays. Those hellos were vastly more important.

Time would continue to slip through her fingers like sand, steady and unstoppable. But the girls never would. She would never lose her daughters; she would only find more of them to love.

Showtime.

EPILOGUE

SEPTEMBER

Speech, speech, speech!"

The crowd on the front lawn would not let her off the hook about it. After all, more than food had drawn them to the fourplex on a cool Friday evening. They had come for her, at the invitation of her parents.

Chloe waved, accepting their offer. Cheers resounded as she climbed the steps to the front porch, a makeshift platform that allowed a clearer view of the many faces and a closer proximity to the gift bag she had tucked behind the first post.

Up on the smooth concrete she had crossed countless times before, often behind schedule, she faced the people gathered. Family, friends, coworkers, church members, librarians, and a few MBA students. Many still savored bites of Seymour's brisket, coleslaw, antipasto, or protein balls.

What a meal it had been. What a celebration. What a summer.

"I owe you all a lot of gratitude," she began. "I could talk for hours and still not name all the reasons why, but I won't do that because my landlord wants you all out of here by eight."

Laughter bubbled through the crowd. Seymour nodded, stone-faced.

"I'm sure you all don't want to hear me drone on for that long anyway. I would be remiss, though, if I didn't say a special thanks to those who have been the biggest part of this chapter of my story. While all of you have supported me in some way, prayed for me, or counted down the days with me, a handful of you have lifted me up as only you could have. I'd like to thank you individually, and since I've already called him out once, I'll start with Seymour."

Heads turned toward the elder statesman of the group, who lifted his chin higher, poised.

"Mr. Bove, you have given me the gift of food so many times. You have also given me a good kick in the pants when needed, and always the God's honest truth. You are so much more than a landlord to me, and I pray the next person who rents apartment 4 from you will hold you as dear as I do."

The old man lifted his cup in cheers. "Thanks for not making me take that lizard."

More laughter.

She gave him a wink and turned to the person who had agreed to take Jeremy. "Sori."

Her friend smiled and took a step forward.

"Thank you for pushing me to do hard things, for telling me when my ideas were crazy but helping me figure out a way to make them happen anyway, and for giving my sweet boy a home where he is loved. I have learned to be a better friend and entrepreneur because of you. The world has no idea what's in store for it when you graduate next year."

Sori placed both hands over her heart and mouthed, *I'll miss you.*

The woman standing behind Sori got the spotlight next.

"Aunt Gab."

Her aunt slipped her hands into the front pockets of her jeans, readying herself.

"Thank you for helping me understand people in new ways. Your advice will serve me well in my new role as a teacher, just as it has in my roles as daughter and sister. Thank you for making a special trip to Kansas City to be here for the weekend. Above all, thank you for loving well the broken things in need of healing, creatures and otherwise."

Her aunt peeked across the crowd at Chloe's mom and grinned. It was the second time the sisters had gotten together since Omaha.

"Go get 'em, kid," her aunt called.

Tears began to push up to Chloe's eyes. The last three people would be the hardest of all to thank, and the hardest of all to hug goodbye. Even good farewells stung.

"Popsie."

Her dad draped his arm around her mom's shoulders and puffed out his chest, though anyone standing nearby would have noticed the tremor of his bottom lip.

"Over and over, you've given me a reminder to trust, to breathe, and to focus on what I know is right. You have taken care of our family so well, and you've ensured I have all that I need—and yes, I did double-check that I have the right voltage adapters."

To the backdrop of chuckles from the audience, her dad flashed a thumbs-up. "Good girl."

Despite the grin on her own face, Chloe's chest hitched. Her dad, more than anyone, had believed in her from the beginning. "Thank you for your encouragement, for your gentle way, and for your ridiculous GIFs. You are the reason I believe heroes exist."

He blew her a kiss, and she had to pause to steady her breath. Because the speech would only get harder.

On the other side of their mom, Lauren stood with a serving of cake. Her meals had been fuller the last many weeks, and so too had her schedule. Both made the impending goodbye easier to bear.

"Lauren. You have given me unwanted but seriously needed lessons in personal finance."

"Amen," Seymour mumbled.

The crowd chuckled again, including her sister. That lovely smile, so much better than tears.

"You've shown me a better way to raise my support and have

helped me set up a burgeoning Etsy shop. More importantly, though, you've shown me what it really means to persevere. I've been watching my big sister all my life, learning from you in ways I've only begun to appreciate. These last several months, though, I've been studying you closer than ever, and what you have taught me in your journey, whether you were trying to or not, are things I will carry with me. These have been my favorite months with you so far."

Key words: *so far.*

"Here's to more adventures together, Laur, when your new job schedule allows and when Gavin hasn't claimed you for the weekend."

Lauren smoothed her jaw-length hair behind her ear with her healed left hand, wet eyes alight. The lovely smile grew. The look of an older sister finally at rest.

Chloe sniffed against the rise of tears.

Only one person remained to be thanked. Her gaze latched on to her mom's, and she nearly broke. Edie Vance, her flowy top hanging stylishly from her frame, delicate fingertips painted in muted pink, posture perfect.

"Mom." Her voice wobbled. She cleared her throat and started again. "There is so much I wish I knew how to put into words for you. If I were a Cather or a Hughes or a Twain, I could figure out a way to fit it all into eloquent words. But my preferred language is pictures. So that's how I'm going to share with you all I wish I knew how to say." She picked up the hidden gift bag and descended the steps. Coming close to her mom, she held it out. "This is for you."

"For me? We're supposed to be giving you gifts."

"Don't worry," Chloe said, "this is an acceptable break from decorum."

Her mom took the bag and glanced up at Popsie, who nodded his encouragement, then she reached inside. Those standing nearby pushed in closer, attempting to peer over the recipient's shoulder.

Lauren was the first to recognize the image inside the frame. Her lips parted.

Then their mom did. "Oh, wow," she breathed.

Inside the simple wood frame lay a watercolored drawing of the three of them in front of Goldie, the drive-in screen in the distance. It was the final picture of the trip, taken by a fellow patron on Chloe's phone in the golden hour of that June night. They stood in a solid line, arms around each other, facing the camera and the horizon beyond. Lauren on one end, free hand relaxed at her side, confident chin parallel to the ground. Chloe on the other end, wide smile and free hand planted to her hip in playful daring. Rooted in the middle, their mom, sunglasses off, expression sure, and soft wings fanning from her perfectly drawn eyes.

Where words failed, drawings spoke. And the drawing spoke of a family that never left anyone behind, fought for each other's dreams, and believed that the most beautiful part of their story was yet to unfold.

"Chloe Grace." Her mom looked up from the drawing, the light in her eyes the same as what Chloe had finally captured on the page. "Well done."

For more from Sara Brunsvold,
read on for an excerpt from

The Divine Proverb
of Streusel

Available now wherever books are sold.

1

The message left little reason to believe Nikki Werner still held significance in her dad's life. After four months of the little girl inside her heart crying for her dad to come back, four months of wondering if he could hear those cries, she had received her answer. It was loud, clear, and immortalized on social media.

She reread the text from Hannah. The words had not changed.

Thought you should know.

The picture underneath had not changed either. A screenshot of a post. Their dad in a light gray suit, boutonniere pinned to the lapel, standing next to a white-clad woman neither of his grown daughters had ever met.

She replied to her sister.

It's like he doesn't care.

Did he? About any of them? At all?

Outside her classroom window, a gray-bellied cloud swelled in all directions, inflating like a balloon against the steel-blue morning sky. An unwelcome blemish invading a tranquil sea. It billowed and rolled, blown by the same invisible wind that churned the treetops. The world advanced at a dizzying pace, no thought to the weary or brokenhearted.

Four long months had passed since her dad had packed a bag and walked away from her mom—from all three of them. They were hollowed of everything they thought they knew of him, of family, of love. How much more would they have to unlearn?

Billow and roll.

The classroom door whined on its hinges. Tracy Brown stepped through and thrust two paper coffee cups above her head. "Raise your praise, Miss Werner, it's the last day of school! Woo!" She'd donned those canvas sandals middle-aged women like her loved so much and a "Salvy for Perez-ident" T-shirt. Both spoke to her summer dreams of no dress code and plenty of Kansas City Royals baseball games.

Nikki roused a smile in response, but there was no point hiding anything from Tracy. A high school calculus teacher for seventeen years, Tracy spotted consternation in the younger set the way a hawk spied a mouse.

Predictably, Tracy's expression mellowed. She lowered her arms. "That's not the face a teacher should be making five hours from final bell. What happened? Is it Jacob's mom again about his grade?"

Nikki shook her head then held up her phone.

Tracy padded over. Her mouth dropped as she read. "He got married?"

"Apparently."

"When?"

"According to this post of his new wife, this past Saturday."

"Oh, sister. I'm so sorry." Tracy sank into the chair next to Nikki's desk—the same spot she claimed every Thursday morning before students arrived—for a "Gab and Grace session," as she called it. The life-giving thirty minutes of prayer and mentoring that had sustained Nikki through her first year at Northwood High.

Nikki gave a shrug. "His choice, right?" A throb pressed against the backs of her eyes.

"Doesn't make it right, or easy."

No, it didn't. Nikki chewed her bottom lip and laid her phone facedown.

"Want your latte?" Tracy asked.

"No, I'm not in the mood." Quickly she added, "Hand it over."

With a sideways grin, Tracy slipped the cup into her hand.

The first sip went down smooth, a warm, centering presence reminiscent of those hopeful days of first semester, back when her only prayer request was how to whet her sophomores' appetites for the nation-shaping literature of Faulkner and Ellison and Twain. Back when she was oblivious to her dad's affair.

"Want to talk about it?" Tracy asked.

Nikki thrummed her fingers on the cup sleeve. She shook her head.

"Want to scream about it?"

A small smile tweaked her lips. "Kinda."

"I would too. Think your mom knows about that?" Tracy gestured toward Nikki's phone.

"Not sure."

"Hopefully she doesn't find out through social media."

"She's been off it for a while. We both have. Ever since—" The rest of that sentence tasted too sour.

"Since the truth came out," her friend finished.

Nikki nodded. That day had been the heaviest of her life.

"You can't do anything about his choices," Tracy said. "Only your own. And I suspect this summer is going to be filled with bright and glorious choices for you. Especially with a certain beau." She winked, a clear diversion to other topics. To Isaac.

The throbbing behind Nikki's eyes speared into her chest. It happened every time he came up. Like the pain her mom felt had suddenly transferred to her. "We don't know that Isaac is going to propose."

Tracy peered at her over the rim of her glasses. "Don't we?"

Nikki pulled her cup closer. "It's not a guarantee, anyway."

"Do you want him to?"

"Yes," she replied a little too quickly.

Tracy tilted her head to the side in that tell-me-more posture she had perfected.

"I do love him. And I have thought of us being married. But . . ."

"But it's a lot on top of a lot?"

"Yeah."

"Have you told Isaac this?"

Nikki shifted in her seat. "No."

Tracy reached over and cupped Nikki's hand. "Probably a conversation to have sooner rather than later. Men are the worst when it comes to mind reading."

"You'd think they'd evolve past that."

"You'd think." Tracy chuckled and glanced at her watch. "Nearly time for the circus to descend. Let's get you fully caffeinated and reasonably cheerful." She raised her cup for a toast. "To summer."

Nikki grinned, tapped her own cup against Tracy's, swallowed another fortifying drink. But the depths of her soul remained as clouded as the sky.

Billow and roll.

 ⸺ ⸺ ⸺

Weeks had passed since his brother had answered any of his calls, but that didn't stop Wes Werner from dialing Chris's number again. "A brother is born for a time of adversity," Proverbs 17 taught, and if what Aunt Emma said she saw on social media was true, his kid brother sank deeper every day. The spiral was evident even from Wes's vantage point clear on the opposite side of Missouri.

Had Lydia seen the photo? Had the girls?

The divorce was barely a month old.

He placed the phone to his ear and stepped out onto his front porch. The midmorning sun coaxed melodies from the winged singers in the century-old oak tree at the edge of the yard, a source of endless adventure when he and Chris were boys. The gentle slopes of the Werner farm rolled into the distance.

The other end of the line rang. And rang. Ignored.

Voicemail picked up. Again.

Wes filled his lungs and held the air in place as he waited for the beep. He prayed the words would come with at least moderate coherence and grace.

Beep.

"Hey, Chris. Wes. Think about you every day. And your family. Spoke with Aunt Emma. She told me you and, uh, Sheryl? Is that right? That you all moved to Oklahoma and you're about an hour from her." He paused. "She also said you may have . . . bigger news. Hoping we can talk. Give me a call."

As soon as he hit the red End button, more words rushed to his lips, a half minute too late.

I want you to be happy—and whole.

I love you.

My heart is heavy.

Words that would be unheard by anyone other than God. At least until—unless—Chris called him back.

— — —

The final bell rang. Nine hundred high schoolers roughhoused and laughed their way to summer freedom. Soon after, Nikki slid into her Malibu. Tracy wanted her to go out for a "celebratory and completely unhealthy amount of spinach dip," but Nikki declined. The ache in her head begged for a quiet place.

She intended to drive to her apartment, crawl under the covers, and sleep off the day—the semester. Instead, she ended up parked behind her mom's car in the driveway of the two-story colonial in the heart of Kansas City, Missouri's northland. The house that had been home for all of Nikki's twenty-six years. The Werner family hub, and the core from which every branch of her existence stretched.

The For Sale sign in the front lawn had donned a new addition: a red rectangle with bold white letters. Contract Pending.

Her entire Werner life had ebbed away, piece by rotted piece. Nothing left whole. Nothing left untouched.

She stepped into the afternoon sunshine.

The shades of the living room's picture window were open, as if the house grasped at any light it could find to chase away the darkness that had settled over it. One of her earliest memories had happened at that window. She'd been four years old, nose practically touching the pane, waiting for her dad's car to turn into the drive.

She gritted her teeth against the pang and pushed forward, up the front steps. She reached for the handle of the storm door and stopped. The inside door stood open, allowing an unobstructed view into the house. Her mom knelt in the middle of the furniture-less living room. A large cardboard box sat in front of her, a stack of framed pictures on one side and a pile of dish towels on the other. She stared at the picture in her hands. Just stared. Like she tried to believe their family had ever been happy.

Such moments had caught Nikki several times over the last four months too. Moments when she saw a picture or relived a memory and the daunting question rose once more: Would anything from that point forward ever be joyful enough to capture and frame for posterity?

Slowly her mom lifted a dish towel and shrouded the picture. The ripple of grief knew no end.

Nikki drew in a breath, then knocked on the storm door.

The noise startled her mom, whose surprised expression slowly melted to one of confusion. She rose and came to the door. "Nik? What are you doing here?"

What was she doing there? What was it that had made her drive twenty-five minutes out of her way? Was she, too, grasping at any light she could find? Any semblance of the life that had been theirs only months ago?

Her chin began to tremble.

Instantly her mom wrapped her arm around her and pulled her inside. "Come on, baby. Let's have some coffee."

ACKNOWLEDGMENTS

This book would not have been possible without:

The extended Revell team, especially Brianne, Lindsay, Karen, Erin, Laura, and Kimberly. Thank you for your passion for stories, those who tell them, and those who read them. It is evident in all you do.

Rachel McRae, my editor, whose humor makes me smile every time and whose encouragement is unfailingly well-timed. Thank you for caring authentically about your authors. That reference to Jane Austen was for you.

Jessica English, my expert copy editor, who has polished this story until it gleams. You have earned my admiration, my trust, and my commendation for a bonus after all the word confusions you had to correct.

Cynthia Ruchti, my agent, who always has a wise word and an impressive ability to fill in gaps. Thank you for all you invest in my stories, career, and well-being.

Those who made research all the more fun because of your expertise, especially Katherine in Winterset, Iowa; John at Shepherd of the Hills Historic Farm; and the dedicated staff at the Watkins Museum of History and the Laura Ingalls Wilder Historic Home and Museum. A special thanks to Heather Beers for helping me see with an artist's eye.

Ruthie Burrell and Bekki Diefendorf, fellow writers with immense talent for storytelling and critiquing. Thank you for brainstorming and spending time with early versions of this manuscript. Your input brought it into sharper focus.

Rebecca Davie for unwavering prayer support, even when I neglected to give you updated requests. You are the hands and feet of Jesus.

My church for their readership, prayers, and encouragement as this writing ministry continues to unfold.

The readers of this book, whom I prayed for every time I sat down to write. I hope your travels with the Vance women inspire you to share the stories that need to be told.

To my mom, Janice, who instilled a love of books in me and who has been there through every victory and tear. Thank you for your eager support of your children and grandchildren.

My husband, Robert, who helped turn research trips into family adventures and patiently takes on the role of sounding board. You have been the Grant to my Edie more times than I can count. Thank you for keeping me centered on what matters.

My daughters. You get the dedication and an acknowledgment because you two were the ones I had in mind the most as I wrote. It is hard releasing you to your own lives, but I hold fast to my belief that watching you run headlong into God's plans for you will be an incalculable blessing.

Above all and because of all, our gracious heavenly Father. Thank you for bearing with me as I learned to let you lead and to trust you with my dreams of being an author. My single best decision was to trust you with everything, and my greatest purpose is to do all of this for your renown. Please keep teaching me.

Sara Brunsvold is the Christy Award–winning author of *The Extraordinary Deaths of Mrs. Kip* and *The Divine Proverb of Streusel*. She creates stories that boldly engage contemporary issues through the lens of hope and unshakable faith. Her passion is to connect with readers first through books, then through meaningful conversation. She lives with her family in Kansas. Learn more at SaraBrunsvold.com.

CONNECT WITH
SARA

SARABRUNSVOLD.COM

SHARE STORIES THAT SPEAK

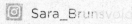 SaraBrunsvoldAuthor   Sara_Brunsvold